The Legends of Matt Baker

A Collection of Short Stories

SABINA BOYER

DEDICATION

This book is dedicated to several people. Mom, most of these pages are for you. Thank you for all of the hard work you did in helping me edit. Nearly all of the rest of the book is for the amazing Flabbits and for Elia, specifically, who helped me hit my deadline. And dad, the last few words in here are for you. You'll know them when you see them

CONTENTS

MAP OF ILDATHORE

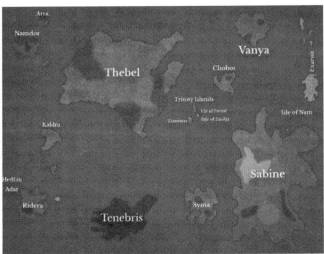

Above: The world of Ildathore. It's odd, but to many, it's home.

Below: A map of the kingdoms of Vanya (if you don't know what that means yet, just remember to check back here when you read about it).

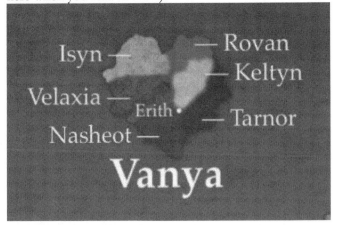

STORY ONE
THE MAPMAKER

THE MAPMAKER
CHAPTER ONE

Matt Baker sat nervously in a chair opposite Mr. Ankletoe, owner of the repair shop on Hensfine Lane. He fidgeted as Mr. Ankletoe looked at him, skeptical. "Name?"

"Baker, Matt Baker," fumbled Matt.

"Age?"

"16 years, seven months, and five days," replied Matt, trying not to sound too desperate.

"Work experience?" asked Mr. Ankletoe.

"Well, I don't have any, yet…." said Matt, trying to stall what he knew was coming, "but I'm good at fixing things….. generally speaking….. most of the time."

"I see," said Mr. Ankletoe, rubbing his temples. "Well, I have your home address. If we ever need you, I'll let you know."

Matt sighed. "I understand. Thanks for your time." Matt stood and shook hands with Mr. Ankletoe, knowing that they would never work together. As he left the repair shop, he looked up at the sky full of storm clouds. Bringing his eyes back down, he saw a stray cat whose desperate appearance reminded him much too much of himself. "Trust me. You're better off far away from me," he said. "I'm probably not even qualified to pet you, knowing my track record." The cat cocked its head, as if trying to understand and then walked off.

Matt made his way slowly around town, watching all the other boys his age running errands and working in shops, and wishing he could be one of them. Without meaning to, he eventually found his way to the edge of town. As he walked, a sign caught his attention. Eagerly he read it, "In need of mapmakers, sailors, explorers, writers, interesting and desperate individuals willing to gamble safety, and handymen."

"Handymen!" he said again, brightening. Maybe there was a job he could do after all.

If Matt Baker had been paying better attention and wasn't so desperate for a job, and was perhaps just a bit brighter of a person altogether, he might have realized that having employers who wanted people desperate for a job wasn't the best idea. However, Matt Baker was not brighter than Matt Baker, so he didn't consider it.

As he walked into the building, a little bell rang on the door. "Hello?" he said to an empty room and a vacant receptionist desk.

Out of a door popped a short jolly man as thin as a stick and as perky as a rabbit. "Oh, hello!" he said, making an enthusiastic bow. "Welcome to Franklin, Franklin, & Smith, Enterprise of Unusual and Extraordinary Events and/or Conquests and/or Business Deals and/or the Buying and/or Selling of Exotic and/or Downright Interesting Objects, or as we have affectionately called it because the full name is much much too long, Franklin, Franklin, & Smith. My name is Mr. Tickleten. How may I help you?" said Mr. Tickleten with a sing-song voice and a friendly smile that brightened the room.

"Hi, I am Matt Baker, and I noticed that your sign said you wanted help from a...."

"Oh yes!" cried Mr. Tickleten delightedly. "You have come just in time to meet your possible employers! Please follow me right this way."

"Um, thank you," said Matt, slightly confused. "Mr. Tickleten, am I meeting...."

"No, you are not meeting Mr. Tickleten. There is only one of me!" said Mr. Tickleten, leading him through the hall with a spring in his step. "And in case you never studied grammar, or just don't remember it, or possibly you don't care and I am just rambling, which I do all the time anyway, the correct way to ask is: Am I meeting Mr. Tickleten, not the other way around. As it is, you are meeting Mr. Franklin, Mr. Franklin, and Mr. Smith, the founders of Franklin, Franklin, & Smith."

"The founders!" said Matt surprised. "But Mr. Tickleten, I'm just a handym..."

"Here we are!" piped in Mr. Tickleten, flinging open some double doors that led into a meeting room. At a table in the middle of the room sat three men. One was old with a grumpy look on his face, another looked like a younger version of him, also with a grumpy look on his face, and the other was between their ages and seemed rather bored. "Gentlemen," said Mr. Tickleten, bowing again, "this young boy is interested in being a mapmaker here."

The bored man stood up with a sparkle in his eyes, "Indeed! A fine looking young man and just when we needed him most! My name is Mr. Smith."

Matt's face went pale, "Mapmaker?"

"Yes he is and a very good one, too!" added Mr. Tickleten proudly.

"WHAT?" hissed Matt into Mr. Tickleten's ear. "I said I was Matt Baker not a map..."

"You look like a nice young man," said Mr. Smith. "As I said, my name is Mr. Smith, and those two happy-go-lucky gentleman are Mr. Franklin and his son. So, how do you feel about sailing?"

Matt's eyes opened wide. *Sailing!* he thought, excitedly. He remembered rowing with his father years ago on a little boat. Those were by far the happiest memories he had.

"Now you must understand the possible dangers of this trip...."

But Matt wasn't listening anymore. He was far away on a beautiful ship, riding the waves and feeling the sun on his face, and best of all, getting paid to scribble some drawings on paper! "I'll do it!" he said as soon as Mr. Smith stopped talking.

"A boy after my own heart!" said Mr. Smith, clapping his hands together. He handed Matt a contract. "Read over this tonight, sign it, and be at the docks tomorrow morning. We set sail at dawn!"

That night, Matt could barely sleep he was so exhilarated. The next day, he hurriedly signed the contract without having time to glance through it and made his way to the dock. When he got there, Mr. Tickleten, the young Mr. Franklin and Mr. Smith were waiting with the crew. "Good to see you, lad!" said Mr. Smith, smiling. "Do you have the contract?"

"Right here!" said Matt, handing it over.

"I can't wait!" cried Mr. Tickleten, bouncing up and down in excitement. "And now, away we sail, to the Isle of Dread!"

"The Isle of what!?"

THE MAPMAKER
CHAPTER TWO

"The Isle of WHAT?!!" cried Matt Baker in horror.

"The Isle of Dread, of course," said Mr. Tickleten. "Why do you sound so surprised?"

"That's the island no ship has ever come back from!!!!" shouted Matt frantically! "I don't want to die!"

"Matt, we told you all about this trip yesterday," said Mr. Smith slowly. "And it was all in your contract. Didn't you read it before you signed? Weren't you listening?"

"Well, um, maybe not as well as I should have…." replied Matt, not quite sure which question he was answering. "I thought this was a sea voyage, not a death exploration!"

"Yes," said Mr. Smith. "A day's sail to the Isle of Dread, and that is where your mapmaking skills will be needed. You really didn't understand that?"

"No!" blurt out Matt.

"Well, in that case…." said Mr. Smith, preparing to rip the paper Matt had given him.

"Wait just a minute!" cried the younger Mr. Franklin, walking up and snatching the paper out of Mr. Smith's hands. "Just because this boy isn't too bright, we can't be held responsible for his stupidity." Matt blushed and hung his head as several of of the crew members jeered. "We need a map maker, and this boy signed our contract. It isn't our fault he didn't know what he was getting himself into, but he IS coming!"

Mr. Smith's eyes burned with anger. "Do not insult this lad like that, and he is NOT coming if he doesn't want to!" he said with clenched fists.

"Gentlemen, gentlemen!" cried Mr. Tickleten, squeezing in between the two men. "That comment was way out of line, Mr. Franklin. You shouldn't pick on people that you don't even know…" Mr. Franklin's face contorted in anger. "But," said Mr. Tickleten, turning towards Mr. Smith, "Mr. Franklin does have a point. We have been waiting a long time to go on this exploration, and we need this lad to complete our goals. I don't want to force him to do something, but perhaps we should ask him what he thinks is fair."

All eyes turned on Matt. "Well," said Matt, sighing, "I definitely don't want to go to the Isle of Dread." The crew hung their heads in disappointment. "However, I gave my word that I would come, so….. I'm in."

Mr. Smith nodded, "Thank you lad." He turned to the crew, "Well men, it's time to sail!"

Matt breathed in deeply, realizing what he had gotten himself into. With a fake grin of self confidence, he followed the others to the ship.

Had Matt fully understood what would happen, our story most likely would have stopped here as he ran away with his tail between his legs. But as no one can ever see the future, quite an interesting tale awaits us.

"Welcome to the *Bella Fawn*," said Mr Tickleten, helping Matt on deck. "May not be the biggest vessel, but in the 6 years she's sailed for us, not once has she let us down... except for that time last year with the giant eel, and several years before that with the storm, and the first adventure we went on with her when her steering got us completely lost, and last week when we found a leak. But, other than that, she's as good as gold."

Matt gulped, "Thanks for the reassurance." Despite the *Bella Fawn*'s misgivings, the day unfolded better than Matt could have hoped. All through the morning and afternoon, there was nothing but smooth sailing. The crew was a very kind group of men overall, and they were so glad to finally set sail that they let Matt believe that his knots and steering were almost sea worthy. By the time night rolled around, Matt had not only become friends with just about everyone on the ship, the exception being Mr. Franklin, but he was second guessing his hesitation to come in the first place.

That night, Matt slept in a room full of snoring, stinky men on an unsafe ship sure that he was by far the luckiest 16-year-old boy in the world. The next morning, he woke early and walked out on deck to find Mr. Tickleten at the wheel.

"Why, good morning, my young fellow," said Mr. Tickleten cheerily. "Hope the snores didn't keep you awake."

"It was great; all of the crew has been so nice."

"Indeed, you couldn't find a better bunch even if you located every banana in Ildathore," he chuckled at his own subtle joke and turned to see Matt's blank face staring back. "You're a very down to earth young man, aren't you?"

"Actually, I'm pretty tall for my age," replied Matt.

Mr. Tickleten grinned, "That's what I thought."

Matt looked up at the crow's nest to see the outline of a man looking out ahead of them. "Who is that up there?"

Mr. Tickleten sighed, "That would be Mr. Franklin. He likes to get away from everything sometimes and take some time to think."

"Oh, can I ask you something?"

"Well, if I were to take your question literally, then yes, you can and you did ask something, but I will permit another." Mr. Tickleten smiled, "What's on your mind?"

"Why didn't you get in trouble for intervening in your boss's business yesterday morning? I don't know anyone who could get away with something like that."

"Well, that is mainly why they hired me," said Mr. Tickleten. "I always speak my mind, and when it comes to important matters, I tend to choose the reasonable approach. I knew the young Mr. Franklin and Mr. Smith long before they started working together. Then one day, each asked me to meet, and each seemed rather upset. So, at noon, I went to see Mr. Franklin, and he told me that he'd met with his new business partner for the first time and he was absolutely terrible! He complained about how his new partner would actually rather help people than make money, 'IMAGINE THAT!' Well, that night, I went to meet my friend Mr. Smith, and before long, he was all fired up about how his two new business partners were dreadful and how they wanted to make money more than be fair, 'IMAGINE THAT!' Well, I'm no genius, but lucky for me, it didn't take one to solve that puzzle. I continued to calm them down whenever I saw them, and before they knew what was happening, not only were they working together, but the business was a huge success. Then, a few months later, I lost my job and my dear friends BOTH offered me one at the company. Now, though it isn't in my job description, I continue to help them compromise since they both respect me." Mr. Tickleten laughed quietly to himself. "What's more is that I am such an old friend to each of them that I don't believe either has caught on. Isn't life ironic?"

Before Matt could answer, Mr. Franklin yelled from the crow's nest, "Land ho, land ho!"

"Well," said Matt slowly. "It's time!"

Mr. Tickleten clapped his hands together happily, "Goody, Goody! Isle of Dread, here we come!"

THE MAPMAKER
CHAPTER THREE

Matt stepped off the *Bella Fawn* onto the Isle of Dread, followed by the young Mr. Franklin, Mr. Smith, Mr. Tickleten, and four other strong sailors. After a brief meeting, it had been decided that only the eight would go: Matt to make the map, the sailors to protect them, Mr. Franklin and Mr. Smith because they were too curious for their own good, and Mr. Tickleten to be an unofficial referee between the company owners. Matt shouldered the pack of mapping equipment from the company, most of which he had no idea how to use, and they set off.

It was a beautiful morning for walking. Birds sung in trees nearby, the occasional rabbit would skip across the path, and deer grazed off in the distance. Before long, the group forgot that they were on an Island no one had ever returned from and began to talk and joke. Indeed, it seemed ridiculous to believe that this was the feared Isle of Dread.

"That's where we're heading, men," said Mr. Franklin

around noon, pointing up at the single mountain on the reasonably small island. "From there, we will be able to get a view of the entire island."

"I disagree!" said Mr. Smith emphatically. "We should circle around it. We don't know what could live up there! Caution should be our first priority."

"NO!" cried Mr. Franklin. "If we are going to make any progress, we must know what we are up against! We must attack this head on!"

Mr. Smith almost replied, but before he could, he saw Mr. Tickleten's pleading glance from nearby. "Very well," he said. "Have it your way."

The whole company relaxed, glad to be rid of the argument. As they walked, Matt made his way over to Mr. Tickleten. "Has Mr. Franklin always been so snobby and stubborn?" asked Matt in a low voice.

"Well, that seems a rather harsh judgement, considering you haven't known him very long."

"I don't have to. It's kind of obvious."

"I suppose you have a point," replayed Mr. Tickleten chuckling. "To answer you question, no he has not. He used to be a very kind man, always generous and loving. But after his wife died, something in him just sort of snapped. For weeks afterward, he wouldn't talk to me or anyone else. He just sat in his house with locked doors and closed windows. Then, he threw himself headfirst into his work, striving for success and fortune. I don't know what happened to him during that time, but he has never been the same man since." Mr. Tickleten sighed sadly, "I've tried to get him to open up and tell me what happened to him, but he wouldn't have it. Now I'm afraid it's too late."

Matt looked over at Mr. Franklin, walking with head held high. "What about his father, the other Mr. Franklin?"

Mr. Tickleten grinned, "No need to worry about him, lad, he's always been a big curmudgeon."

That night, the party set up camp in a little grove of trees not far from the beach. They put down their packs and started a campfire. The full moon cast shadows of the trees dancing around them, and soon, theories of why it was called the Isle of Dread began to surface.

"I think it's because a wielder of dark magic cursed this place," said one of the sailors.

"I think that it's because cannibals are hiding here, waiting for the perfect moment to attack."

"You can guess all you like," started Mr. Tickleten with a twinkle in his eye. "But I say it's a dragon." All grew quiet as they waited for an explanation. "Drakes may be kind and gentle ever since they submitted themselves to the authority of humans, but dragons are another story all together. The true sons of Bethoch! They speak straight into the minds of humans and are made of death itself….." A crash filled the air from somewhere on the island, causing everyone to jump.

Slowly, as night wore on, all finally fell asleep, all except for Matt. After the others were down, he pulled out the mapping equipment and stared at it. He took the two things he knew how to use, a pencil and a piece of paper, and tried his best to draw where they had gone. To his frustration, art was a lot harder than he had anticipated. By the time he put everything he had into it, it was little more than the scribblings of a young child.

"Can't sleep either?" asked Mr. Franklin, propping himself on and elbow.

"No," said Matt, hurriedly stuffing the 'map' in his bag." Just getting some late night work done on the map. What about you?"

"I just can't believe that after all these years I'm finally here. Emily always wanted to come to this place."

"Who is Emily?"

Mr. Franklin got a far away look in his eyes, "My wife, such a dear little thing. As frail and beautiful as a rose without thorns."

"What happened to her?"

"It took her," he said shakily. "The plague. She was so delicate, and it came so fast. I knew I had to get the doctor, but I didn't want to leave her side, so I made a terrible mistake. I paid a boy off the street to run and fetch a doctor. He returned with a man in a white coat and a doctor's bag who said he required payment in advance. I gave the money to him, and he asked me to leave the room while he examined her. A few minutes later, I came back to find the man gone and the window open. And Emily.....was dead." A cold chill ran down Matt's spine. "It was that day I realized that the world is a terrible place. People will do anything in their quest for power. There is no way to change it, only to join it."

Matt stared into the fire, "Not everyone is terrible, you know. Not everyone is a cheater, or a con, or a fake. Some people just...."

"Just what?" snapped Mr. Franklin.

"Some people, Mr. Franklin, just want to help."

After a long time, Mr. Franklin spoke again, "Call me, John."

Matt looked over as John Franklin laid down with his back to him. Matt smiled, knowing he'd made a friend, and leaned against a tree to sleep. As his eyelids drooped, he looked up at the mountain. *Dragons indeed*, he thought, amused. As he drifted to sleep, another thought crept into his mind, **Imagine, a human scoffing at dragons; then again, people can be stupid.**

Matt blinked. Where had that last thought come from? As If in answer, a deep booming voice rang out in his head, **Pathetic creatures. You dare assume that the Creator gave you all of the land and sky and sea to chart and rule. You foolishly believe that humans can stand in sacred places and command all living creatures as if they were slaves, and you imagine that the world would tip out of its orbit if you were not there to watch over it. Mankind stands on but a hanging thread as the world takes its course beneath you. You have carelessly leaned out to take control of power that is not yours to harness, and this time, it will cost you.**

THE MAPMAKER
CHAPTER FOUR

"Ahhh!" screamed Matt, sitting up and panting. He looked around at the blank faces of his companions who were sitting around the fire, cooking breakfast. "Did I fall asleep?"

"Yes, you did," said Mr. Tickleten, smiling, "and from the sounds of things, you had quite a dream."

"It wasn't a dream!" said Matt. The others drew in close to hear what he had to say. "I think I heard," he paused, "a dragon in my head!" His friends snorted with laughter. "It isn't funny!" said Matt panicked.

"Did he growl? Or maybe he invited you in for tea!" said one of the crew members, still laughing.

"No, I heard him in my mind!"

Once again, the four crew members roared with laughter. One of them reached into Matt's bag saying, "I know! Let's label the map 'Dragon Island'!"

"No, don't! It isn't finished yet!" said Matt frantically.

"I'd like to see your progress," said Mr. Franklin. "After all, you were working on it late into the night."

Before Matt could stop them, they pulled out his map and unrolled it. All gasped as they saw the terrible mess of lines that sat on the page. "What is this?" asked Mr. Smith, looking at him.

Matt hung his head, "It's my map." He could feel everyone's eyes on him. "I'm not a mapmaker. I'm just a handyman."

A long pause followed. Matt waited for the harsh words and angry tones, but they didn't come. He looked up to see Mr. Smith's gaze resting on him. "I suppose we could always use a handyman when on the *Bella Fawn*," he said, beginning to smile.

The company nodded their agreement, remembering their 'seaworthy vessel'. Several of them laughed, but this time, it was a kind, encouraging laugh. Matt turned to look at Mr. Franklin. All emotion Matt had seen in him the night before was gone. His face was blank, his jaw set like stone, and he seemed to have grown a foot taller, but his eyes were filled with pain and hurt. He turned away from the others and walked off into the trees and out of sight.

"Just give him a bit," said Mr. Tickleten slowly. "Let him cool off."

Once again Matt remembered their delima, "Mr. Smith, we have to leave!"

"Because of the dragon?" asked Mr. Smith doubtfully.

"YES!" Matt sighed at the crew's muttering. "Listen, just stay here and don't go anywhere until I get back!"

"Where are you going, lad?" asked Mr. Tickleten nervously.

"To find Mr. Franklin!" called back Matt, sprinting into the trees. As he followed Mr. Franklin's path, he found himself getting ever closer to the mountain. *Just great,* he thought. *He went to the mountain.* **Good,** replied a deep cruel voice in the depths of his mind. **He will come right to me; see if you can stop the inevitable, little human. I'd like to see you try.** Matt broke into a cold sweat, and he doubled his pace, running as fast as he could.

***

John Franklin huffed and puffed as he made his way up the mountain. He looked up to see that he was making good progress.

"If we are to ever conquer this insane island, we must know what we are up against. Dangers on the mountain, huh? We'll see about that, Mr. Smith? Stay safe with your handyman as I truly discover the reason we are here. I wonder how much farther to the top," said John Franklin to himself.

As if in answer, his mind replied, **Most likely a while at the pace you are going. See that cave up ahead? If you rest in it a few minutes, you will be able to continue on faster.**

"True," replied John, "but it's so dark in there, almost unnaturally dark."

All the better, a place away from the hot and torturous sun. John nodded and turned towards the cave. As he walked to it, a hand touched the back of his shoulder.

He spun around to see Matt behind him. "What are you doing here, handyman?"

"I'm here to get you!" said Matt. "You can't be up here. It's a long story, but I can sense evil up here. Can't you feel it? It's like a stench that won't go away!"

"Don't be ridiculous," snapped John. "Don't you talk to me about evil. You told me that people were different than I thought. You told me to trust, I trusted you, and look where it got me!"

"John, calm down!"

"Call me Franklin, Mr. Franklin!"

Matt stepped back. Once again, the voice rang out in his head, *Ah, he has come right to me. Die, human!* From the terrified look on Mr. Franklin's face, Matt knew that he heard it, too. A fiery white glow shown out from the cave.

"I'm sorry for what I'm about to do!" said Matt. As fire shot out of the cave straight at them, Matt jumped at Mr. Franklin and pushed him back, sending him rolling down the mountain. Matt flattened himself just in time to dodge the flames that flew at him. When he stood up, he looked down the mountain to see an unconscious, but breathing, Mr. Franklin, lying on his back in some bushes.

Well, looky here, said the same voice Matt had heard

in his head. He turned to the cave to see two glowing eyes. *You seemed to have ruined my good time. Come with me, human. We are going to have a nice long chat.*

Matt sighed. Even he knew it generally wasn't a good idea to refuse dragons. "What are you going to do with me?"

Oh, little friend, said the voice and the eyes seemed to smile darkly. *Trust me, I know how to treat house guests. Especially.... unwelcome ones!*

THE MAPMAKER
CHAPTER FIVE

Come in, said the voice behind the evil eyes. *And see the true Isle of Dread.*

Matt stepped shakily into the cave, and as he did, everything went pitch black. Whatever dark powers were in this cave, they extinguished the sunlight immediately. Shivers ran up and down his spine uncontrollably.

The eyes turned so that their dim light shone further into the cave. *Follow me...* said the voice into Matt's head. Matt stood there, not sure what to do. As the creature began to walk, a scaly tail brushed passed him and made him jump back in terror. *Come, human,* said the voice again, *to see one of the wonders of the world.*

Matt walked cautiously through the dark, always staying close to the glow of his enemy's eyes. *Stand back,* said the voice. Then the eyes rose higher than Matt thought possible, and white flames shot out from just beneath them, deep into the cave. In the white light, Matt could see the creature clearly. It was an enormous emerald dragon, taller than the mast of the tallest ship. He swung his head from side to side, spewing fire around the chamber, and as he did, the light of the fire danced and flickered off his scales until they shone. Matt decided there and then that the dragon was the most beautiful thing he had ever seen.

The white flames shot through the middle of the chamber, lighting forty huge torches, twenty on each side of a long stone pathway. Beyond the path on either side were enormous piles of treasure. Heaps of gold and jewels filled every corner. To the left, Matt saw a huge ship resting in the treasure, its flag hanging low and defeated, as if it were frozen in time right before it sunk.

Matt looked up at the huge beast, "Who are you?"

Valinar, said the dragon. Then, lifting his head and roaring, he sent echoes bouncing off every wall until Matt thought the sound of it would shatter the mountain.

"You're so huge! I never thought a dragon could be so…..majestic."

The dragons you know of are nothing more than fakes, said Valinar. *I assume that even a human like you knows at least a little history, how at the end of the first age, Dahn, the first man killed Bethoch, the first dragon, and brought about the fall of mankind. What the legends do not say is how, after the fall, Bethoch's wife became the first Drake and subjected herself to the human scum!* Valinar spat. *In her desperate state, she doomed herself and all of her descendants to grow into the weak worms that they are. Now they are nothing more than the other worthless kindred of Bethoch, who have slowly become more docile over the ages. Even the ones that call themselves dragons are nothing more than grumpy housepets. But Gelidor, Bethoch's son, did not let his hate be lessened by time...* Valinar grinned. *He did everything he could to teach his descendants the truth about humans and the evil they can cause. Most of his descendants are gone now, hunted down by the humans. I am one of the last left.*

"Just because Dahn killed Bethoch, it doesn't mean all humans are bad!" said Matt.

You remind me of a young reckless dragon I once knew, said Valinar, a faraway look in his eyes. *His name was Valley. He lived with his grandfather, here on this very island. Though Valley was not his birth name, when he stretched out his wings on this land, his grandfather said he seemed more like a part of it than a living thing.* He smiled. *His grandfather did everything he could to protect Valley, even confining him to this desolate island for his safety, far away from the evils of man. The young dragon did not take heed of his grandfather's warnings. He believed it was wrong to judge a race for one human's misgivings. If only he knew how wrong he was.*

As he had spoken, the two had walked down the chamber between the torches until they reached the far wall, where a single painting hung.

"What happened to them?" asked Matt, forgetting caution in his curiosity.

The grandfather suffered what he had always warned about. Valinar's eyes looked sadly at the painting. *He suffered the same fate as his father.*

Matt looked closely at the painting. It was truly a

masterpiece. On the left lay the dying Bethoch, blood seeping from his chest. In his last moments, his head was lifted to the sky, eyes closed taking in one last breath of precious air. On the right was Dahn's hand, stained with blood, and on the top of the frame was written two words: Bethoch's Demise. Across the painting lay a scratch mark trying in vain to hide the hand from view. For the first time, Matt noticed a terrible truth: the dragon in the picture looked almost exactly like Valinar.

I take after my great grandfather, don't you think?

Matt gasped, "But that means that the grandfather was Gelidor, Bethoch's son, and you are…."

One day, interrupted Valinar. **Gelidor was out near the shore, but Valley had gone to the other side of the island, to enjoy the forest and watch its creatures. Suddenly, Valley heard a roar. The roar turned into a screech of agony that was cut off unnaturally. Valley raced to the top of the mountain as fast as he could to see what had happened. He looked down to see his grandfather, dead on the shore, with humans celebrating around him. He rushed down to them and became their last nightmare…… That was the last anyone ever saw of Valley. The docile Drake was gone forever. He returned to his birth name, Valinar, and vowed to avenge his grandfather.**

"It was you," whispered Matt. "You were Valley."

I have kept my vow. I have destroyed every human that has come anywhere near this island, and I will not let Gelidor be forgotten. Now, tell me that I am wrong in what I am about to do. Tell me that I am wrong for killing you… Valinar looked down at Matt to see a single tear make his way down his cheek. **Pathetic**

*human, crying that you shall never leave. Be a man
and face your fate.*

"I'm not crying for me. I'm crying for you."

*Ha! How could you possibly cry for me, you
murderer?!* scoffed Valinar.

Matt met the dragon's gaze, "Because I know how you
feel…. to lose someone you love and not be able to stop
it." The evil glow in Valinar's eyes dimmed just a bit.
"When I was little, my dad was an amazing sailor. He used
to take me out on his little boat and teach me what to do
to keep it afloat. But, when my mother died, the boat trips
stopped. Then a few months later, he told me we were
going to go boating. I was only four, but I still remember
how excited I was. He walked with me to a grey building
and told me to wait there while he left to get something. I
sat down on the steps and watched him walk away. When
he was almost out of sight, he turned and waved one last
time. Then he was gone.

"I waited and waited. That night, someone came out of
the grey building and took me inside. The next day, they
told me that this place, the orphanage, would be my new
home. I told them they were wrong, that my dad WAS
coming back for me, but they just smiled sadly. I lived
there until two years ago. No one would hire me because I
was never taught a trade. My father left me with nothing.
A few days ago, I was ready to give up. I woke up and told
the Creator that if I didn't get a job that day, there was no
use getting up the next morning at all…." Matt sighed.
"That was the day I met Mr. Tickleten and signed on with
Franklin, Franklin, & Smith."

*I am so sorry, young human, but don't you feel
hate for your father? Don't you understand why I*

made my vow? asked Valinar. **Don't you want to make him pay?**

Matt paused, "My father made a decision, a wrong one, and I had to pay the consequences for it, but I have made mistakes, too, and my friends and the Creator have forgiven me more times than I could ever deserve. If I didn't forgive my father for what he did, what kind of person would I be, what kind of son? I learned to forgive a long time ago, but you still haven't." Matt locked eyes with Valinar, "Now it's up to you, Valinar. You can kill me or forgive humans and put the past behind you. The choice is yours."

Outside of the cave blinking in the sunlight, Mr. Franklin lay dazed. Matt's words had carried all of the way down to him, echoing off the cave walls. Though he couldn't hear the dragon, half the conversation was all he needed to know. He dragged himself to his feet, trying to process what had happened. Though his leg was twisted at an angle that worried him, he knew what he had to do.

Dragons don't show mercy! John thought, *I HAVE to warn the others before he destroys us all!*

THE MAPMAKER
CHAPTER SIX

"We have to do something!" said Mr. Smith, pacing back and forth.

"Matt said to stay here until he got back," said Mr. Tickleten. "I'm sure he knows what he's doing."

"Oh yes," replied one of the crew members sarcastically, "leave our lives in the hands of a handyman, that's a great idea."

"You shut up, or I'll have to come over and do it myself!" snapped Mr. Smith. The crewman took one look at Mr. Smith's huge hands and shut his mouth.

"Run! RUN!!!" came a voice from the trees. Out limped Mr. Franklin into the camp, frantically waving his arms.

"What, why?" asked Mr. Smith, running over to help him.

"My word!" cried Mr Tickleten, looking off in the direction of the mountain. "There, on the mountain.....a giant scaled creature, with terribly huge and scary claws and teeth at least as long as me, is rapidly on his winged way here, most likely to devour us! I suggest we escape as fast as we can by whatever means possible!" The others paused for a moment, trying to unpack what he just said. "Incoming dragon, RUN!!!!!"

In a panicked frenzy, they all sprinted as fast as they could for the shore, Mr. Smith with Mr. Franklin slung across his back. Before long, only two hundred feet lay between them and the ships. Then a hundred seventy-five. The dragon quickened his flight. A hundred twenty-five. A hundred. The dragon swooped down and grabbed for Mr. Tickleten, missing him by mere inches. Seventy-five. Fifty.

The sailors who had remained on the ship stood on deck, jumping up and down desperately. Before the others could reach the ship, the terrible dragon swooped past them and shot out rivers of white fire at the *Bella Fawn*. Though they could hear screams from the deck, the steam from the fire hitting the water completely hid both the boat and the dragon from view. Then suddenly, all went silent.

As they watched, afraid of what they might see, the steam cleared. To their utter astonishment and joy, the *Bella Fawn* bobbed happily in the water. The crew members on the boat looked around, blinking in confusion.

"What on Ildathore?"

"Boo!" shouted a voice from behind Mr. Tickleten. The company nearly jumped out of their skin. Behind them stood Matt Baker, grinning at their skittishness.

"My boy, you must never scare a man of my age!" scolded Mr. Tickleten. "You nearly gave me a heart attack!" Then, forgetting to be angry, he laughed. "How did you get away alive?"

"It's a long story," replied Matt, still smiling. One by one the others welcomed him back, until he came face to face with Mr. Franklin. "I am so sorry for everything Mr Frankl..."

"Stop," cut in Mr Franklin. "It's John, remember." Then, he did something that Matt never would have expected. He hugged him, whispered, "I'm sorry about your father," and then quickly pulled away. Matt looked at him questioningly, but he only smiled. Together, the company walked onto the ship.

"What happened!?!?" Mr. Tickleten asked the still quaking sailors.

"I've never seen anything like it!" said the captain. "When that dragon shot fire, I thought we were done for. But, he just shot the flames in a circle around the boat so we couldn't see. I figured he was just playing with us before the kill, but by the time the steam cleared, he was nowhere in sight. Extraordinary!"

***

All that night, rumors filled the boat as to the dragon's odd behavior, but whenever someone asked Matt what had happened, all he would say was that there was no cause to be afraid of the Isle of Dread anymore. Every time Matt and John caught one another's eye, they gave each other strange looks, but always kind ones. It was decided that they would go back to gather more men and supplies before returning. One by one, each of the crew members fell asleep in the cabin as the boat made its way back home, all except Matt. He went up on deck and made his way to the edge of the boat.

"I know you're here, Valley."

Slowly, a huge majestic dragon, scales shining in the moonlight, rose out of the water and rested its gaze on Matt. *Do they know?*

"I think that John has suspicions, but no one else," replied Matt. "Man, when you said you wanted to leave with a bang, you really meant it. You know, you don't have to leave the island for our sake."

A glow came into his eyes, *I want to leave Valinar forever. Let people say that he disappeared from his hoard, never to be seen again. It will suit me just fine.*

"Where will you go?" asked Matt.

Perhaps I'll find a new island, beyond the maps and the watchful eyes of man... A sad look crossed his face, *Perhaps discover the fate of my kin...* They both turned as footsteps thudded in the hold. *I should go.*

"Goodbye, Valley, and good luck," said Matt, looking at him. He smiled, in the way only a dragon can smile, and dove back into the water in a graceful arc, just before John stepped out on deck.

"Matt, are you okay?" asked John. "It's freezing out here."

"Yes," said Matt, "I'm just coming back in." John nodded and stepped back through the door. Matt followed, but right before he went in, he turned. Out, almost farther than the eye could see, Valley rose out of the water, framed by the moon. Matt waved, and though he could never explain how, the creature waved back.

That was the last time Matt saw Valley. It was not, however, his last time on the sea. He continued on at Franklin, Franklin, & Smith as an apprentice and later a business partner once he had become a true sailor. Eventually his skills were noticed among the royal family and he left the company to serve as the admiral of their fleet. He went on many more adventures in his days, most much more significant to the world than this, but he always said that his first was his favorite. Were his stories about speaking to dragons and the conversion of Valley true? Many say no, that no dragon could ever change. Some, however, myself included, believe that with the help of forgiveness, anything is possible.

STORY TWO
FATHERS

FATHERS
CHAPTER 1

Matt Baker sat on the crossbeam of the *Bella Fawn*, pounding a nail into a loose board. On the deck far below him sat John Franklin and Mr. Tickleten, two of his closest friends.

"You know," said Matt with another pound of the hammer, "we could probably get this beam fixed a whole lot quicker if the two of you would climb up here and help me."

"Don't be absurd!" said Mr. Tickleten with a laugh. "That is what young bones like yours are meant for, not old ones like mine." It was true; the little man's hair was almost completely white now, but he was still as jolly as ever.

"So what's your excuse, John?" Matt asked, grinning.

"Hmm..." was his only reply.

"John!" called down Matt. John jumped and looked up. "What are you doing?"

"I'm reading *The Trinity Gazette*."

The Trinity Gazette was the national newspaper for the Trinity Islands where they lived. It was called the Trinity Islands because there were three small islands grouped together, and so the founders had gone with the obvious choice in a name. The island where they were now was called The Isle of Emily (formally known as The Isle of Dread) and was only just starting to be settled, so The Trinity Gazette was pretty much their only option for news.

The Trinity Gazette

STRANGE NEWS FROM TENEBRIS HAS AUTHORITIES ILL AT EASE

After hearing strange news about the happenings in Tenebris, Queen Ella and her officials are beginning to question the island's motives. Though not ready to give an official word on what their next steps are, they have made it clear that they are prepared to do whatever it takes for the good of The Trinity Islands.

WALLACE HOLLINGWOOD FOUND DEAD

After a full investigation into the whereabouts of Admiral Wallace Hollingwood, he along with his crew and his beloved ship, The Shark, were found wrecked against the Rocks of Hearth. His funeral will be held at the palace on the 22nd of this month. All are invited.

TIRED OF UNSIGHTLY NOSE HAIRS?

Try Carter and Jones' Extra Super Duper Scissors, the nose hair clippers of the future.

"It's quite interesting!" said John. "Did you know that the Admiral of Trinity's navy was just found dead?"

"What?" exclaimed Matt. "Throw the paper up to me."

John rolled it up and threw it. It was a good toss, even if Matt had to reach out a ways to catch it. Mr. Tickleten gasped as he did so. "You worry too much!" said Matt with a laugh; then he unrolled the gazette, reading it slowly.

"Wow," said Matt. "I remember seeing Admiral Wallace when I was just a little kid. He was my hero."

"He was a lot of people's hero," responded John. "And you may have a shot at being my hero if you pass the gazette back down."

Matt grinned, "Why don't I just bring it down?" He slid down one of the ropes and landed with a thud next to his friends.

"Are you done with the mast?" asked Mr. Tickleten.

"Oh yeah. The *Bella Fawn* is worth its weight in gold again."

"I have no doubt," commented John. "With how many times it's sunk, it practically *is* its weight in gold. I don't know why we keep repairing it."

Matt smiled "Oh, come on, don't be so heartless. Our first adventure together was in this thing; I could never abandon it."

"You've changed a lot since then, Matt Baker," said Mr. Tickleten, patting him on the back. "Ten years can do a lot in turning a boy into a man."

It was very true, and Matt knew it. Ever since he was

sixteen, he had been a sailing apprentice in the company Franklin, Franklin, & Smith. Now he was twenty-six, and his long scrawny arms had most certainly had time to fill out. Some could call him a dashing young man, with sandy, brown hair and steady blue eyes, but Matt didn't think of himself as dashing. Instead, he hoped that the name 'sailor' could be branded on him for the rest of his life.

Together, the three men left the *Bella Fawn* and returned to the dock. As they did, another kind face greeted them. "Hello, fellas. How's she looking?" asked Mr. Smith, one of the owners of Franklin, Franklin, and Smith.

"Alright," answered Matt, "but did you hear that the Queen's admiral was found dead?"

"Yes, I heard." Then a mischievous twinkle came into his eye. "I have a letter for you, Matt. It's from Queen Ella on Head Island."

Head Island was the most important of the Trinity Islands, where all of the rich people lived and the best universities could be found.

"Queen Ella?" asked Matt surprised. "Why would she write me?"

He tore open the letter and read:

To the person of Matt Baker,

Please come to the palace of your own accord on the night of the twenty second of this month. I have important matters that I wish to speak to you of.

Her Royal Highness,

Queen Ella

"She wants me to come to the palace on the twenty second of this month!"

"Lad, today is the twenty first!" cried Mr. Tickleten in alarm. "What could she ever need in such hastiness of haste?"

"It's obvious what she wants," responded John, trying to hide his wry smile with the gazette.

Matt looked at him curiously. "What is it then?"

"Well, Mr. Tickleten practically said it a minute ago. You've gotten older, Matt. After all, the queen is single." Mr. Smith burst out laughing at this thought, and even Mr. Tickleten couldn't help but chuckle.

"Oh, give it up," said Matt, smiling too. *They knew that although he was a good man, he would be a terrible king.* "When should I set sail to get there on time? An hour or so?"

Mr. Smith nodded, "That seems about right. I would expect you could get there in a day as long as you tack *The Adventurer*'s sail well. It will be faster than the *Bella Fawn*. You best go get your things so you can be off."

Matt grinned and set off to the bunkhouse, a rudely constructed little building in the middle of the uninhabited island where the crew slept. He grabbed his few clothes and his copy of *The Sailor's Prayers to the Creator: Singing, Sailing, and Swabbing, Deluxe Edition.* He put them in his satchel and slung it over his shoulder. Patting one of the bed's three legs *(no one is actually sure what happened to the fourth, but it was not unusual for Matt to wake to the thud of his own body hitting the floor),* he turned and left the bunkhouse to find *The Adventurer.*

Though Matt would never admit it, *The Adventurer* was a much better boat than the *Bella Fawn*. It was small and light, made for one man on a mission of speed. When he reached the place where it was docked, it greeted him like an old friend. He stepped onboard, tacking the sail to catch the most wind possible. He was so consumed by the task that he didn't hear Mr. Tickleten walk up and stand on the dock, watching him.

When he finally did turn around, Mr. Tickleten was smiling at him. "You be careful out there, all right. Don't tip the boat over out in the middle of nowhere."

"Don't worry, I won't!" He stepped back onto the dock and gave the kind little man a hug. "I'll be back soon. Tell the others bye for me."

"Will do," said Mr. Tickleten. "Goodbye."

"Bye!" said Matt, untying the the boat from the dock and sailing off. As the wind sped past him, he remembered the first time he sailed away from this island. Out of habit, he glanced down into the water for any sign of his friend with large wings, emerald scales, and a forgiving heart, but he saw nothing but his own distorted reflection looking back at him. The wind was perfect for a day out on *The Adventurer,* though, and the nice cool water sprayed him as he flew over the waves.

Before sundown, he pulled up to the dock in the capital city of Tamers.

"Good Evening to ya, sir," called a man in his fifties, helping Matt to tie up his boat. "How long will you need the dock for?"

"For now, let's plan for two days," said Matt. "Though it may have to be extended. I'm not sure how long my business here will take."

"Why are you here?" asked the man, helping him out of the boat.

"Honestly, I'm not sure yet. I was summoned by Queen Ella and..."

"So, you're the one!" said the man with a grin, patting Matt on the back. "Could I have your autograph before you leave?" He pulled out a paper and a pencil from his pocket as if he'd just been waiting for him.

"Um, sure..." said Matt, taking them and writing his name. "But, I don't know why you'd want it. What do you mean 'before I leave'?"

"All guests of her majesty go to her personal dock at the palace," he said, taking back the piece of paper with reverence. "I'll lead you there!" Before Matt could protest, the man had already tied *The Adventurer*'s lead rope to another much finer looking vessel and was beckoning him onto the new boat. Matt sighed and stepped on hesitantly. "There we are. Time to set sail!" They set off.

"What's your name?" asked Matt, trying not to feel so nervous.

"Hecter," he answered. "Have you ever seen the palace?"

"Um, no, I can't say I have," said Matt, standing up and adjusting the sail slightly out of habit.

Hecter grinned. "This is going to be fun, then."

As if on cue, he turned the boat around a bend in the shoreline, and what Matt saw took his breath away. Towers after towers after towers! Steeples that rose into the sky and seemed to defy all laws of gravity. Silver rooftops and pillars shimmered in the last light of day. The enormous structure's reflection danced on the rippling water.

"Is that the capital?" asked Matt in astonishment.

"Nope, that's just the palace."

Matt stared as they pulled into the queen's personal dock and pulled the two meager ships up next to huge navy vessels whose masts towered up into the sky beside them. "Welcome to the Palace of Silver Nights," said a well-dressed man on the dock. "You must be Matt Baker."

FATHERS
CHAPTER TWO

Matt sat on a bed (with four legs this time) fit for a king, in a room fit for a king, in a palace that could fit a kingdom! The bedroom that he had slept the night in was huge, with its own fireplace, living room, and an indoor toilet! (He had asked the butler, who had brought him here, where the hole in the toilet went to, but the man had just smiled and advised not to go down to check.) Next to his giant bed, there was a window that looked down on Tamers from the eighth floor. *The eighth floor!* He had sat there watching the city since the sun had risen over the rooftops. Suddenly, there came a knock at the door. "Come in!" said Matt, turning around.

"Um, no need, sir," said a voice on the other side. Matt got the impression that the man thought he might be changing. "Here are the garments you are to wear when you see the queen." A hand came through a little flap at the very bottom of the door and laid a bundle wrapped in velvet cloth on the floor. Matt bent over and picked up the bundle. When he unwrapped it, a sense of childlike delight washed over him. In it were a pair of black pants with several golden designs stitched on them, high stylish brown boots, and a white shirt with frilly cuffs and a collar. He couldn't help but wish that he had some kind of jacket to finish of the look, but he couldn't complain, these were much finer clothes than any he had ever owned before!

Before he put them on, he made sure to shave (the few wispy brown hairs on this chin and upper lip just wouldn't leave him alone these days). Then he dressed and combed back his hair, which is something he often forgot to do. When he was done, he took one last look in the mirror. Mr. Tickleten had been right when he said Matt had changed a lot in the last ten years, but then again, hadn't they all? Mr. Smith was more open to John's ideas these days, John was all around more agreeable, Valley was off having whatever adventure he was having, and Mr. Tickleten was… well, he hadn't changed much.

Matt was just wondering how he would find the queen in this huge palace when there came a knock at the door. He opened it to find the same butler who had met him at the dock the day before. "Are you ready to see her majesty, sir?"

"Yes," Matt said, taking a deep breath, and then added a hasty, "thank you for getting me."

A slight smile played over the man's lips, "You're welcome."

He led Matt through long decorated hallways, up and down elaborate spiralling staircases, and to a large door at the end of a hall. The man gave him one last look and nodded. "Good luck, Mr. Baker." Then, he opened the door.

Matt gasped at the size and splendor of the room in front of him. It was a wonderful throne room, with paintings on the walls and guards lining the pathway to the throne, all standing at attention, none of them looking at him. He walked forward, head high and back straight, until he reached the steps leading to the throne. He had seen many paintings and cameos of Queen Ella, but not one did her justice. She was beautiful, from her golden hair and blue eyes to her light blue dress. Her crown was as silver as the the roof of her palace, but decorated much more beautifully, with golden flowers woven into it.

Matt bowed low. Queen Ella smiled and nodded, indicating he should rise. "Welcome, Mr. Baker. I hope that you have found my home accommodating."

Matt marveled that, even though she was the queen and nearly twice his age, she called him 'Mister' "I have never slept in a better bed, but if I may be so blunt: why am I here?"

Queen Ella laughed softly. "I was told you were a down-to-earth man." Matt blushed. "I brought you here to ask you a question. I am sure that you heard of the death of Admiral Wallace Hollingwood."

"It is a terrible loss," he replied, as was custom when someone died, though he truly meant it.

"Yes, it is." A sad look came over the queen's face. "Step forward, gentlemen!" Out of nowhere (at least that is what it seemed like to Matt), a group of sailors came and stood next to the throne. One man in particular caught Matt's eye. He was a tall man, with black hair that came down to his shoulders and eyes so dark that one could barely see where the pupil ended and the colored part began. Matt smiled at him; the man only stared back coldly.

"These men," said the queen, "are some of the finest sailors I have ever known. They sailed under the admiral's right hand man, but with the admiral dead, and his right hand man retiring, they have no leader." The man with dark eyes didn't once take his gaze off Matt as she spoke.

Matt took a step back. "Your highness, correct me if I'm wrong, but are you asking me to be the new admiral's right hand man?"

Queen Ella smiled. "Not at all, I'm asking you to be the admiral."

Matt's jaw dropped. "I have heard nothing but praise about your sailing abilities," the queen continued, "but also about your leadership. If all I have heard is true, you are just the man I need."

Matt didn't even have to think about his answer; it had been hammered into him ever since he was a small child. He put his hand to his heart and stood a bit straighter as national pride flowed through his veins. "Your highness, if I, your loyal subject, can at all offer my service to you and my beloved Trinity, let nothing but death or the Creator's hand hinder me."

The queen nodded soberly. It was a grave thing to repeat this age-old oath. She pulled out from behind her a red admiral's jacket, complete with the signs of office and matching red hat with a plume sticking out of it. She stood and came down off of her platform. Then she put the coat on his shoulders, and placed the hat on his head. "Your ship sails in two hours, Admiral Baker."

***

Nearly two hours later, Matt stood on the queen's dock next to the huge ship that only yesterday he had marveled at, preparing to set sail. In his hand was a letter to Mr. Tickleten and the rest of his friends on The Isle of Emily, explaining what had happened and promising to come and visit them as soon as he could. He looked around trying to find someone in the hustle and bustle of the dock. "Hey, can anyone a letter for me?" he asked waving it above his head.

"I could mail it for you; I probably know the address already."

Matt turned around to see Mr. Tickleten along with John and Mr. Smith standing behind him. "Guys!" he said, hurrying towards them. "How did you know to come? And how did you get here?"

"Last night, they sent us a message to let us know what was going on, and we knew you would say yes," said Mr. Smith, patting him on the back. "As for how we got here, we took the *Bella Fawn.*"

"You look so spiffy in the uniform!" said Mr. Tickleten, grinning at him.

Matt looked down at his coat and laughed. "Maybe a bit!" He looked from face to face, not wanting to say what he knew he had to. "Admirals aren't allowed to work for other businesses. I can't be part of Franklin, Franklin, and Smith anymore." He hung his head and waited for the disappointment, but it never came.

Instead, they laughed. "My boy," said Mr. Tickleten, "we didn't come because we were angry or we wanted to stop you... We wanted to see you off! This is a great opportunity for you. Heaven knows I'll miss you, but I know you'll make a magnificent admiral." The two others nodded in agreement.

Matt grinned harder than he ever had before. They had come to see HIM! They weren't just his employers, they were family. "Thank you for coming to see me!" said Matt.

"Well, I must admit, we had an ulterior motive," said John Franklin. Matt cocked his head. "We wanted to give you a gift to remember us by."

Matt smiled. He knew that now that he was the admiral, he could buy pretty much anything they could afford on his own, but he was prepared to treasure whatever it was dearly. "What is it?"

"It's over there," said Mr. Tickleten, pointing at the dock.

Matt looked. The only thing that looked remotely familiar was the *Bella Fawn*. "Is it on the *Bella Fawn*?"

The men laughed. "No, lad," said Mr. Smith. "It isn't on the *Bella Fawn*. It IS the *Bella Fawn*."

Matt stared in shock. "The *Bella Fawn*?"

"Yes, Matt," said Mr. Tickleten. "We know how much it means to you, and we want you to have it."

"Now you can be the one to fix it next time it sinks," mumbled John Franklin.

Matt had to push down the lump in his throat. No matter what he said, they would never know how much this meant to him. He shook hands with Mr. Smith, felt a pat on the back from John, and turned to Mr. Tickleten. There was something almost fatherly in his gaze, like a mix between love, pride, and heartache. Matt bent down and hugged the little man so long that when they let go, they were nearly out of breath. "Good luck, Matt," he said, wiping away a tear. "May the Creator protect you."

"Thanks," said Matt. Then turning for the ship, he said, "I'll be back!"

He walked up onto the deck of *The Steed* with an air of someone who was going on an adventure. Well, he didn't know exactly where he was going, but that didn't surprise him. He'd read many books about the admirals of Trinity. Royalty didn't just tell you what your mission was; no, after all, what if someone was listening and the word got out? Instead, admirals were given sealed envelopes with instructions inside that they were only allowed to open once they got out of sight from land. Matt patted the envelope in his pocket as the crew worked to raise the sail.

He walked up the steps to the poop deck where the steering wheel stood and grasped it with both of his hands. Then, as the wind picked up, *The Steed* pulled away from the dock. As it did, Matt looked back at the shore where Mr. Tickleten stood, waving. At the sight of him, a memory surfaced - his father, walking away from him as he sat on the steps of what he later learned was an orphanage. His dad had stopped when he was almost out of sight and turned, framed by the setting sun. He had waved, too, but it was a very different kind of father who waved to him now. Matt waved back.

The wind was in *The Steed's* sails, and it seemed that nothing in the world could stop her now. The man with the dark eyes came and stood beside him as he steered. "So, you're the admiral now," he said in a low voice. "I was in line to take the admiral's place before you came around."

"I'm sure you were." Matt looked over at him. So it was true. It really was him. The man's dark eyes searched him in just the same way they had several years before.

"How long have you been sailing?" asked the man.

"Ten years," answered Matt.

"Ten years?" the man repeated, obviously not impressed. "I've been doing it since I could reach the steering wheel on my father's ship."

"I don't doubt it," said Matt, smiling at the befuddled look on the man's face. Matt glanced back in the direction they had come from. The land was out of sight. "Tell you what," he said. "since you obviously know how to steer well, you take the wheel while I speak to the navigator for a minute." He stepped away and watched the man scowl before taking the wheel. Some people were just harder to make friends with than others.

Matt stepped down onto the lower deck. "Who here is the navigator?"

A thin man wearing a pair of glasses with a book under his arm stepped forward."I am, Admiral Baker. Navigator James Lend at your service."

Matt smiled. "Would you mind joining me in my quarters while I take a look at what this mission is all about?"

James smiled back like a child receiving a long awaited pleasure. "Yes, sir!"

Together they went into the captain's quarters, or the admiral's quarters in this case, and sat down at a table. Matt looked over at the other man, curiously. "What's your story, James? Have you always been a navigator?" asked Matt, pulling the envelope out of his pocket and taking off his plumed hat.

"Oh no!" said the man, pushing his glasses further up his nose. "I used to be a mapmaker, but it seems that most of the places to be mapped these days are all inland, and I know I don't look it, but I'm a sailor at heart."

He truly didn't look it with his light red curls and scrawny arms, but Matt didn't say as much. "A mapmaker, huh? I was a mapmaker once." James looked at him curiously, but Matt just shook his head. "It would take too long to explain, but trust me, I wasn't a good one." He broke the seal on the envelope and pulled out a handwritten letter:

Dear Admiral,

You might have read in the paper that we have recently heard disturbing news from Tenebris. Some say that a dark lord is rising to power; others say nay. Either way, we must do something to protect ourselves. Although it hurts my pride to do it, I am sending you to the Isle of Vanya to speak to King Rhonder about signing a treaty with us. If he agrees, we are strengthened; if he disagrees, then let us hope that my fears will never come true, either for us nor our descendants. He is one of the only kings we are still on good terms with (my apologies); let us pray to the Creator that he helps us.

Her Royal Highness,
The Queen

Matt had not read the letter out loud, of course. James

watched nervously as he read. He slowly folded it up and put it back in his pocket. So this would be his first mission, meeting with a random king about an alliance. Sounded exhilarating!

"James," he said, "map out a course to the Isle of Vanya!"

FATHERS
CHAPTER THREE

That night, the crew brought two large metal fire pits on deck and roasted fish over them. When Matt sat down, he noticed with dismay that the entire crew crowded around the other fire, all except James, who followed Matt to his seat like a loyal puppy.

Matt saw the man with dark eyes sitting in the middle of the other group. "Who is that man?" he asked James once their fish were cooked.

"That's Riggins," James said, taking another bite of fish. "He's sort of the ring leader on this ship. We were all stunned when he didn't become admiral. After all, he's six years older than you and has a lot more experience. No offense."

"None taken," answered Matt. "So his name is really Riggins? That's kind of odd, don't you think?"

"Oh, no! I have no idea what his real name is. He

earned that nickname long before I joined. It started out as Riggings because he could climb up the riggings of a boat faster than anyone else. Over time, it morphed into Riggins."

"I see," Matt said as he watched Riggins eat. Most sailors he could win over pretty easily by just being friendly, but Riggins seemed deeper than that. Matt figured he could still work on him, but when Riggins looked up and met his glance with an icy stare, he wasn't so sure.

That night, Matt slept in his own room on the ship. He couldn't help but miss the snores of his fellows back at the bunkhouse on the Isle of Emily. There he had been rallied around; here he was shunned and avoided. He woke before dawn and went up on deck to find the sailor who was supposed to be steering asleep. He sighed, took up is spot behind the wheel, and sailed ahead.

The next five weeks continued in the same way. Most of the time, when Matt told someone what to do, they just stood there until Matt went and did it himself. At night, he was avoided by all except James.

Finally, one afternoon, they spotted land off in the distance. "There it is!" cried James in excitement. "Vanya!"

"Where are we on the map?" asked Matt, jogging over to him.

"You see this?" James asked, pointing to an island. "This one is Vanya, the one that looks like a heart."

"Yes... with the river running down the middle, it looks more like a broken heart."

James smiled. "There are many stories that tell that tale,

but that's beside the point. We are here at the bottom of the heart, where the river touches the sea."

"So if we sail up the river, then it will take us right into the heart of Vanya?"

"In more ways than one," James said, laughing.

"Then that's where we go!" said Matt, making his way to the wheel. When he reached it, he took it in his hands and pulled to the left, steering the ship straight for the river.

Riggins came up behind him and shook his head. "This isn't a good idea. I think that we should..."

"No one asked your opinion, Riggins!" It came out more harshly than he had meant it to, but his treatment over the last few days had really been getting on his nerves. Riggins didn't reply.

They entered the river slowly, and before long, Matt was beginning to question his idea. The shore on both sides was unnaturally silent and not at all like the Isle of Dread had been with chirping birds and skittering mice. No, there was only complete and utter silence. Matt didn't like it, and yet, in a way, he loved it. He sensed that there was something drawing him further in. It felt like they had entered an abandoned paradise that both shunned and welcomed them at the same time. It was the strangest, most confusing, feeling he had ever had. As they sailed on, it felt as if the huge hulking war ship was somehow trespassing in sacred waters. Eventually, he felt so wrong sailing up the river that he laid anchor to continue on foot. He didn't explain it to his men but instead told Riggins and three others to come with him while the rest minded the boat.

It feels like a lost place, thought Matt, *but one that shouldn't be found.* He could tell that the others had sensed it, too.

Together, the five men rounded a bend in the river and came into a clearing. Matt gasped at what he saw. Far off on their side of the river, seven scarlet towers rose into the sky, silhouetted by the sun. The fiery rays seemed to lick at them lovingly. On the other side of the river was a fortress, so old that Matt thought it could have stood since the beginning of time. It's sapphire walls were crumbling and caved in with vines and flowers growing from them. There was a little cottage on the other side of the clearing, and Matt wondered if the occupant would be home and able to answer a few questions about this strange place. Just as he was about to head towards it, Riggins stopped in his tracks, staring off over the river. Matt looked, too. On the horizon was a line of men, all of them wearing flowing blue, green, and indigo garments. One man in blue stepped forward, and two catapults were rolled up on either side of him. Then, twenty men in indigo raised their arms, and light swirled around them. When the light faded, eagles, dragons, and other winged creatures swarmed over the heads of the men who had called them into being.

"Gifteds," Matt breathed.

Gifteds were special men and women who the Creator had given incredible powers.

The Trinity Islands had always prided themselves on being powerful without the help of gifteds, but to see such power unleashed was breathtaking all the same.

The man in blue stood stock still between the two catapults. He stared above the heads of Matt and his crew. Matt looked behind him and saw another line of men that had formed without him noticing. Then, the man dressed in blue raised his fist and shouted in a booming voice. The catapults on either side of him fired on cue, and huge stones whizzed over the river and smashed into the line of people on the other side. Matt realized with sudden horror that they had walked right into the middle of a war zone.

"Get down!" he shouted. The five men hit the ground as chaos erupted around them. Boulders fell down around them. Water sprayed. Dust filled the air and momentarily blinded them. Terrible screeches, roars, and cries split the air as the winged creatures flew over the water and attacked. After about ten minutes - though it felt like an eternity - the chaos stopped, the dust cleared, the clouds lifted, and the two armies were gone.

Matt rose shakily to his feet. "Is everyone alright?" The three men nodded and stood slowly.

Matt reached down to help Riggins up, but the man swatted his hand away, "Nobody asked for your help."

Matt's cheeks flushed red. "Right..." he said, dusting himself off. "Well, that was an experience." One of the men chuckled; Riggins did not.

Suddenly, a wail rang out, and they looked around in confusion. Matt was the first to spot a little girl sobbing outside the cottage. The hut had been crushed by a large boulder during the battle. Without knowing how much those next few minutes would change his life forever, Matt ran towards the girl.

When he reached her, the poor thing, no more than three, buried her face in his coat. He patted her unsual gray hair gently and ducked into the now broken door of the cottage. There on the floor, her legs smashed underneath the fallen roof, lay a woman, in a pool of her own blood. Another girl, with the same gray hair as the first, only about seven, sat next to the woman, her face streaked with tears. Matt bent down close to the dying woman's face. She was still gasping for breath, but it was clear to see there was nothing he could do.

"Ta... take..." struggled the woman between painful breaths.

"Take?" repeated Matt, leaning in close.

"Take them to their father," the woman said, clutching his arm with her shaking hand. "Promise me that they'll be cared for! Promise me!" Tears streamed down her cheeks.

The sight broke Matt's heart. He took her hand in his and gave it a gentle squeeze. "I promise you."

Her grip loosened as he said it. In later years, he liked to think that those were the last words she heard, that she died knowing her daughters would be safe. He had to lead the older girl away from her mother's side, her eyes still staring at the limp body that only seconds ago had been alive. When they came out, the younger one tried to go in, but Matt stopped her. No child should ever see a sight like that. He picked her up, and she cried into his shoulder. When he turned back to the older girl, she was staring at the cottage in a daze.

"Staying here won't bring her back," Matt said softly, stroking her long gray hair. The seven-year-old looked up at him with her remarkable lavender eyes. He knew there was nothing in the world that could erase what they had seen.

Matt's four companions didn't say a word when he

returned from the house with two little girls and a blood stained coat. They could see in his face what had happened. By the time the got back to the ship, the smaller girl had cried away all of her tears, and the other was nearly asleep on her feet as the light of day faded. Matt took them to his quarters.

"You can sleep here tonight," he said, for there was nothing else to say.

Once he left them alone, the older girl wrapped her arms around her little sister. "It's okay, Lily," she whispered. Lily looked up, and when their eyes met, they were like reflections of each other, lavender eyes and long gray hair. But Lily noticed there was something different, something broken about her older sister that hadn't been there before.

"What will happen to us, Helen? Who are these men?" Lily asked softly.

"Pirates," said Helen, a chill running up her spine.

"Pirates?" Lily scooted closer to her.

"Yes, pirates," said Helen. "Mother told me all about them. We mustn't say anything, Lily, do you hear? Not a word. Mother said that girls who don't speak have a better chance of being bought by some nice man when the pirates sell them."

"But I don't wanna to be sold, Helen. I wanna go home," said Lily, yawning. "Don't you wanna go home?"

Helen didn't answer for so long that by the time she said something, Lily was already asleep, "We can't go back to mother; she's gone now. And if we go to dad," she paused, "I might get him in trouble again." When she fell asleep, her dreams were filled with high curtained windows, a veiled woman on the street, and blood, lots and lots of blood.

***

As Matt left the two girls, he heard several members of this crew murmuring behind him. "Great, now we're stuck babysitting, and the admiral will stink up our sleeping quarters tonight."

It was getting late by that time, and the stars were shining overhead. No one brought out supper; no one seemed to have an appetite. Matt stationed himself behind the wheel of the ship and watched the rest of the crew go down to their bunks one by one. He had decided to lead *The Steed* back out of the river the way they had come. There seemed nothing else to do.

When he was finally alone, he looked up at the stars. There were so many of them up there, and every one had been made by the Creator. "Help me," he said quietly. "I don't know what to do. I can't abandon either of my promises. I can't not do what I was sent here to do, but I must find the father of those two girls. None of my crew will listen to me. I've made a mess out of things, Creator. Please, just tell me where to go!"

Nothing.

Matt hung his head. What had he been expecting, some kind of sign?

The Steed glided out into the open water. Then, without warning the wind changed. The sail billowed out further than Matt had ever seen before. He looked at the trees on the bank, but not a single one swayed. Then he looked back up at the sail. With sudden resolution, he pulled his hands off the steering wheel and watched in awe as it began to move on its own. The ship turned right and sailed along the coast.

Matt couldn't help it: he grinned. "By George! I didn't know that the Creator was a sailor." As if in answer, a large clump of something white and squishy landed on his arm. A seagull cawed at him. Matt glanced up at the sky sheepishly. "Sorry."

FATHERS
CHAPTER FOUR

When the men came on deck the next morning, a grinning Matt sat near the wheel, which was still turning itself. Throughout the night, *The Steed* had been guided by an invisible force around every large rock and shallow bit of water. Riggins didn't say anything when he saw what was happening. He just stared like a man afraid he was going mad.

By noon, the smaller of the two girls gently pushed open the door and crept out of the captain's quarters. She came up on deck and watched, wide eyed with wonder, as the steering wheel moved on its own. Matt walked over and knelt down beside her.

"Do you like the wheel, princess?" The girl nodded, not taking her eyes from it. Her brown dress, which reached down to her ankles, was torn and tattered at the bottom. "What's your name?" he asked. The little girl shook her head. "Are you not talking to me?" She nodded. He stuck out his bottom lip and made a ridiculously pathetic face. She smiled at him.

"How old are you?" asked Matt, picking her up and setting her on his lap. He held out one finger, then another. "One? Two?" The little girl pulled her eyebrows down low and shook her head hard. Then she held up three fingers. "Three!" Matt said in playful astonishment. She hid her smile behind her hands. "Three is a really good age! Much better than one or two." She nodded sincerely.

That afternoon, Matt showed her around the boat, and everything seemed to fascinate her. In the crow's nest, she stared out over the sea like she had never seen such a wonderful sight. When Matt asked her where her sister was, the little girl lay down on the ground and closed her eyes. Sleeping, then. Matt half wanted to wake her up; who knew what terrible dreams she was having after the night before? But he didn't want to scare her.

When supper time came, the boat was still steering itself, and the older girl (her sister had signed she was seven) still hadn't come out yet. There were still only two men at Matt's fire, but this time he had a little girl on his lap. Matt was just trying to figure out where they were when a loud splash caught his attention. Matt and Riggins jumped to their feet at the same time and ran toward the sound. They reached it just in time to hear the chain go taut as the anchor hit the ocean floor. Matt looked in wonder from the chain to the place the anchor had been sitting only moments ago. What was the world coming to when boats steered themselves and anchors jumped overboard? He caught Riggins's eye and smiled. "Would you like to join me?"

Riggins said nothing but followed him to one of the row boats. Just as they were about to step in, Matt paused, "We should take the girls."

Riggins looked at him, incredulously. "Great idea, we take the two most vulnerable people in our crew down a possibly dangerous path in the middle of the night."

"I just have a feeling that we should," Matt said. Riggins scoffed at this but made no move to stop him when he went to fetch them.When Matt reached the little girl, he got down on his knees in front of her. "Would you like to come with us, princess?" She nodded. He then stepped over to the door of the captain's quarters and opened it softly. There was the older sister, curled up on a bed which was much too big for her, sleeping peacefully. He felt guilty taking her, but every time he considered not doing it, the same nudge he felt earlier came to him. He picked her up, wrapped her in a blanket, and walked out into the night air. The girl's little sister looked at him questioningly, but he only smiled at her.

So the little row boat set out from *The Steed,* filled with an admiral, his first mate, and two little girls, one of them fast asleep. When they got to the little dock, they tied up the row boat and climbed out. Matt led them down the path, still carrying the child in his arms.

"This is a stupid idea," Riggins said softly. "We don't even know where this path is going. It might lead us right off a cliff."

"It won't," answered Matt, though he had been thinking exactly the same thing.

After a few minutes, they saw a man walking across the path from one side of woods to another. "Hey!" said Matt, giving the girl to Riggins and running towards the man. "Hey, stop!"

Stopping, the man turned to look at him, or, at least, Matt was pretty sure he was looking at him. He had his brown cap pulled down so low that Matt couldn't see his eyes. "What do you ask of me, my lord?" asked the man, bowing so low that his hat nearly fell off.

It took a few seconds to get past the odd greeting. "Where does this path lead?"

"It leads to The Library, my lord," he answered. "Surely you have heard of it. It is run by Silas Evans."

"A library?" asked Matt, befuddled.

"Not a library, my lord. *The Library*. The librarian keeps accounts of every king, every court case, every birth, and every execution that has ever occured in the entire kingdom of Nasheot!"

"Every birth?" said Matt, satisfied. "So if that's true, then he would have family records for say, a lost child?"

"Indeed, my lord!" During the entire conversation, the man had remained bowed. "Now if you please, my lord, I must be going." He shrunk back a bit, as if he were afraid of being struck for saying so.

"Umm… yes, yes of course. I'm sorry for keeping you."

The man rose and bowed three more times before running off into the woods. When Matt rejoined the little group, Riggins looked at him questioningly.

"Down this road is a place that keeps family records," Matt said with a sly smile. Riggins just rolled his eyes and gave the girl back to Matt.

Before long, they came upon a large mansion. It was at least five stories tall, and it looked as if it had been standing there since the beginning of time. Huge oak beams ran horizontally and vertically between patches of brick. Vines crept up the sides and corners of the building, and a candle flickered behind every window. Dozens of sunflowers lined the path leading to the door, and the little girl picked a seed out of one of them.

"Are you going to eat it?" asked Matt, smiling at her. She shook her head solemnly. Lovingly, she put the seed in a little ditch, and covered it with a few inches of dirt. She spoke to it softly, lovingly, and slowly a tiny sprout poked up out of the ground. When she whispered, several birds flew down beside her, completely unafraid, and a rabbit hopped out of a bush nearby and cuddled up to her leg.

"A gifted," Riggins said quietly. "Let's be glad none of the rest of the crew are here. Trinitads don't generally like gifteds."

"And you?" asked Matt, nervously.

"To me, she's just a little girl, but many of my friends wouldn't feel the same way. What about you?"

"To me..." Matt didn't know how to answer. He wanted to say she was just a little girl, but she was more than that. "I don't think badly of her because she's a gifted, if that's what you mean." Riggins didn't question his words. "What I want to know now is... is her sister a gifted, too?"

Matt looked down at the sleeping girl in his arms. Gazing into her face, so peaceful and still, it didn't seem likely, but who could say? Gifts were said to run in families.

"No time to think about that now," said Riggins, pulling Matt out of his thoughts. They had reached the door, and Matt hadn't even noticed. Without giving him time to second guess himself, Riggins knocked. For a second, nothing happened. Then a young man, no older than eighteen, opened the door.

"My lord!" said the man, bowing suddenly. "What an honor to have you here!"

"Lord?" asked Matt. "There aren't any lords here."

The man raised his head slightly and bowed again without warning. "Do not taunt me, my lord. I can see it in your eyes."

Riggins rolled his eyes and glanced over at Matt. "What? You think he's a lord because he has blue eyes?"

"All of those with eyes of blue are lords and gifteds of this kingdom of Nasheot," said the man.

Matt put his hands on the man's shoulders, and he straightened a bit. "I'm not sure how it is here on Vanya, but where I come from, any average Joe can have blue eyes."

The man finally stood up straight. He stared at Matt's eyes like they were something from another planet. "Are you the head librarian here?" asked Matt.

The man shook his head hesitantly, still staring at Matt's eyes. "Me, my lord? Nay. I am simply here to let in our most honored visitors, such as yourself."

"Then why do you keep us waiting at the door so long?" asked Riggins, annoyed as usual.

The man blushed. "My deepest apologies, my lord. Come in, and I will take you to 'the husher'."

"The husher?" asked Matt.

"Yes, that is what we call Silas Evans, the head librarian."

"Oh, I get it. Let me guess, if you make noise in the library, he'll hush you, right?" said Matt, grinning. Not even a flicker of amusement crossed the young man's face. Matt cleared his throat awkwardly.

"Good going, Admiral. You've already offended our host," muttered Riggins under his breath.

"This way to his office, my lord," said the young man, glancing at the two girls. "They can't go in his office, though; he isn't fond of children."

"Then where will they go?" asked Matt.

"Leave them here," the man said, bending down to the younger one. "Would you like to see some books with big pretty pictures?" She nodded, smiling. "Here," said the man, taking a book off of the shelf. "This one has pictures of flowers in it. Do you like flowers?" Her eyes widened as she took the book from him and sat down on the ground to look at it.

"See, they'll be fine. You can just set the sleeping one here," the man said, pointing to a comfortable-looking armchair.

Matt gently put her down, the blanket still wrapped around her, and then stood tall. "Alright, now, take us to the husher."

The man nodded and led them to an old door with a brass knob that shone in the lamplight. He knocked softly. "Oh, what do you want now?" called an annoyed voice on the other side.

"Some men are here to see you."

"Well, tell them to go away. I'm busy!"

"But sir, they aren't from Vanya! They're foreigners."

Instantly, the door opened, and a large, roly-poly man stood on the other side. Although he wasn't old, the man's hair was straight and white, his features rounded, and his eyes gray.

"Oh, forgive me, sirs!" he said, without bowing or looking at Matt's eyes, and then beckoned them into his study. It was a rather messy place. Books littered the shelves, the desk, and towered in stacks on the floor. "I'm sorry it's such a wreck, but I wasn't expecting visitors. It isn't often that people come here from other parts, and when they do, I typically like to have things a little more presentable. My name is Silas."

"No worries. I'm Matt," he said smiling.

For the first time, Silas looked him up and down and gasped as he noticed the admiral's emblem on his coat. He gulped hard. "Henry," he said quietly, "leave us, and close the door behind you." The man obeyed.

Silas sunk into an armchair with a sigh but didn't take

his eyes off of Matt's jacket.

Matt cleared his throat. "I see you've noticed that I am the admiral of Trinity." Silas only nodded. "We came to Vanya because we have some official business to conduct with your king. Could you tell us where to find him?"

Silas sighed, and Matt could see his hand shaking a bit. "Vanya doesn't have a king," he said softly.

"Yes, it does. His name is King R-"

"Rhonder," said Silas, his voice was hoarse. "Admiral, please forgive me. I am King Rhonder."

FATHERS
CHAPTER FIVE

"You are King Rhonder?" asked Matt, confused.

"Yes," said Silas. "I'm King Rhonder."

"Impossible," said Riggins under his breath. "King Rhonder is a king of splendor, not a roly-poly librarian."

Matt gave him a warning glance, then turned back to Silas. "Please, explain."

Silas put his face in his hands. "There never was a King Rhonder! Vanya doesn't have a king. I wrote the letters to Trinity." His voice was barely audible, but Matt listened carefully to every word. "My mother was from Trinity. She always told me that Trinity was a land where mothers let their children walk through the streets without fear, a place where the only magic in sight was the way the birds sing and crickets chirp. I always dreamt of a place like that. I may live in Vanya, but I don't like it. All the people do now is hate; they fight long endless wars, brother against brother and father against son."

"Why are they fighting?" asked Matt.

"It isn't something that I feel right telling you, you being a foreigner. It's more of a family matter, but even an old librarian like me can see that it has gotten out of hand! If these power-hungry people knew that Trinity had a huge navy that could be used in this accursed war, I hate to think what might happen to my mother's homeland. A few years ago, I was brought a box of old books for my collection, and stuck inside one of the pages was a letter from the queen of Trinity. The queen of Trinity! It said that she would like to begin friendly correspondence with us. At the end, she said that if we did not reply soon, then they would send their fleet to make the message 'more clear'. I...I panicked. I wrote a letter and made it look as official as possible, I said that we would be pleased to do that. When it came time to sign a name, I knew I couldn't sign my own, so I made one up - King Rhonder. I thought that was the end of it, but then another letter came, and I was cornered into responding. Letters kept coming and coming, and I knew that I had ridden the waves too long to get out of it." Silas was shaking again, so hard that his glasses nearly fell off his face. "Please, punish me by the laws of your country for my crime, but don't hurt my family or my servants. They know nothing of this!"

"Your family?" asked Matt quietly. "You have children?"

"Yes," said Silas. "Two boys, one four and the other six."

An image came into Matt's mind - himself, as a young boy, sitting on the orphanage steps, watching his father walk off into the distance. He hadn't been scared then; he had known that his dad would come back soon. How wrong he'd been! Then the picture changed. Suddenly, there were two boys on the steps, not one. They watched silently as their father was taken away by a man in an admiral's coat, his sandy brown hair blowing in the wind.

"Sir, send me back down to the boat," said Riggins, glaring at him. "With the help of a few more crew members, we can have a gallows ready by sunrise." Silas put his hand to his neck.

"No," said Matt slowly. "No, I must think." He put his hand to his mouth, as he did often when deep in thought, and paced up and down the room. Then he stopped suddenly. "Silas, do you have paper and something to write with?"

"Yes, Admiral," said Silas, his hand not leaving his neck.

"Stop clutching yourself, or you might choke! Now get the things to write with." Silas scrambled to the table and snatched up a pen and some paper.

"What are you doing, Matt," said Riggins coldly.

Matt ignored him. "Are you ready, Silas?" The quivering man nodded. "Write down what I say. 'Dear most exalted Queen Ella, Greetings from Vanya. My name is Silas..'"

Silas's pen dropped. "But, Admiral..."

"Keep writing!" said Matt, and Silas picked the pen back up. Matt continued, "My name is Silas, head advisor and scribe to King Rhonder. You may find my handwriting familiar for it was through my hand that he sent his wishes." Riggins was about to cut in, but Matt didn't give him a chance. "I regret to have to be the bearer of bad news, but just recently, so recently that it feels like scarce seconds ago, King Rhonder met an untimely end." Matt pulled his letter from the queen out of his pocket and held it over one of the lamps. The paper caught immediately and within a few seconds the whole thing was ablaze. Soon it was nothing more than ashes and a tiny puddle of wax from the royal seal. "His home burned to the ground. He shall never be heard from again, I'm afraid." Silas stared at the little puddle in disbelief but never stopped writing. "The country has been in turmoil ever since. There are many things that must be tended to; some would call them family issues. At this point, we aren't able to enter into an alliance, though I hope that all of your troubles may quickly come to an end and your enemies gravel at your feet. I hereby end this correspondence until we are strong enough to be of use to you. Signed, your humble servant, Silas."

Silas looked like a man who had risen from the dead. Riggins looked like a dejected dog. "Admiral, the law is the law. I cannot allow you to..."

"Yes, the law is the law, and here I am the highest form of Trinity law! You will not command me, Riggins! Now leave us!" The words stung his own mouth as he said them, but Riggins left them, dutifully.

"Admiral," whispered Silas. "How can I repay you for this?"

Matt smiled, "You know, there might be one thing you can do."

"Name it!" cried Silas, relief and joy dancing every his features.

"I was told you keep family records. I have two young girls with me that I found. Their mother is dead, but their father is not. They won't speak to me. I think they're still afraid of me, but I have to take them to their father."

"Well, it sounds like a difficult challenge, but the trickier the challenge, the better the reward," said Silas, rubbing his hands together excitely. "Tell me everything you know about them. How do they look? In this country, looks are the easiest way to narrow it down. There are six great houses on this island. If they are from the family of one of the great houses, unlikely as it is, they will have the eye color of that house. I have no doubt you got some rather strange reactions from people on your way here. This territory is under the kingdom of Nasheot, and all of the gifteds of Nasheot have blue eyes. You must have given people quite a start, but I know better. You have brown hair, so it's obvious you are a foreigner. You see, in Vanya, you either have white hair or black hair. All the people on this side of the river have white, and all on the other have black, don't ask me why."

"But that can't be true," cut in Matt. "The girls don't have white or black hair."

"Really!" said Silas, obviously intrigued. "What colored hair do they have?"

"Gray."

"GRAY!!!!! What is their eye color?"

"Um, violet or something like that."

"Lavender perhaps?" asked Silas, his eyes twinkling.

"Probably, why?"

"Because of a very sad story that happened here not many years ago," said Silas. "As you might have figured out by now, all of the people on this side of the river have white hair, and on the other there are only black-haired people. It's said that a young man, one of the gifteds of Nasheot, began crossing over the river in secret just to see what was there. He met a beautiful young lady who was a gifted from the kingdom of Tarnor, just across the river from here. They fell madly in love, and he took her into his home. She stayed inside nearly all day to hide her identity, and when she left, she wore a veil to hide her scarlet eyes and conceal her identity. The two of them had a child, a girl, with lavender eyes and gray hair, a perfect mix between the two of them. But when the girl turned four, she saw her mother out on the road. She didn't want to stay inside anymore; she wanted to go out like her mother could, but she forgot her veil. She and her mother were discovered and thrown into the river. They washed up on the bank here. Though they were still in the kingdom of Nasheot, the people let her build a little hut on the beach to live in. After that, she gave birth to another child, all alone on the bank of the river, another girl with the same gray hair and lavender eyes as her sister. They made a little home on the bank. I see it from time to time when I pass by. It's a dangerous place to be, right between the two fighting peoples."

"Yes, it was," said Matt quietly. "In a recent battle, a boulder crushed it. The mother was inside."

"Did she have white hair and scarlet eyes?"

"Yes, though by the time I reached her, most of her hair was dyed red with blood." He didn't say anything for a while. "Was the father ever found?"

"No," said Silas. "No one ever discovered who the father was."

"So we're right back to where we started,' said Matt, sighing.

***

Helen slept. Her dreams tossed and turned from one thing to another. Finally, she was sick of it. "Tommy!" she yelled at her dream. "Stop it!" The dream went black as it typically did when she addressed it. She had first learned how to command her dreams years ago. Her mother had told her to name the dream itself so that it could know when she called it, and as a very little girl, she had decided on the name Tommy. "Tommy," she said again. "I've had enough of this! I am Helen. You know that! Stop carrying me around! This has gone on long enough!" She loved how she sounded in her dreams, so brave, so loud, so sure of herself, everything that she wasn't in real life. "I'm tired of all of these shadows, these fleeting flickers. Show me my father!" It obeyed. He was standing in a road, talking to someone she didn't know. His blue eyes were filled with all of the kindness of her memories. She watched him for a long time. Then, finally, "Tommy, show me my mother." There was some resistance to this. "Show me my mother!" Reluctantly, it obeyed. In the dark, she could barely see the body lying on the ground. The blood around her had gone brown. Her face looked… "Tommy," whispered Helen. "Take me away from here." It swept her away like the little cottage had never existed. "Show me the pirate!" she demanded. Nothing happened. "Tommy, show me the pirates who took me and my sister away!" Still nothing, but it wasn't being disobedient. She knew that. It was almost as if her dream were confused. "Show me the man who took me and my sister!" This time, there was no pushback. The man with the fancy coat was standing in a small room where a lamp flickered uneasily. Books littered the room. Another man, a bigger one that Helen had never seen before, was sitting in an armchair.

"I don't know how to help you, Admiral," said the bigger man. "I don't know who their father might be."

The man in the fancy coat sighed, "You don't understand. Their mother made me promise; I have to find their father! One way or another, I have to find him!"

Find her father? They really wanted to find her father. No matter how unruly her dreams had been before, they had never lied to her. "Tommy, let me go." Her dreams held her tighter as they always did when she had played around with them too long. "Tommy, I promise I'll come back, but I've been here too long already. Let me go."

Helen opened her eyes. She was wrapped up in a blanket in a comfortable armchair. She sat up. Where was she? Lily was turning the pages of a picture book on the ground nearby. "Where are they?" she whispered softly, all the authority and command gone from her voice. As if in answer, a door at the far end of the room caught her eye. She rose, brushed her hair from her face, and straightened the wrinkles in her dress, then walked to the door and pushed it open. The two men she had seen in her dream turned to look at her. Lily came up behind her and held her hand. "You said you wanted to find my father."

"How did you hear..." started Matt, but the larger man cut him off.

"They're gifteds," said Silas. "You can see it in their eyes."

"I dreamt of you." Both men stared at her. "I heard you say that you wanted to find my father. Is it true?"

Matt nodded, though he didn't know what to make of her.

The younger girl tugged on her arm, "But Helen, you said that we shouldn't talk to them because they were pirates."

"I was wrong, Lily, or at least I hope I was." Helen stared up at Matt. "I know his name, but I don't know how to find him."

Matt turned to Silas, "Silas, do you think you can find a the home of a gifted man in Nasheot if you have his name?"

Silas cracked his knuckles determinedly, "Give me the name, and I'll run the game!"

Matt looked back to Helen, "If you tell us the name, we can find him. Please tell us."

Lily looked up at her. Helen had never told her little sister what their father's name was and neither had their mother. Helen sighed, "Derick, his name is Derick."

FATHERS
CHAPTER SIX

"Found it!" cried Silas excitedly. After two whole hours of tearing through his books of genealogies in Nasheot, he pointed to a page triumphantly. "Derick, a gifted of Nasheot."

"Let me see!" said Matt, looking at it. "This says he was never married and never had children. How could that be if he is Helen's and Lily's father?" The two little girls were sitting in a chair in the corner of the room. Lily had long ago curled up with her head on her sister's lap, but Helen remained wide awake.

"Like I told you, Admiral," said Silas. "The father was never discovered by the people of Nasheot, but this is the only Derick the right age to be him!"

"Where does he live?" asked Matt.

"In the palace of Nasheot. He has his own quarters there."

"Good, we can take it from here." Matt went over to Lily and wrapped her up in the blanket that Helen had come in and picked her up. "Are you ready, Helen?" The girl only nodded.

"Thank you again for, well, you know," said Silas, fingering his throat.

"No worries," said Matt. Then an idea formed in the back of his mind. "Silas, on the way here, I met a man whose hat was pulled down over his eyes. Is doing that uncommon?"

Silas shook his head, "No not at all. Many peasants are ashamed of the gray color of their eyes so they would rather they aren't seen at all."

"And what age did you say your two boys are?"

Silas looked puzzled. "One is four and the other is six."

Matt glanced down at Helen, then at Lily. "I don't think Lily will mind clothes a little too big for her when we get there, and Helen is a bit small for her age." Helen was about to protest but changed her mind.

"Ah, yes," said Silas. "Certainly, I'll go fetch a pair or two and meet you at the front door."

A few minutes later, Matt left with two pairs of boys clothes, two little girls, and a letter from the scribe of King Rhonder, The Nonexistent. When they reached the rowboat tied to the dock, Riggins was already sitting inside it. He didn't say anything when they got in but simply took up the oars.

That night passed, slowly but surely, and the next morning, it was up to Matt and not the Creator to sail the ship towards the capital of Nasheot. Mid-morning, while Lily was playing with a little carved doll that one of the men had made, Riggins came up and sat behind Matt, working knots out of a rope. "You know," said Riggins without looking at Matt, "last night was the first time I ever really respected you."

"Last night?" said Matt glancing back. "But I was so rude to you."

"Don't look at me," said Riggins quickly glancing at one of the nearby crewmembers. Luckily, he hadn't noticed. "Last night was the first time you didn't let me take charge. It was the first time you acted like an Admiral. Ever since you got on this boat, you've acted like just another sailor. You have tried to make friends by being kind, but you aren't just another sailor."

Neither of them said anything for a few minutes, then Matt nodded. "You're right, I've made a mess out of things, but now I'm not sure how to get out of it."

Matt didn't look back, but he could almost feel Riggins grin at him, "In order to lead a pack, you have to lead the leader."

Matt thought about that for a second. *Does he mean now? Like, right now?* He took a deep breath. "Riggins," he said rather loudly, "I need you to go up the mast and adjust the sail."

"Do it yourself," said Riggins, not looking up. Several crew members stared at them. Matt wondered if he had misunderstood.

"Riggins, maybe you didn't hear me. I told you to go and adjust the sail."

"I heard you," said Riggins, still not looking up. There was an icy chill in his voice. Lily, who was sitting nearby, sucked in her breath.

What was Riggins doing? This was his idea! Why was he sabotaging it? "Riggins!" said Matt. "I heard you got that name because you were good at climbing and fixing a ship's riggings, but I'm yet to see much work out of you. Now do it!"

"Make me!!!" said Riggins. He sprang up from his seat and met Matt's astonished gaze. His face was hard as stone and yet as fiery as his words. The two men stood so close, they could smell each other's breath. Then, Riggins eyes twinkled with a mix of amusement and mischief. He leaned forward just a tiny bit, and their noses touched.

Matt clenched his jaw. This was ridiculous, absolutely and completely ridiculous. Matt's mouth twitched up and down uncontrollably. He started breathing harder; it took all he had to keep from cracking up. They stood there like that for what felt like hours. *Creator,* he prayed silently, *help me not to blow this now.* Everyone on *The Steed* was staring at them. Matt knew he couldn't do this much longer. The motionless expression on Riggins face only made it harder to stay serious. Then, Riggins pulled away and hung his head. He walked away, off the poop deck, and silently climbed up to the top of the sails. The crew murmured to each other in low voices. Matt sighed in relief and turned to Lily who clapped for him quietly.

***

That night, when Matt sat down at his own fire with

Lily, Helen, and James, everything had changed. Riggins came over and sat next to them. Then others slowly joined them one by one. A long silenced followed. Riggins rolled his eyes, "Come on, people. Talk, murmur, laugh, be normal! Well, as normal as you can be. This isn't a freakshow, so stop staring!" The group laughed nervously, but before long, the night was filled with chatting and joking. Matt turned to Riggins and gave him a grateful nod.

After the meal was over, one of the young sailors took out a banjo and started playing a lively tune. Matt stood and bowed to Lily, "My lady, would you give me the honor of dancing with you?"

Lily smiled broadly. Ever since her sister had confirmed his nonpirateness, her shyness had vanished. She stood up and curtsied back in her brown torn dress. "Of course!"

He grinned and took her hand. Together, they stepped out onto the deck where several other sailors were already doing the jig. "What type of dance should we do, my lady?"

Lily pondered this for a moment and rubbed her chin with her little hand. "One where I can stand on your toes!"

"Oh really?" said Matt laughing. "Well, I think that's a very good idea!" Her violet eyes twinkled, and holding tightly to his hands, she stepped up onto his boots. Soon, they were prancing around the deck with little jumps and skips right when she least expected them. With every new twist, Lily burst into peals of giggles and held onto him all the tighter.

Once the song was over, the two of them finally tumbled over each other and collapsed on the deck. "Sorry I'm not much of a dancer," gasped Matt still laughing. He picked himself up and then glanced at Helen. She was standing at the edge of the boat, staring off over the waves. "Helen, would you like to join us?" She didn't respond. Her gray hair blew out in the wind beside her. "Helen?" She turned slightly. "Would you like to dance?"

"No thank you, Admiral," answered Helen. The politeness in her voice made her words sound cold.

The night hushed, and all eyes turned to Matt. "Well," he said, trying to sound carefree, "maybe that's enough music for tonight. Riggins, you think these sailors have any good stories to tell?"

Riggins couldn't help smiling when Lily looked up at him. "Definitely."

So, story after story was told, but eventually, most of the crew retired for the night until just Riggins, Matt, Lily, and Helen were left on deck.

"Just one more story!" begged Lily. "Please, just one more story!"

"I don't know if I have any more good ones," said Matt grinning. "What kind of story?"

"A story about dragons!"

Instantly, Matt's eyes lit up. "A story about dragons, hmm... I don't know... are you sure?"

"Yes yes yes!" cried Lily in delight.

So Matt told her the story of a young man named Matt Baker (whether it was really about him or not, one couldn't tell) who met a dragon and helped him see that forgiveness is always the best choice.

By the time the story was done, Lily was nodding off, and Matt had to carry her back to her bed. Helen went with him but didn't say goodnight when he left the room. He sighed. Some people were just harder to get to. By the time he got back to the wheel, Riggins was standing there, looking at him skeptically.

"You know, that story couldn't have been about you," said Riggins.

"What makes you so sure?"

Riggins rolled his eyes. "My father was a sailor and merchant, so I've heard what dragons are really like. They would never forgive, especially not for as dumb of a reason as you said in your story."

"And what was so dumb about my story?" asked Matt, generally curious.

"You told the dragon that you understood how he felt and that it was better to forgive. No dragon would take that for a reason. It would at least need to know HOW you understood. A dragon wouldn't believe just any pathetic excuse. What was your reason, Matt Baker? What was your reason..." His voice trailed off.

"Maybe I told him and just didn't put it in the story," answered Matt.

"Then what was it?" His stone hard eyes stared at Matt.

"I understood him because I..." He stopped and looked away. In a lower voice, he started again, "Because I had to forgive my father for leaving me." Riggins didn't say anything. He just stared at him. "Trinity's my home; it's where my heart is, but let's face it, Trinidads can be idiots." Riggins nodded hesitantly. "Honor, honor, always honor. We need honor for our country, and we need it for ourselves." Matt had to lower his voice again to keep it from cracking. "It leads to single fathers who would rather get rid of their responsibilities than ask for the help of their neighbors. It leads to little boys sitting on orphanage doorsteps every afternoon for years, waiting for their fathers to come back, like they promised they would! It leads to wondering for twenty years if it was because of something that they did!" He paused and took a deep breath. "Because of something that I did."

A long silence followed. Matt wanted to punch himself for getting so carried away. Then, the last thing Matt ever would have expected happened. Riggins put his hand on Matt's shoulder and kept it there, only for a few seconds, but that touch spoke louder than any words. "If you would like, I can steer the ship, and you can get some rest."

Matt sighed. Then he smiled slightly, "No, you go. I'll be fine here."

FATHERS
CHAPTER SEVEN

Matt woke with a start as a boot hit his side. He was lying on the deck of *The Steed* near the wheel. There stood Riggins, gripping the steering wheel. He wasn't looking at him, but Matt could practically sense his amusement.

"Hope you enjoyed your sleep."

Matt stood up, boot in hand. He glanced down at Riggins's one bare foot. "I did," said Matt, grinning. "You want your boot back?"

"Yep," said Riggins turning. He wasn't smiling, but that now familiar twinkle in his eyes gave him away. Matt tossed the boot back, and Riggins put it on with a grunt.

"Funny," said Matt, "I don't remember you coming up last night to take my place at the wheel."

"You were out cold by then," said Riggins turning back to the wheel. "I came up at about one to see how you were doing, and you were slumped over the wheel. I never realized I'd have to babysit my new admiral."

Matt couldn't help but laugh. "Well, at least your resume just got a bit more impressive. What time is it?"

"Almost seven. We'll be arriving at the capital of Nasheot soon, so I suggest you do something with that bird's nest on your head."

Matt nodded and went over to a barrel filled with rain water and checked his reflection. What he saw looked very different from the man who had met with the queen. This man's hair was standing up at odd angles as if he were standing in a strong wind, and his admiral's coat, which had seemed so splendid only days before, was caked with dried mud and blood at the bottom with a small rip at one of the seams. His face had gone unshaven for so long that it was covered in peach fuzz. Even the ploom on his hat seemed to sag a bit. *Well, what did I expect?* he wondered.

He took off his hat and combed through his hair with his fingers, then smoothed it back with some water. Turning from the barrel, he took off his coat and dipped it in the sea. With some scrubbing and squeezing, he got most of the mud and a bit of the blood off. As he hung it up, he noticed that Lily had come out and was watching him.

"What do you think, Lily," he asked, picking her up. "Do I look any better?"

She reached out a small finger and touched the few whiskers on his face, then jerked her hand back and giggled, "You look funny when you're fuzzy!"

"I do?!?" asked Matt, laughing. He glanced over at

Riggins nearby who was trying to conceal a smile. "Well, we'll have to do something about that, now won't we?"

The little girl nodded happily, "Yes, we will, Mr. Baker."

Matt smiled, "You know, you can call me Matt if you want to. I'm not a very good baker after all."

Lily giggled again, "Okay, but then you have to call me something else, too!"

"What's wrong with Lily?"

"Nothing," said Lily, "but everyone calls me Lily! I want something that only YOU call me!"

Matt felt something in his heart dance with joy. He set her down and kneeled in front of her. "How about, Illy?" She shook her head. "Blossom?" She shook her head again. "Frank?" She laughed. "What about, Lil? My Little Lil?"

Her eyes brightened, "Yes please, Matt!"

"Well, then, Little Lil, I suppose I should go shave before we arrive at the lovely capital, don't you think?"

"Definitely!"

He chuckled and turned to Riggins, "Riggins, if all I've seen is right, I don't think that we should enter the city as representatives for Trinity. That would draw far too much attention. Would you happen to have a pair of clothes that I could borrow?"

Riggins nodded, then paused, "What do you mean

'we'?"

Matt locked eyes with him, "I mean we: me, the girls, and my right-hand man."

Riggins stood straighter at the sound of that. "Then I suppose 'we' was the right word."

Matt grinned, and then, before heading down to another room to change, he handed Lily the boys clothes that old Silas the librarian had given him. "You and your sister put these on okay, Little Lil?"

She practically jumped up and down with excitement and ran to the captain's cabin where Helen was still sleeping. She closed the door behind her and tiptoed up to the bed, "Helen? Helen, wake up!"

***

Helen stood on the edge of a tall cliff. She wasn't sure what Tommy's point was in bringing her here. She looked out over the horizon, nothing but clouds and sky for as far as the eyes could see. When she looked closer, she could see another mountain far away in the distance and could sense two overwhelming powers within. "Tommy," she said in a loud and commanding voice, "take me to them!"

In answer, the dream swirled for a moment, then cleared again. She was now standing in a dark cave. She could barely see a finger length past her nose. "Let me see, Tommy!" she cried, and again the dream obeyed. She was in a very long cavern. At the other end were two hulking creatures - dragons. One had emerald green scales, the same color that the one in the admiral's story had had. The other lay further in the shadows, and though Helen couldn't see him well, she could sense him there.

Then without warning, the green one spoke telepathically to the other, and yet Helen found she could hear it as clear as if he had meant it for her. *I have searched for many a year to find another of my grandfather's descendants. It appears that he had more than I'd previously thought.*

It has been a long time since I've seen one of Gelidor's kin, replied the other, his voice low and deliberate. *It is comforting to know they are still alive upon this earth. Have you found others?*

Indeed I have. Most had already retreated beyond the maps of man before I did the same. I had located seven before today: five dragons and two drakes.

And what are you, Valley? He looked the green dragon up and down. *Do you still follow your grandfather's convictions? Do you hate people as much as he did?*

The green one, Valley apparently, sighed, *If you would have asked me years ago, I wouldn't have needed a second to answer that I was not only a dragon but one who had earned great respect and fear. However, a young man once taught me how to forgive, and so I have forgiven the humans for what they did to me. I cannot say that I love them or that I would serve them if they asked me to, but I am willing to leave them in peace. What have you decided?*

The one in the shadows laughed, a long low laugh that seemed to shake the stones of the mountain. *You ask me which I am, but I am neither. I serve the one true god of Ildathore. I serve only... myself.* Helen didn't know what to make of the voice, but she could sense that there were many secrets hiding behind it. Suddenly, the creature raised his head. *Do you feel what I feel, Valley? We are no longer alone.* Helen's blood ran cold.

Valley sniffed the air. *You're right. A gifted is watching us.*

Yes... it must be... but it's a young one, replied the second. Helen panicked. All her life, she had been able to see things happening in the present through her dreams, but no one had ever known!

Cousin, said Valley softly. *I wish nothing to do with humans, let alone with a gifted. I must go.*

Yes, perhaps it's for the best, replied the one in the shadows. *Go, but come again another time when we may speak alone. I have matters that I wish to discuss with you.* Valley nodded and left the cave, his wings sending him up in a wind that tossed Helen's hair.

Then the remaining dragon turned his attention towards her. *Don't be afraid, child,* he said kindly. *I have no hate for you. On the contrary, I believe that gifteds are to be respected and honored.* His voice held none of the coldness it had only a minute before but instead seemed to sing to her with sweetness and grace. *All I wish is to give you your heart's desire. Would you deny me that? I could give you all of the riches of the world. I could make you into the most beautiful being who has ever lived. I could turn back time for you.* As he spoke these last words, her heart skipped a beat, and the dragon seemed to feel it. *I see in you a longing, child. You seek a loved one who can't return, or at least, not by your power.* His words seemed to be seeking her out, trying to pinpoint where in the room she was. With every word he spoke, the more sure she felt that he meant no harm. *I shall do it all for you, give it all to you, if you do only one thing for me in return.*

No one could save her mom, right? Surely this was just some kind of trick, a cruel joke. She tried to leave the dream, but it was too late now. The dragon's attention was too focused on her. She didn't like it. All she wanted was to leave. All she wanted was for Tommy to spit her out of this strange dream and let her go, but she didn't want to speak. She didn't want the dragon to know where she was. As kind as he seemed, she wasn't about to go searching for a dragon in the vain hope that he might turn back time. Then she heard a voice from somewhere far away, echoing off of some hidden part of her mind, and she thanked the Creator for her pesky little sister.

***

"Helen? Helen, wake up!" said Lily.

Helen sat up slowly and wiped the sleep from her eyes, "Oh, thanks for waking me up, Lily. Was having a..."

"A nightmare?" asked Lily.

Helen smiled slightly at how different this was from what she almost said. "Yeah, a really, really bad nightmare."

Lily frowned in sympathy, "I hate it when I have bad dreams." Then she perked up again, "We're almost to the capital where daddy is! Matt said to put these on." She put two pairs of boys' clothes on the bed.

After a few minutes, they had the clothes on and headed back out on deck. Matt was standing there already. He was wearing sailor's clothes, with a cap covering his hair pulled down so low that when he tilted his head it was impossible to see his eyes. But they could still see his freshly shaven chin, which Lily seemed quite happy about. "Hi there, Little Lil," said Matt, coming over to them. "My! You look fine in those clothes."

Lily giggled, "Why is your hat so low? I can barely see your eyes."

"Well, because we are going to Nasheot's capital, and I would rather not be thought of as royalty just yet. Because of that, we are all going to play a little game."

"I love games!" cried Lily in delight.

"Good! So you and your sister are going to put on these hats," he said, giving them each a hat, "and we are going to make sure that all your hair is in them and pull them down low over your eyes. That way, no one there knows where you're from. After all, secrets are fun, right?"

"Right!" agreed Lily, then she frowned and beckoned him closer so that she could whisper a secret into his ear, "I'm not the best at keeping secrets, though, so I just won't talk."

"That sounds like a good idea," he whispered back.

He helped Lily get all of her beautiful hair in her hat and then pulled it down over her eyes. After that, he turned to Helen. He knew in an instant that she wasn't buying any of the game nonsense. He had never met a kid that was so grown up.

Before long they reached the dock, and stepped off *The Steed* into Nasheot once again. Towers and houses rose up higher than any in Trinity. Matt sucked in his breath at the beautiful sight of it. Turning to Riggins, he said, "You take Helen's hand; I'll hold Lily." My head will be down, so you'll need to lead us to the castle; I'll follow your feet."

Riggins nodded, his long black hair and dark eyes were normal enough for him to hold his head high. Together, they left the dock and went straight into a busy town square. Matt struggled to keep his eyes on Riggins as hundreds of other feet shuffled past. Several times, he had to call out Riggins's name when they got seperated, but every time, Riggins came back for him. After a while, they got further and further from the bustling crowds. Soon, Matt got the impression that they were hurrying through back alleyways, but he never raised his head despite his growing curiosity. Finally, Riggins stopped.

"We're here," he said quietly.

Matt looked up. They stood in an alley near two large blue gates that kept the commoners away from the palace. Matt took a deep breath. "Thank you, Riggins, for everything. Now, you'll wait here while I go in."

Riggins nodded, "As you wish, Admiral."

Matt smiled and pushed up his hat a bit so that his eyes could be seen, but not enough to show his hair color. As casually as he could, he walked out of the alley and straight up to the guards at the gate. They bowed. "Let me into the palace, men," he said commandingly.

One of the men cocked his head at him, "Your accent seems... different, and why are you dressed like a sailor?"

"Don't question me, man, or I shall... uh, report you to... people!" The man didn't seem satisfied with an answer like that, but the other one nudged him, and together they opened the gates. Matt strolled in, trying not to seem as awed by the giant blue palace as he felt. He walked over to a servant who was tending a garden in the courtyard. "Um, excuse me, would you mind taking me to the Derick that lives here?"

"My Lord!" said the man with a start. "My apologies! I didn't see you approach. Yes, I will indeed take you to him."

"Thank you," said Matt. The servant led him into the palace and through the many halls until they finally came to a blue door.

"The duke is through that door."

"Duke?" asked Matt surprised, then, when the man looked at him strangely, he added, "Oh, yes, that duke." The man cocked an eyebrow but left him there and went back down the flight of stairs. Matt took a deep breath and knocked.

"The door's open!" called a friendly voice from inside.

Matt opened it and entered a large bed chamber decorated with every shade of blue you could imagine. At the end of the room sat a man with black hair and blue eyes in a beautiful robe. "Derick?"

The man turned to him, "Yes, what do you need?"

"I'm here to talk to you about your wife and daughters."

FATHERS
CHAPTER EIGHT

"I'm sorry, I must have heard you wrong. For a second, I thought you said I had a wife and daughters," said Derick, staring at him incredulously. "I'm not married."

Matt paused and closed the door behind him. "Whether you're married now or not, I have two little girls with me and my crew who have your nose and their mother's smile."

Derick looked taken aback. "I see." He rubbed his temples with his forefingers and bit his lip. "So she was pregnant when they took her?"

Matt didn't know how to answer a question like that, but he nodded. Derick stood and stepped closer to him. "Why do you have my daughters?"

Matt sighed. "Derick, your wife is gone." He cleared his throat awkwardly before continuing. "Her hut was right next to a battlefield. As boulders were being catapulted back and forth, one of them landed on it. I'm so sorry."

Derick just stared at him, then he rolled his eyes. "Yes, I figured she was dead and gone if you had my daughters. I'm not some simpleton, but why did you bring them here?"

Matt stared in shock. "What did you ask?"

"You heard me. Why did you bring them here?"

Matt felt anger bubbling up inside, but he pushed it back down. Surely this was just some kind of misunderstanding. "I brought them here because they're your daughters, and their mother is dead."

"Well, you can't leave them here," said Derick quickly. "I hope you know that. Do you know what happened the last time they were here? My reputation was nearly ruined. It's a good thing no one saw where they came from, or I would have been done for."

Matt stared at him in unbelief. "Yes, I do know what happened. A pregnant woman and a little girl got thrown into a raging river and had to fend for themselves for years!"

"Look at it however you, but it ended badly," said Derick bluntly. "I can't take them now, not when my promotion in the army is so close. This simply is not the time to think about family issues."

Matt stepped forward and grabbed his shoulders hard, "Now, Derick, is the perfect time to think about family because right now, your daughters are standing outside this palace waiting to see their father."

Derick spoke softly, but his voice was the most demanding thing Matt had ever heard, "Let go of me." For a second, he looked so threatening standing there that Matt was taken back to another time, another place. He was standing in a field next to a small hut where a woman lived with her two daughters. On the other side of the river stood a figure whose blue robe whipped in the wind. His fist was raised, and he shouted a battle cry as two catapults were fired on either side of him.

Matt took a step away from the man, and Derick seemed to sense what he was thinking. "Sometimes, sacrifices have to be made in times of war." Then, he lowered his hands and stepped closer to Matt. "Listen, it isn't that I don't want them. I just can't handle them right now. They are products of foolish choices that I made as a kid and nothing more. I'm sure if you look around, you can find a good home for them." For a split second, Derick's features seemed to change. He was no longer a gifted from Vanya but a man that Matt had always looked up to as a small child. He was putting him on the orphanage steps and walking away, never to return.

Matt looked straight into the man's eyes. "You're their father, and whether you know it or not, for you to leave them will break their hearts forever. You don't know what you're missing, not seeing them grow up. Helen has done what she can to be strong, but she's still so vulnerable. She needs you. And Lily wants nothing more than to have a special man in her life who will love her more than anyone else. Please come with me, and be their father again."

***

Riggins used his knife to carve a stick he'd found in the alley. Lily hummed quietly to herself and ran her fingers over the bricks on the building beside her. Helen didn't make a noise. She just stared at the palace in silence. Finally, the guards opened the gates, and Riggins rose to see who was coming out. One of them was wearing a shirt and trousers that Riggins knew well, and the other was dressed from head to toe in blue. They stood for a moment, just outside the gate. Riggins watched in anticipation. The man in blue put something in Matt's hand, and Matt nodded. Then the other man turned and walked back into the gates. The guards closed them behind him.

As Matt came closer, Riggins saw on his face what had happened. "Hello, princesses," he said, picking up Lily when he reached them and twirling her around. "I think you two got even more beautiful while I was away." Lily giggled. Helen stood, wide-eyed, and stared first at Matt, then at Riggins. As she saw their faces, she stood straighter, her back rigid, and lowered her eyes.

"Who was that man?" Lily asked as Matt put her down.

"Well, Little Lil, I don't think that's the right question to ask. The right question is: what did he give me?"

Lily's eyes sparkled. "Okay, what did he give you?"

Matt opened his hand to reveal three shiny coins. Then, he pointed to a pastry shop across the street. "He said the two of you were so beautiful that you should have the sweetest, most wonderful sugar pastries that you've ever eaten!"

Lily squealed with delight and clapped her hands together in joy. "Can I go now to pick some out, Matt!"

"I think that's a wonderful idea. In fact, why don't you

and Helen go together to choose some. Riggins and I will be there in a minute to help you buy it." Lily nodded and turned to Helen hopefully. Helen had gone white as snow, but seeing Lily's pleading face, she took her sister's hand and went with her.

Riggins and Matt watched her go. She didn't shed tears as Matt expected, but her lack of tears told her grief even more. "She's a brave girl," said Riggins quietly.

Matt was still looking after them, and when he spoke, his voice sounded worn and tired. "She shouldn't have to be. No seven-year-old should ever have to be so brave."

Riggins put his hand on his friend's shoulder and turned him around. "Are you alright?"

Matt shook his head slowly, almost as if it hurt. "No. No, I'm not."

Riggins looked at him, but in a different way than he ever had before. He wasn't trying to figure him out. He wasn't trying to outdo him. He wasn't trying to undo him. He simply looked. Then he nodded and took the coins out of Matt's hand. "Why don't you go down to the shore and take some time to think. I'll help them get them the candy, and we'll catch up to you later. Then we can figure out if there are any good orphanages in town."

"No!" said Matt suddenly. "No orphanages! I won't... I can't." He took in a deep breath as the unspoken thought passed between them: *But you don't have a choice.* "I'm sorry, I shouldn't have snapped at you like that. Maybe I will go down to the shore."

Riggins nodded and watched as his admiral walked away through the crowd, not stopping to hide his eyes from the passersby.

***

Helen hardly tasted the sugar pastries that she ate on the way to the shore. She hardly smelled them, either. Her father, the man who was always in her dreams at night, the man who had twirled her around every night after work, didn't want her. What had she done? What had she said?

It was nearly nightfall by the time they got to the shore. Matt was sitting on an old abandoned dock down the shore. Lily began to play in the sand nearby, and Riggins set to work whittling the same poor little stick that he had found in the alley. Helen wanted to cry, she wanted to so bad, but she had used up all her tears over the last week, and no matter how hard she wished they would, no more would come. Riggins didn't look up at her, and she appreciated it. Sometimes, you just don't want to be seen.

"You know," said Riggins quietly, "I'm sure your father loves you."

Helen stood in a sudden rage. Even if she couldn't cry, she could shout. "You're sure? You're SURE?! If you're so sure, then why am I here? Why's my father still in that palace acting as if I never existed? Why doesn't he come for me?! You know why? Because I'm not worth it! No one could love me!" Helen was glad that Lily was far enough away not to hear her outburst, but she wasn't about to take anything back. With her eyes, sSe dared Riggins to try to disagree with her.

"Matt loves you." He said it so calmly, so naturally, that Helen was taken aback. "You can see it in his eyes," he continued softly. "Every time he sees you or your sister, they light up like they were seeing you for the first time."

Helen's fists unclenched of their own accord. She stared at Riggins as if he'd said elephant could fly. Then she sat back down with a sigh. "Well, I'm not looking for a substitute father. I can handle life well enough on my own."

"Of course not, of course not," said Riggins, but the way he said it didn't at all make her feel belittled. "You're a brave girl, and I'm sure you're right when you say you don't need one. But does Lily?" Helen looked over her shoulder at what he was looking at. Lily was slowly approaching Matt from behind. Riggins rose suddenly. "Well, if you talk to Matt, tell him that I went back to the ship."

"To the ship?" asked Helen in surprise. "Why are you going back now?"

He put the stick in his pocket and slid the knife into its home inside his boot. "As much as I'd like to stay and find more twigs to torture, I got up at about one o'clock this morning to babysit our beloved admiral, and I'm pooped."

***

Matt sat on the old dock as he had for hours. The stars reflected down into the water, and not far away, several water lilies danced up and down as the tide rolled in. Every time he saw them, he pictured Lily's face. His own Little Lil. How he wished he could take them into his life, that he could be their father, but every time he thought of it, a hundred doubts crept into his mind. Could he care for them? Didn't they need a mother in their life, too? Where would they live when he had to go out to sea? But one thought plagued him most: would they even want me? A twenty-six-year-old who barely knows how to make oatmeal and has no idea how to be a father?

From behind him, he heard a small noise and turned his head just in time to see Lily sit down beside him. They didn't say anything for a while, but Matt was glad she'd come. Finally, she spoke up.

"Was that man in blue my daddy?"

Matt nodded slowly. "Yes, he was. How did you know?"

Lily smiled sheepishly, "He had Helen's nose." Then she looked up at him questioningly. "Does he want us?"

Matt sighed. "Lily, he doesn't think he can take care of you."

"Oh," said Lily, but there wasn't any sadness in her voice. "Who will be our daddy then?"

"I don't know," Matt said. "I just don't know."

She looked up at him again, and he met her lavender eyes with his own blue ones. "Could you be our daddy?" she asked.

Matt felt tears spring to his eyes, but he pushed them back. "Well, I don't know, Little Lil. Do you really want me to?"

Lily put her hand to her chin thoughtfully. "Well, you act like you love me, and you're a lot nicer than that weird blue man, but you do have a bigger nose."

Matt couldn't help it laughing. "Is that a yes?"

"Yes," said another voice coming up beside him. Helen slid down on his other side. "That's a very definite yes, but only if you promise to never leave us or stop loving us."

There was no use in trying to hold them back any more. The tears came streaming down his cheeks and straight into his smile. "I promise! Oh, I promise!" He grabbed the two girls and hugged them so long and hard that by the time he was done, Lily was on his lap instead of beside him. She didn't seem to mind.

***

This, my dear friend, is the end of the second legend of Matt Baker but by no means the end of the story. Matt went on to serve many more years as the admiral and was one of the most loved heroes that Trinity has ever known. No matter where he went, you could nearly always recognize him as "the handsome hero with the shadowy companion at his side." Near the end of his life, he was interviewed by The Trinity Gazette and asked one simple question: "If you could have one name to describe you for all of history, what would it be?" His answer came without hesitation: "Daddy."

STORY THREE
PILLAGERS AND PARENTHOOD

PILLAGERS AND PARENTHOOD
CHAPTER ONE

Matt Baker walked alongside Helen into the little town of Halingem. Neither of them said much, as was typical when they were alone. A bird chirped over head, and Matt turned to see it flutter away.

"You know," said Matt absentmindedly, "No matter how hard I try, I have never found a bird that sings prettier than the ones on Vanya."

"Vanya is overflowing with life," said Helen in response. *Unlike Trinity,* she added in her thoughts. Matt seemed to sense what she was thinking. Helen didn't mean to seem ungrateful, but it was the truth. Ever since Matt had taken her and Lily in five years ago (Helen was now twelve and Lily eight), Helen had felt the deadness of Trinity in everything she did. Then again, maybe all places felt like that to someone who had grown up in Vanya.

Matt sighed. He never knew how to break the ice between him and Helen. No matter how hard he tried, it simply didn't work. "So how do you think Danny will be today?" he asked, changing the subject.

"Fine," said Helen. "Though he might be mad that we didn't bring Lily, I'm telling you that they are going to marry one day." She smiled as she said it. Talking about Lily was one of the only times she smiled anymore it seemed.

Matt grinned, "I don't know. He'll have to get through me if he wants to court my daughter." As they rounded a corner, the little gray building came into sight. An orphanage. The same orphanage where Matt had grown up, and the current residence of Lily's crush, a nine-year old boy named Danny. But something wasn't right about the picture. In fact, something was very very wrong. A crowd of reporters stood restlessly around the front door. Matt handed Helen the basket of sweets he was carrying and rushed forward, pushing his way into the chaotic crowd.

"What is this?" he asked, making his way to the front step and barring the way to the crowd. Several people grunted their disapproval.

"If you don't know, then you're an illiterate dunce. Now out of our way!" said a larger man, trying to push through him, Matt however was not the type of man that could be pushed through easily.

"Actually, I'm the Admiral," said Matt, grinning. The large man cleared his throat and stepped back. "Now, someone tell me what's going on?"

"A missing gifted!" said a lady near the front of the crowd. "It's in the Trinity Gazette." She handed it to him.

The Trinity Gazette

YOUNG GIFTED CHILD KIDNAPPED

Last night, in a local orphanage on Albeton, nine-year-old Danny went missing from his bedroom. After a thorough investigation of the room, authorities are officially labeling it a crime scene. We have been told they are following several leads. As Danny was the only gifted in our largely anti-gifted society, there is quite an uproar from all sides. While all agree it was a despicable act, many are also relieved that the child is gone. Head advisor to the queen, Levin Contbon, said, "Though it's a tragedy, I believe that overall it's better for the citizens of Trinity."

TRADING SHIPS GONE MISSING

Many merchants sailing to trade with Syan have gone missing. Among them are Sergeant Monucer, Captain Peterson, and Clire Staple along with their crews. If you have any information about their whereabouts, please contact the authorities immediately.

HAVE YOU EVER WANTED TO BE A COW?

Ever wanted to be more like a cow? Now, for a limited time, you too can own the all new Moo-O-Matic. For more information, send your question to our headquarters at Moo's "R" Us.

"Danny taken?" he asked, when he had skimmed the article. He glanced at Helen. Standing just out of the crowd, she stepped back in shock. Matt sighed. "Well, if it is already in the newspapers, what are you all doing here?"

"To see if the caretakers know anything," replied a slim man with a pencil stuck behind his ear.

"Now that is just ridiculous," said Matt. "The women who work here are loving and kind. If you are looking for a conspiracy, I suggest you check politics, but as for right now, I am asking you to leave." The crowd grumbled a bit at that. "Now!" Slowly they dispersed.

Helen rushed up to the door as soon as she could make it through. "Danny is gone?" she asked, wiping away a tear.

"It seems so," said Matt. "But I'm going to talk to the women who work here before jumping to any conclusions. Can you take the sweets upstairs?" Helen nodded and turned towards the stairs. "And Helen?" She turned around hesitantly. He grinned at her, "It'll be okay."

She nodded coldly and went up the stairs. Matt went into the little gray building slowly. Huddled in the corner sat a few of the caretakers. One of them let out a sigh of relief when she saw who it was.

"Matt," she said, coming to him. "Thank you so much. We didn't know what we were going to do when they got in."

"Don't worry about it," he said. "Can we talk, Sally?"

Sally's eyes got big, "You don't think we did it, do you?"

"No," said Matt, "but I do want to know what happened to Danny."

"Oh Matt, he's gone." She looked almost as if she were going to cry. "We knew when we took him in that we would have to deal with controversy, him being a gifted and all, but I never thought something like this would happen."

"Something like what?"

"He was kidnapped!" said Sally hoarsely. "Last night."

"Well, I read that much in the news," said Matt. He smiled to try to cheer her up, but it didn't work. How could he possibly be this bad at comforting women?

"Oh Matt, but it is worse than what the news said," explained Sally, holding onto his arm. "Before the police came, we took something out of the room."

"What is it?"

"A note," said Sally, taking a piece of paper out of her pocket and handing it to him.

He read it quickly, then cleared his throat. Immediately he looked around for any sight of Helen, then he remembered she was upstairs. "I'm sorry" he said, pulling away from her, "but I think we will have to cut out visit rather short."

She looked at him oddly, but he didn't stop to notice. He ran out the door to the outside stairs leading up to the second floor. "Helen?" he called up. "Helen!" He was just about to sprint up the stairs to find her when she finally opened the door. He sighed in relief.

"What's the matter, Mr. Baker?" asked Helen, quickly coming down to meet him. "What happened?"

"I think it's time to head home."

They walked together, much more briskly than on the way there, to the dock. There, waiting for them, bobbed the *Bella Fawn* in the tide. Matt hastily led the way onto it and tacked the sails for the swiftest way home. "Mr. Baker, what is wrong?" she asked. She hated how incredibly feeble she sounded in real life. Oh how she longed to always sound as strong and commanding as she did in her dreams.

"Nothing," said Matt, steering the *Bella Fawn*. He could tell from her gaze that she didn't buy it. "I just had a little scare, that's all, we'll get home soon and everything will be okay."

Helen didn't try asking again. After all, she would probably just get the same answer.

"I'm going below deck."

"Okay."

"Tell me when we're getting close, alright?"

"Okay, Helen."

***

Helen looked around. Where was she? Everything was black, and yet somehow, even without light, there were shadows. She didn't like it at all; something wasn't right. Then, off in the shadows to her far right, she saw a figure. She rolled her eyes. Not again, not the same dream AGAIN.

"Tommy, take me somewhere else." Nothing. She sighed. Her dreams always seemed to lead here recently. She studied the figure. He was the same as the other times, a young boy, about her age, with a very confused expression on his face. He didn't look at all like Danny; Danny would have at least waved or stood on his head or something.

"Who are you?" she asked, but as always, there was no response. It was such a frustrating dream. "Tommy, take me somewhere else." Nothing. Again. "Don't get ancy with me, Tommy!" She felt a slight stirring in her dream over to the left. "I know you are listening, Tommy, and I'm tired of your games. Show me something else, ANYTHING else."

The darkness spun around her, merging and twisting. Helen was used to it by now. Tommy was finally obeying. When the haze cleared, she was kneeling next to her mother's side. She could feel the lump in her throat rising and tears stinging her eyes. She felt someone take her hand, probably Matt. This dream was far worse than the last. "No," she whispered, as her mother's blood puddled around her. "I'm sorry, I'm sorry Tommy, but please don't leave me here."

A warm feeling passed through her, like the dream was somehow trying to comfort her, and the little cottage with the broken roofs spun together and vanished. Once again, she was back in the dark. "Okay, okay, you win," she said, wiping away her tears. The boy in the shadows just stared at her. She rolled her eyes.

***

Matt smiled as the *Bella Fawn* neared The Head island and his own little private dock. He locked the steering wheel in place for a minute and went over to the entrance to below deck. "Helen, we're almost home!"

He heard a stirring as she got up then went back to the wheel. *When he had first taken them in, he had been a bit concerned with Helen's strange sleeping habits, but he had gotten used to them by now. After all, she was a gifted, and gifted tended to have strange tendencies.*

He looked over as Helen, climbing the ladder out of

the hold and straightening her hair. "Thank you for waking me up, Mr. Baker."

Matt cringed -- Mr. Baker, so formal, so cold, yet that was about as much affection he had ever gotten from her. "You're welcome, Helen."

She came up and stood beside him as they neared the dock. Hesitantly, she asked, "Do you ever have the same dream over and over?"

"Well, it depends on the dream, I guess," said Matt, looking down at her. "Why do you ask?"

She sighed, "Recently, I've been dreaming about a boy..."

"Tommy?" asked Matt with a playful grin. "You say his name in your sleep. Don't worry Helen. Imaginary boyfriends at your age are completely normal, just stay away from real men alright? They're animals!"

Helen shook her head. "Never mind." There was no reason he should be able to understand.

As they neared the dock, they looked beyond it, at a lush green hill, where the Baker Manor sat. Lily ran down to meet them as they came, waving like it would go out of style.

PILLAGERS AND PARENTHOOD
CHAPTER TWO

"Daddy!" shouted Lily as she jumped over the side of the *Bella Fawn* and latched her arms around Matt's neck.

"Hey, Little Lil!" said Matt, swinging her around. She laughed as the air flew past her skirts. Helen smiled slightly and stepped past them onto the dock. "Man, have you grown?" asked Matt, putting Lily back down.

"It's only been three days!" she said smiling. "But yes! I'm sure I did!"

"Really? Reach up tall!" she reached up on him as high as she could so that her fingers tickled his chest. "No tiptoes!" he cried, prodding his fingers under her arms until she had to retreat with squeals of delight.

"Why did Helen get to go to the other island with you and not me, Daddy?"

"Because Helen was done with her school for the

break," said Matt. "How'd your last math test go, Little Lil?"

"Well, I got a 89..... but that isn't too bad, is it?"

"Not at all," he said, stepping out of the boat with her "In fact, that is so good that I think you and Helen should run up and get changed into your favorite dresses so that we can go out for dinner tonight."

"Alright!" cried Lily. She took Helen's hand and began pulling her toward the house. "Can I wear one of your dresses, Helen?"

"What's wrong with your own?" asked Helen.

"They aren't yours!"

"We'll see."

Matt smiled broadly as he watched the two girls run to the Baker Manor. From the garden gate, a figure sauntered up to him. The man had black hair that fell down to his shoulders, and though he wasn't smiling, you could almost feel his smile from the twinkle in his dark eyes. "So, you're back again."

"Well, Riggins, I see nothing wrong with returning to my own house," said Matt, patting his friend on the back.

"I see one thing for certain. It's far too nice for you."

Matt nodded thoughtfully, "Very likely. Whoever would have thought that I, of all people, would not only become an Admiral but also have my own manor."

"Not anyone who knew you very well, that's for sure."

Matt grinned, "Thanks for that! I do love getting insulted by my right-hand man."

"Well then, you can be sure that is the reason I do it." said Riggins. There was something about the first mate that Matt liked, even if they had been practically enemies when they first met.

"Thanks for watching Lily while I was gone." Matt sighed.

Riggins looked at him, concerned, "What's the matter, Matt? Don't you think I've known you long enough to know when you're worried?"

"It's nothing. Well it is something, but not something to discuss right now. Did I get any mail while I was gone?"

"Yes actually, here," said Riggins, pulling a letter out of his pocket and handing it to Matt. "It's from the queen's court."

Matt took it and opened it, the first thing he saw was another envelope inside, sealed with the queen's seal. *Just great,* thought Matt. *I need an assignment right now like I need a hole in the head.* He read the loose piece of paper carefully.

"What does it say?" asked Riggins, looking at him. Matt just stared at the letter incredulously.

"It says that you and I are being called to a mission tomorrow at noon, and that we should bring five ships with us… Riggins," he said softly. "Did you read the Gazette today?"

"About Danny? Yes, it's quite sad."

"In the article, Levin Contbon, the head advisor to the queen, said that in the long run it was a good thing that Danny was kidnapped."

Riggins rolled his eyes, "You know very well I don't agree with him on stuff like that."

"Yes, but he wrote this commision."

"So? He writes a lot of commissions. Have you really never noticed that?"

"I've noticed it, but I never payed attention to the handwriting," started Matt. "This isn't the first time I've seen his handwriting today." Riggins stared at him incredulously as Matt dug his hand around in his pocket. When he pulled out his hand, he was holding a piece of paper. He handed it to Riggins. "This note was found in Danny's bedroom."

Riggins read it slowly, then went pale. On it were four words: *Death to the GIFTEDS!*

"Give me the commission from him." Matt obeyed. Riggins was much better at this type of thing than himself. Riggins held up the two papers one after the other against the sun. He squinted at it a minute or two, then nodded. "Well, either someone is a very good trickster or that is definitely the same handwriting." Riggins handed the two papers back to Matt. "But, if he wants to get rid of gifteds, what would he want with you?"

Matt looked up to the manor where the two girls were just going inside. "Have you told anyone about Helen and Lily being gifteds?"

"No! I would never!" said Riggins, in an almost offended tone. Then he added in a hushed voice, "Did Danny know?" Matt nodded. Riggins sighed, "I would stay to protect them if I could get out of going with you. You know that, don't you?"

"Yes," said Matt. "I know, but I am wary of asking anyone else to do it, just in the sense that everyone knows you don't need a guard without something to guard. I'm scared to draw attention to them." Then he paused and glanced sideways at Riggins, who was obviously having the same thought.

"No, Matt, don't even think about it. We were asked to take five ships with us on the voyage. It will probably be dangerous." said Riggins, staring at him.

"I know, I know. But what would you do? Would you keep your kids by your side in danger or send them into it alone?"

"One of the reasons I don't have kids," muttered Riggins, "Too many difficult decisions."

Matt smiled, "Come on, old friend. It will be like our first adventure. What do you say?"

"I say you're insane," said Riggins, obstinately, a mischievous twinkle in his eyes. "But then again, that never seemed to stop you."

***

"What do you think, Helen?" asked Lily, posing like an archer in one of Helen's best dresses.

Helen smiled slightly. "I think it looks fine, but how

will you be able to hold onto the arrows while my sleeves are flopping over your hands?" Lily scrunched up her face in thought. "Maybe you should just leave the bow and arrows at home tonight, and when we get back, you can get in your own clothes again and can defend us from goblins."

"That works! I guess when we go to dinner, I can settle for..."

"A princess?"

"No!" said Lily stubbornly. "Princesses are for girly girls, like Cindy Delane..... Hmm.... I'll be a duchess!"

"Quite different," agreed Helen.

"Girls, can you come down here for a minute?" called Matt from the first floor of house.

"Coming!" said Helen as the two hurried out of the bedroom and down the stairs. Once they had gotten down, Helen instantly recognized the look on Matt's face. It was the look grownups always had when they were trying to hide worry behind fun. Helen didn't like it much.

"Little Lil, would you be disappointed if we didn't go to dinner tonight?" asked Matt, lowering himself beside her. Lily nodded, unsure of what he was leading to. "Would you rather go to dinner tonight or come with me on an adventure tomorrow morning?"

"Adventure!" cried Lily, jumping up and down in excitement.

"Good!" said Matt, grinning. "We'll have to go first thing tomorrow morning, so run and get packed!" She squealed with delight and ran back up the stairs. Helen just looked at him incredulously. "This really is the best thing, Helen."

"As you say, Mr. Baker."

Matt watched, dejected, as Helen went upstairs after her sister. "So, I assume that the attempt to get closer to her these last few days didn't go well?" asked Riggins, looking at him.

"Not in the slightest," said Matt sadly. "I just can't connect with her like I can with Lily."

"Maybe because she isn't Lily," said Riggins quietly.

"I know, I know, but I'm failing her as a dad. It's a terrible feeling to have, like you can't fill a gap you were made for! It hurts."

"Don't worry, Matt. In time, I think she'll come around. I did," he said, patting Matt on the back.

"You're probably right," said Matt, sighing. "Who knows, this trip might be the perfect opportunity."

PILLAGERS AND PARENTHOOD
CHAPTER THREE

Matt walked behind the two little girls as they came to the dock. Each had a bag under her arm. Lily was dressed in her most free-flying clothes, the best for climbing in, with a navy jacket draped around her shoulders. Whether she was walking or skipping, it was hard to tell. Maybe it was both. When she reached the dock, she looked around in surprise at the five ships. Four were wonderful, towering warships with cannons, but bobbing next to them, quite innocently, sat the *Bella Fawn*. "We're taking the *Bella Fawn*, Daddy?"

"Yes," said Matt, helping her into the boat. "We will ride in this one. She may be smaller, but she'll get us there all the same." He turned to Helen who had come up beside him. He smiled at her, but there was no response. She looked worn and tired. "In you go, my lady."

Helen took his hand and stepped in, "Thank you, Mr. Baker." Riggins, however, completely ignored his hand and hopped into the *Bella Fawn* on his own. Matt grinned.

"James, come on over here!" called Matt to the scrawny redhead navigator. "The *Bella Fawn* will be the lead boat!"

"Yes, sir!" cried James.

"Which crew members would you like with you, Admiral?" asked Cork, the captain of one of the other ships.

Matt thought for a second. "We'll take George's group over there. It's the smallest."

"Maybe," said George, joining them with his little crew, "that's because we're the best men."

"I never said you weren't!" laughed Matt. "Okay, that's all the weight we need over here. We'll go ahead and start off slowly so the rest of you can trail behind."

"But, Daddy!" said Lily. "What about the cannon shot?"

"Oh, that's right," said Matt. George looked at him puzzled. "It is sort of a family tradition that before we go on a boat adventure, Lily gets to shoot the cannon. Hmm… but the *Bella Fawn* doesn't have any cannons."

"She can use one of mine, Admiral," said Cork, grinning. "I have plenty."

"Thanks," said Matt. "Come on, Little Lil, let's go kill a poor fish." Hand in hand, they left the *Bella Fawn* together.

Helen didn't go with them. Instead, she sat down on the deck of the *Bella Fawn*, utterly exhausted. Bad nights, bad nights! Nothing but bad nights recently. Out of the corner of her eye, she saw a concerned look from Riggins. She acted like she hadn't seen it. There were too many things in her head for Riggins to help with.

Suddenly, he heard a cannon being fired. She stood up with a start before she realized it was only Lily. A few seconds later, Matt and Lily returned, laughing together about something. But then again, weren't they always laughing?

"Well, Little Lil, I am now convinced that you could outshoot the whole of Trinity's Navy on your own, myself included," said Matt, stepping into the *Bella Fawn* with her.

"Does that mean I can fire the cannon on my own next time, Daddy?"

"NO!" said Matt, Riggins, and George at the same time.

"Okay!" said Matt. "The cannon has been fired. Now, we're off. Catch us if you can, Queen's men!" With that, Matt and Lily got behind the wheel, Riggins scurried up the mast like a squirrel on a mission, George went to work making sure all else was in order, and James sat idly watching beside Helen.

Soon the *Bella Fawn* was sailing through the ocean with the wind in her sails. Helen looked on as Matt let Lily take the wheel while he and James went in the captain's quarters to discuss their destination.

***

Matt opened the sealed letter from the queen with James watching anxiously. It read:

Admiral Matt Baker,

You are being sent to the island of Syma. Syma has been, for many years, a peaceful trader with Trinity. Recently, however, many trade ships in that area have disappeared. Your mission is to go there and scout out the situation.

Her Majesty the Queen

"James, map out a course to Syma, will you?" said Matt, closing the letter.

"Yes, sir!" said James, obviously glad to finally be doing something. Within a minute or two, he showed the map to Matt.

"Hmm… not bad, but is there some way we could come in sight of Thebel's coast on the way?"

"Um, if you say so, sir," said James, reworking their course of action. "May I ask why you want to see the coast?"

"Just personal reasons." Matt stood. "When do you expect us it to be visible?"

"In a few days, sir," answered James.

"Good!" All that day, Matt stood beside Lily, helping her steer, but when they came close to Thebel, he vanished into the hold of the ship for a few minutes and came out with a quilt in his arms. The whole crew looked puzzled as he approached the mast with it.

Riggins, who had been talking to another sailor at the bottom of the mast, went silent when he saw what Matt was carrying. The two stood there for a minute, staring at each other. Then, Riggins turned his head away and went into the hold, closing the door behind him. Matt sighed. "Little Lil, would you like to climb the mast with me?"

"Oh, yes!" cried Lilly, giving the wheel to George. Together, she and Matt climbed the mast. "Why are you taking a quilt up the mast, Daddy?"

"You'll see, Little Lil, you'll see." When they finally reached the top, Matt took down the Trinity flag and hoisted the quilt in its place. The ragged old thing flew in the wind. "Now do you see, Little Lil?"

Lily nodded slowly. "You are trying to signal someone, aren't you?"

"Yes," said Matt smiling. "You're very clever."

"But who are you trying to signal? Someone on Thebel?" Matt nodded. "Who?"

Matt looked almost as if he would answer, then shook his head. "I'll tell you someday, Little Lil. Not now, but someday." In a few minutes, when Thebel was once again out of sight, Matt raised the Trinity flag and took down the quilt. Together he and Lily slowly made their way down the mast again.

As they did, Lily asked, "Daddy, you say you'll tell me someday. When is someday?"

Matt smiled, "Sooner than you think." Matt went back into the hold after that, and when he came out, the quilt was gone. By that night, the crew had practically forgotten his strange behavior. They caught a tasty batch of fish and fried them with mushrooms and herbs from home. By the time it was ready, the whole crew was five times as hungry as when they'd started it.

They stood in a rather frayed line to shovel the delicious looking food onto their plates. When they had all filled up their plates, the sailors pulled off their hats, bent their heads, and Matt prayed.

"Creator, we thank you for this food and for the fellowship you have given to us. We ask your blessing on this food and on the adventure that awaits us. Amen." The men began to scarf the food almost before the prayer was over. Soon they were all quite drunk on good food and laughter, though not on wine itself as the queen didn't allow it for her navy men.

Soon, someone called for music and a whole little band had gathered together with a harmonica, a makeshift drum, and a banjo. "What song, little ladies?" asked George, stroking his banjo lovingly.

Helen ignored the question, but Lily seemed to be getting quite in the spirit of the evening. "Do 'The Captain's Jig'!"

"Alright, little captain," replied George with a wink. "But who will you choose as your partner?"

Lily tapped her finger to her head several times making a big show over her thinking. Then, she walked over to where Matt stood. She slowly put her hand out for him to take, then jerked it back with playful rejection. Several of the sailors whooped with laughter. When Lily put out her hand again, Matt didn't give her a chance to pull it back. He pulled it close to him and hugged her.

"What about the other little lady?" called a member of the crew.

Helen turned to look at the crowd. She had been staring off over the water. She looked from one face to another, then rested her gaze on Lily. She was so... playful, innocent, hopeful. How could Helen say no to that face? She forced a smile and walked over to Riggins, holding out her hand. Riggins looked like he was going to choke with surprise. "Come on, Riggins!" cried a few of the crew.

Riggins' eyes twinkled at her. He stood slowly and bowed till his long black hair nearly swept the deck. When he stood back up, he was was looking at her so lovingly that Helen was almost startled. The music started, a lively boot-kicking tune, and soon single sailors were jumping in to join them.

"Are you alright?" asked Riggins when the noise was so loud that no one could hear them.

"No," said Helen quietly. "I'm not." She turned her face away from Riggins hastily. "Why do you even care? Matt's always pretending to be my dad, our old nanny tried to make me think she loved us before she ran off with a shoemaker, but you don't have a reason."

"You're like my niece," said Riggins, spinning her around with the music. "Isn't that enough?"

"I'm sorry! I know you care. I just had a bad night's sleep the last few days."

Riggins looked at her skeptically, then nodded. "That's okay, I like to keep my secrets, too."

"What kind of secrets could you have?" asked Helen.

"Well, my name is a pretty big one," admitted Riggins. "Not Riggins, but my real name." Helen looked up at him, asking the question with her eyes. Riggins glanced left and right before slowly bending down next to her ear. "Alfred Clive." That night was the first time since coming to live with Matt that she burst out laughing.

PILLAGERS AND PARENTHOOD
CHAPTER FOUR

The next three and a half weeks were much the same. There was work in the day, fishing in the evening, and dancing through the night. If you had been like Lily and had just gotten out of school, you would have probably agreed with her that it was the perfect life. But for Helen, every night was a battle against Tommy and the terrible scenes he would offer her. I, myself, heard the stories of these days many times as a child, but I shall spare you of the day to day adventures they enjoyed, and instead go to the day they reached Syma.

Helen's head ached. Another fitful night, another long morning, and now, just around the bend was another dreary afternoon of fishing. Lily sat beside her, doodling the sail and the clouds in her sketchbook. Helen sighed. Would this never end? Just then she noticed James, the navigator, walking by.

"James!" she called to him. He turned to look at her. "When do you think we will get to Syma?"

"By evening, I'd say," replied James, pushing his

spectacles further up his nose.

"Oh, thanks," said Helen. Only a few more hours until they reached land. This greatly lightened her mood. Soon, not seeing much else to do, she went up to where Matt was steering the ship. "Hello, Mr. Baker."

"Hi, Helen. How has your day been?" asked Matt, putting his arm around her.

"Fine," said Helen, pulling away. They stood there silent for a few minutes. "Do you remember when I told you I was having the same dream over and over again?"

"About Tommy, right?" asked Matt playfully. Helen was about to disagree, but something suddenly stopped her. Slowly the wheels in her head started turning. "Don't worry, Helen. I dream about purple elephants quite frequently, but that doesn't mean anything."

"Thanks, Mr. Baker," said Helen, starting down and across the deck.

"Where are you going?" asked Matt, puzzled.

"You gave me an idea. I'm going to take a nap now, but… wake me up when we get close to land!" With that, she disappeared into the captain's quarters where she and Lily were staying.

***

Tommy had whizzed around excitedly from the moment she arrived. He had taken her zipping through time here and there, in such a frenzy, that it took her a little while to get her bearings.

Finally, she said, "Tommy, take me there." He seemed confused. "Take me to your favorite place." Instantly, he jumped at the chance. Everything around her spun for a second, then settled down into the place she had come to know so well. Over in the corner, huddled with his arms wrapped around his legs, was the boy.

Helen stared at him for a while, lying there. By the time she moved again, she didn't know how long it had been... minutes, hours, it was hard to tell in dreams. She walked over to the boy slowly. He didn't look up. She bent down and put a hand on his shoulder; he didn't stir.

"Hey," she said softly. "I've thought about you a lot recently, and, I think I know who you are." She smiled slightly to herself at the fact that it had actually been Matt who had figured out. "I was thinking about how I have only ever had one boy in my dreams." She sighed. "I don't know how I didn't figure it out before, now that I have it seems so simple, yet still so complicated."

She patted his shoulder. "Is it you, Tommy?" There was no response. "Please tell me, I can't do this anymore. I can't keep getting dragged here night after night without knowing, without understanding. Please tell me!" The boy didn't move. "Tell me!" she repeated. She shook him hard.

Finally he looked up at her, tears streaking his face, "Was that my name once? Tommy?" The boy asked in wonderment. Then his face hardened. "No, I am not Tommy! I was never Tommy! Get out of my head!" The boy stood up, and shoved her hard. Tommy was wanting her to leave? Her thoughts of confusion turned to panic, and she screamed as she fell away from Tommy and into a great darkness...

***

"Helen, wake up. Syma is in sight," said Matt Baker, shaking her slightly.

Helen blinked sleepily, "Oh, um, thanks Mr. Baker. I'll get myself presentable and head right out."

"Okay," said Matt, patting her arm.

He went back out on deck to stand next to Lily, who had, by this time, given up on her drawing and taken over the wheel. "Do you think there could be pirates on the island, Daddy?" asked Lily when he got there.

"I don't know, Little Lil, but I doubt it. I haven't heard anything about pirates."

"Exactly!" said Lily. "Because they are trying to hide here!"

"I see," said Matt. "So I suppose every time we don't hear about pirates, they are involved?"

"Right!" said Lily. "Now you got it!"

Matt chuckled. He looked over at Riggins. Riggins was staring out at Syma with an emotionless look on his face. Matt wondered if he was always as calm as he looked or if he just had a mask that he could pull out to hide his feelings whenever he wanted to. Just as they got close to Syma's shore, Helen came out and stood on deck.

"Men, let's sail right up onto the the white shore. It looks as if we can get that far with these boats. I want them all docked together so that there is no chance of getting separated! Signal that to the other boats behind us, George!"

"Yes, sir!" called George from the crow's nest.

Within a few minutes, the boats were harbored near the shore. "Riggins, George, come with me. The rest of you, stay here and mind the boats."

Matt was just getting ready to step out of the *Bella Fawn* when he felt a tug on his sleeve. He looked down to see Lily, her arms crossed, staring up at him. "I'm coming, too!"

"No, Little Lil, not right now."

"Yes, right now. I know you don't have time for this, and I'm telling you I'm not going to be left here while you have that adventure." Several of the sailors smiled. Matt did, too.

"Alright, alright, but just this once." Lily squealed with delight and hopped over the side of the boat and onto the sand.

"I'm coming, too!" said Helen, stepping out. She could feel the eyes of the entire crew staring at her. Matt glanced at her. "If only to look after Lily."

Matt nodded, and with that, they were off, the three men and the two little girls. They explored the bank until they went quite far to the right and out of sight of the ships. As they walked, the men talked in hushed voices while Lily entertained herself by swashbuckling a shipful of imaginary pirates with a stick. Helen felt completely out of place with either.

Finally, Riggins pointed at something up ahead, "Look."

He was pointing at the dark opening of a cave. In the sand, six sets of tracks led in, but none came back out again. Lily instantly ran for it.

"No, no, no," said Matt, grabbing her and holding her tight. "I'm sorry, Little Lil, but you can't go in there, not until I have at least checked it out to make sure it's safe."

Lily sighed, "Alright, but can you do it quickly? I'm dying to check it out!"

"You heard the little captain!" said Matt, grinning at George. "Let's go check it out! Riggins, can you look out for these two?"

"Yes, admiral," said Riggins.

So Matt and George went in, and the three others waited, and waited, and waited some more. Helen stood next to Riggins, talking quietly to him, but Lily didn't care much for talking at a time like this. Instead, she went over to the entrance to the cave to inspect the footprints like an official investigator.

"Well, Mr. Whatsend, I'd say we have a mystery on our hands," Lily said, looking over at an imaginary person to her right.

"It sure is, Sir Lock," she answered herself, turning to the left. "What do you make of it?"

"We must look at the evidence, Mr. Whatsend," replied Lily, turning to the right again. She bent down to look at the tracks. "Obviously a man's tracks," she said absent-mindedly. "How is it that they can tell the age of the tracks in books? Oh, that's right, they taste the sand." She licked her finger, stuck it in the sand, then tasted it.

"Well, how did it taste, Sir Lock?" she asked, turning to the left a bit.

She turned back to the right and scrunched up her face. She spit it out, "Like sand." She stood up and wiped her tongue with the back of her hand, then looked back down at the tracks. Something about it looked wrong. Three sets of tracks were just imprints in the sand while the other three had left some darker dirt in their tracks, too, the same dark dirt that was in the cave.

Suddenly, the truth of it struck her, and she turned to tell Riggins and Helen. As she did, she realized for the first time that she hadn't heard them talking in a while. When she laid eyes on them, what she saw terrified her. She froze and stared, trembling. Face down in the sand lay Riggins, a knife buried deep in the back of his shoulder surrounded by a puddle of his own blood. Beside him stood Helen, held by a huge, hairy man with his knife to her throat and a hand over her mouth. Helen's eyes were huge and staring right at her. A muffled sound came out between the man's fingers, but by then, it was too late.

A hand clamped down on Lily's mouth from behind before she had time to scream. "A man never regrets walking out of a cave backwards, does he lass?"

***

"Well, that was disappointing," said Matt as he and George got close to the cave's exit. "We walked all that way for nothing. It would have been at least interesting to have found an empty beer bottle or something." George nodded.

As they walked into the light, they both stopped dead still. There, only a few yards away, lay Riggins, blood soaking his clothes with a knife sticking out of his shoulder. Matt ran to him as fast as he could and dropped down beside the man. With a jerk, he pulled out the knife and used it to cut his own ruffled shirt in two. Quickly, he wrapped it around Riggins's wound and tightened it as much as he could. "Come on, Riggins," Matt whispered, turning his friend over on his back. "Come on, don't leave me now!" Matt pressed his ear to the man's chest.

"Is he dead?" asked George, sliding down beside him.

Matt shook his head, relieved. "No, not yet, but he's close." Matt stood and hauled Riggins over his shoulders. "Helen and Lily probably already went to get help, but in case not, run and tell them to get ready for him."

"Right," said George. But, he'd only just ran around the next bend when he stopped in his tracks.

"What is is, George?" called Matt, struggling under his friend's weight.

"Admiral, I think Riggins is the least of our worries." Matt hurried as fast as he could up beside him, and when he got there, he stared, too. On the shore, where the five ships had been not long before, rested the *Bella Fawn* alone. The other five ships were out away from the shore with pirate flags hoisted on their masts. Bearded men crowded them like bees on a honeycomb. On the white sand, next to the *Bella Fawn,* lay a line of struggling squirming human bodies, the crew members of all five Trinity ships, bound and gagged.

Matt sighed, "Just great."

PILLAGERS AND PARENTHOOD
CHAPTER FIVE

Helen watched from the little window in the boat she had been taken to. After the pirates had snatched Lily, they had blindfolded them both before carrying them off to this dark, stinky hold and putting them in separate rooms. Helen had already tried banging on the wall to try to discover where Lily was, but it was no use. As she peeked out the little round window, she saw the line of ridiculous-looking, tied up sailors on the shore.

"Our brave heroes," she whispered to herself. But then again, she had gotten captured, too. She watched as two figures approached the line, one with a burden on his back. From where she was, she could see they were speaking, but she couldn't hear anything. *Maybe that is for the best,* she thought. *You never know what men might say in a situation like this.*

No, Matt wouldn't curse, came another thought, and she knew it was true. *George might, though.* She tried to angle herself better to see what they were doing, but just then, another boat came in view. She sighed. From behind her, she heard a click. She turned just in time to see the door swing open and a large beast of a man smile down at her.

"Ack mad farnuuuf," he said, "EEk man elkanad vat bushen?" He motioned for her to follow him.

Helen hung her head. If only they were in a dream. She could be so overpowering and commanding in dreams, not at all like the real Helen. "I'll come."

The apish man smiled, "Malman. Helrit ba bashnad!"

Helen sighed. She walked in front of him, always with the point of his spear urging her on. As they reached the deck, two things suddenly struck her. The first thing was that they were on one of the ships that had sailed with the *Bella Fawn* from Trinity. The second was the reason it had smelled so bad in the hold. Whiskey. The deck was full of pirates, as they hollered and stumbled about she realized most of them were drunk. The smell practically made her gag.

On the far side of the deck, a stage of sorts had been set up, and on the stage, stood the captain. His coat was sewn from what looked like pure gold itself, embedded with hundreds of gems and his hat was adorned with three, tall, exotic plumes, but the worst thing of all was his face and his eyes. As she got pushed past the rest of the pirates, one after another, she saw the difference. The ones she passed were fools, drunken cutthroat fools, but the captain was no fool. His eyes shone with brilliance, with strategy, and with complete and utter hatred for everyone he saw.

He smiled at Helen as she got prodded onto the stage beside him. "Welcome, my lady. Tell me, how do your new surroundings suit you?" He spoke in Mayren, a common merchant language. Matt had insisted on teaching it to Helen and Lily as soon as they came to live with him.

"Oh, wonderful," muttered Helen. The man laughed.

"A quick tongue, I see. No matter, that can be easily fixed." He looked up at the others. "Afred mal agnuted ratha?"

"Berde ba bahradanee," said one of the men hastily.

As if in answer, at that moment, Lily was carried out of the hold, kicking and screaming. As she was brought closer to the stage, she landed one good kick right between the legs of one of the pirates she passed. The man stumbled back drunkenly, howling with pain.

"Mayne furd lakman," said the captain, annoyed. "Out done by an eight-year old girl, are you?" With one swift motion, he brought his sword out of the scabbard and placed it gently against Helen's neck. Lily looked up at them with horror and instantly stopped kicking. "There," said the captain. "That wasn't so hard, was it? Learn the truth, boys. The weakness in women is always their soft hearts. Efned anosoon alcobath reath almood leeken!" Several of the pirates laughed.

Soon Lily was standing beside Helen, terrified. "What are you going to do with us? Kill us?"

"Oh, goodness no!" smirked the captain. "If I wanted you dead, I could have done that a long time ago. No," he said, crouching down next to their faces, "you get to play the part of my bartering chips."

***

Matt sat next to the motionless form of Riggins. He was lying flat on his back in the *Bella Fawn*. Every once in awhile, the physician they had brought with them would ask Matt to do this or that, but mostly he just worked in silence. George sat next to Matt, staring at the floor.

"I've done all I can, but I'm afraid I might be too late," said the physician, turning to them.

"Of course you're too late. If we hadn't have had to cut all of you stinking idiots free on the shore, he'd be fine!" snapped George, staring daggers at the physician. *To be fair, George didn't actually say 'stinking', but this is a children's story.*

Matt didn't respond. He had his eyes closed, his head in his hands, wishing that somehow he had seen this coming. Then, unexpectedly, a voice brought him out of his own thoughts, "Admiral?"

Matt looked over to see Riggins's eyes half open, staring at him. "Hey," he said, putting a hand on his arm. "How do you feel?"

Riggins almost smiled, "Somewhere between 'eh' and an 'ugh'….." Matt chuckled, softly. His friend's face was as red as fire even as his arm was freezing. Bad signs. "Where are we?"

"The *Bella Fawn*," replied Matt. "The captain's quarters, to be specific."

"But..." started Riggins, his voice trailing off.

"But what?" asked Matt.

"But if I am in the captain's quarters, where are the girls going to stay?"

"Don't worry about that, Riggins," said Matt, patting his arm.

"Yeah," said George, "Leave the worrying to people who can stand up."

Riggins smiled slightly, "Only if you insist."

"We do," said Matt. "And I also insist you get some rest. We'll leave you to it." Riggins nodded and was already fast asleep by the time George and Matt left the room.

"It looks like he's on the mend," said George, relieved.

"Sounds like it," agreed Matt, "but I don't want to take any chances. No one is to tell him about the pirates or the ships being gone or anything. Is that understood?" George nodded. Matt chuckled, "Gets stabbed with a knife, and the first thing he asks about is sleeping arrangements. Speaking of that, where are Lily and Helen. I haven't seen them in a while."

"They are probably around here somewhere," said George, shrugging. "You know kids."

Matt nodded absentmindedly. Then something behind George caught his eye. One of the Trinity ships was sailing closer to them. On it stood one pirate above all the rest. His coat shimmered like gold, and his eyes smoldered with hate. His sword was drawn, but he held it up in the peace position.

"Hail, Trinidads!" he cried in Mayren as his ship stopped a few feet away from the *Bella Fawn*. Matt stared at him hard. The man only smiled back. "Let me introduce myself. My name is Silam the Severer. Please don't ask me how I earned it," he said, caressing the blade of his sword lovingly.

"And mine is Matt Baker, and I think it is fair to say that I am not your biggest fan right now," replied Matt in Mayren, studying him.

"Indeed! I don't have many victims as fans," laughed Silam. "But then again, who needs fans when you have fear on your side?"

"What's your game?" asked Matt warily.

"It is simple really, and it starts with a little persuasion to cooperate." Silam smirked. He reached down with his right hand to grab the hair of two little girls and pull them on stage. Matt gasped at the terrified little faces. "So you do know them?" said Silam in mock surprise. "It isn't often that I am witness to such a touching reunion scene. I'll have to paint a picture."

Matt had to use all of his will not to jump over the side into the other boat and murder the villain, but here were far too many pirates there for him to fight. "What do you want?"

"Not much really," he answered, pushing the girls back off stage. "I want you to fight." Matt looked puzzled. "There is no fun in simply killing! Why do you think we left most of your men unharmed? No, but killing in battle is something different all together. There is a kind of thrill about it, isn't there? Tomorrow at sunrise, the battle will begin. Try to escape by land or sea, and the girls will die instantly."

"You're bluffing," said Matt through gritted teeth.

Silam laughed so hard his hat nearly fell off, "Bluffing? Why would I need to bluff? We have more people, more boats, and more skill. I have nothing to lose by killing them now in front of you, right now, if you would rather."

Matt sighed. He looked out over the boats that swarmed around them. Most of the non-Trinidad boats were simple long boats and could be easily destroyed. One, however, was five times the size of the *Bella Fawn*, plated with metal, an iron mast holding up the sail. Silam caught him looking at it. "Yes," he said, "I found that beauty beyond the maps. Gorgeous, isn't she?"

Matt looked the captain in the face and glanced down where Lily and Helen were standing. "I guess we will see you at dawn."

Silam smiled, "Yes, dawn." With that, the formally Trinidad ship pulled away into the oncoming darkness of night.

George nodded, "Well, I will go get the cannons ready for dawn."

"The *Bella Fawn* doesn't have cannons, George," said Matt quietly.

George sighed, "Creator help us!"

PILLAGERS AND PARENTHOOD
CHAPTER SIX

All was completely dark in the little room where Helen had been put. With nothing to do, her mind continually wandered to the boy in her dreams. What did he say his name was? Not Tommy? But if he wasn't Tommy, then who could he be? Only one boy had ever been in her dreams, but was Tommy really a boy at all? Had her naming the dream somehow created the boy? Something Matt said floated to the top of her mind, "Sometimes I dream about purple elephants." Maybe the boy, Tommy, was a purple elephant in disguise. She smiled at the thought.

Suddenly, she heard a creaking from the lock on her door, and it swung open. In the doorway stood a woman that Helen had seen on deck. Helen looked away.

"Miss?" said the woman in Mayren, the merchant language. "Are you alright?"

"Yeah, I just love getting kidnapped by pirates," said

Helen. She knew it was harsh, but she wasn't in the best of moods.

"I know how you feel," said the woman, sitting down beside her. She placed the lantern on the ground, too.

"How would you know?"

"You aren't the only one in this room who was kidnapped by pirates at a young age." The woman stared off into space as if reliving horrible memories.

"What happened?" asked Helen. She hadn't meant to, but it was so good to be talking to someone.

"They raided my town when I was five," answered the woman wistfully. "They killed my whole family and took me with them. Since then, I have been given from captain to captain."

"I'm so sorry," said Helen, trying to comfort her.

"My parents were fools when they named me," said the woman, starting to cry softly. "Emily means 'strength' where I come from, but I'm not strong. I can never seem to stand up to those pirates. I couldn't dare!"

"I think Emily is a fine name," replied Helen, smiling at her.

"Thank you," said Emily softly, wiping her tears away. "But I must go. I only came to bring you the lamp. It can get terribly lonely to sit in the dark." With that she left, locking the door behind her.

Helen sighed. It felt ten times lonelier with Emily gone, even if it was lighter. The hours dragged by. Helen stayed wide awake. She didn't feel like dreaming. She didn't feel like anything. She just stared at the wall, wondering if she would live her life like Emily had. Finally the gray that comes before dawn came to the outside world. Helen stood and looked out the window. There was a longship just a twenty yards away from where she peeped out. On it, stood Silam the Severer, shouting at several of his men.

"Arshana molcen ally va!" he shouted. "I tell you, I want to see the slaves on this ship and you deny me? Bring them out on deck now! Oclee enmech artenmerfad!"

"Saks firener!" said the frightened pirate. Helen watched as he unlatched the door to the hold. The first two chained prisoners were two huge creatures. The man looked so crushed and depressed that Helen felt sorry for him even though she had never seen him before. The other was a.... woman? Was it possible? Did women come in that size? Her arms were as muscular, if not more so, than the man's, and she had an impressive scowl plastered across her face. After them, several other much scrawnier ones followed, glancing about nervously. One in particular caught her eye.

He had brown hair and a small frame. His cheeks were tearstained, and his eyes...... there was no mistaking those eyes. Instantly all sounds, the whip, the chains, the shouting, vanished. He seemed to experience the same. He looked around for the cause, until his eyes met Helen's. They stared at each other for what seemed like years. "No," whispered Helen. "It's not possible! Tommy?"

Even though they were too far to hear each other, she knew he had heard her. He walked slowly, as if mesmerized, in her direction. All else seemed to fade. "No, this can't be happening. This can't be happening." But her words didn't slow him down. He continued to walk across the deck in her direction. "No!" she screamed at him.

"You're nothing but a purple elephant!"

"Huh?" asked the boy, puzzled. In that split second of confusion, he tripped over the side of the longboat. His chains rattled as he flailed over the side, hit his head, and fell unconscious into the water. As he hit his head, Helen crumpled to the ground. She could feel Tommy trying to suck her into a dream after the boy.

"No," she said hoarsely. "I won't go." Those were the last things she remembered saying before she fell asleep.

***

"Well, Matt, it's nearly sunrise," said George, coming up and sitting beside him. The two had their swords, but that was it. No armor, no arrows, no bows, no cannons.

"I think I can safely say that was the shortest night of my life," replied Matt, trying to smile.

"How's Riggins doing?"

"Not great. He hasn't woken up again, and the fever is raging. I don't know how much longer he can hold out." The two were silent after that, watching the sunrise together. "I'm sorry," said Matt.

"Sorry about what?"

"I'm sorry that we have to do this for my daughters." Matt nearly choked on his words. "Ever since I talked to Silam, not one sailor has complained that they might end up dying because I was stupid enough to bring my daughters. Not one has told me to get a grip and let them go."

"That's because none of us would do that to our

daughters," said George, putting his hand on Matt's shoulder.

"Here they come!" shouted a man from the crow's nest. Matt stood in alarm and pulled his sword out of his sheath. George did the same.

The first thing Matt noticed in the growing daylight was that the longboats were gone, probably off to some market to sell the things they had plundered. Unfortunately, though, the Trinity ships and *The Metal Giant* (as Matt's men had nicknamed it) were still there, and those were the real problems. Matt and the 18 other men on the ship (the rest were waiting on the beach so that the *Bella Fawn*'s deck wouldn't get too crowded during the battle) stood at their posts preparing for the attack.

When the first wave hit, it was worse than they had thought. Arrows whizzed past their heads. As one body, they flattened themselves to the deck. An arrow struck Matt's hat, and another lodged itself in his boot, but other than that, he was fine. As soon as the arrows stopped, he leaped to his feet and brandished his sword in the air.

"For Trinity, in Liberty!" he shouted at the top of his lungs.

"For Trinity, in Liberty!" answered the brave sailors around him in one voice. With that, their energy doubled. Several of the men bent down to pick up the arrows and hurl them back at the ships. Some of them hit their mark, but it did very little good. A thrown arrow might sting, but not in the same way as a shot one. *The Metal Giant* slowly made its way closer to the *Bella Fawn*.

A few of the sailors jumped over the sides and tried to climb up the sides of the other boats, but they were swatted away like flies. *The Metal Giant* came ever closer.

"For Trinity! IN LIBERTY!" shouted Matt again.

"For Trinity! IN LIBERTY!!!!" shouted the crew back. They weren't defeated yet. Finally *The Metal Giant* came within a few yards of the *Bella Fawn* and halted. Pirates swung on ropes across the gap, and the hand to hand combat began. Matt watched as a plank was set between to two boats. On it, stepped Silam, dressed in gold armor and smirking at Matt.

"Come along, my dear man. Captain against captain. Make my day enjoyable, why don't you?" said Silam, glaring at Matt.

Matt grinned, remembering how this man had laid hands on his daughters, and stepped up onto the plank, "Gladly."

PILLAGERS AND PARENTHOOD
CHAPTER SEVEN

Lily watched, from the cage she had been put in, as her guard's head slowly drooped. She held her breath as the first long snore echoed past his lips.

"Too much whiskey makes my job easy," whispered Lily quietly to herself. She had listened to the shouts of battle for a while now, and it was about time she do something about it. She glanced from the sleeping man's face to the keys on a ring hanging partially out of his pocket.

Carefully she reached her small hand through the bars of the cage. She stretched her arm as far as she could until the tips of her fingers could just barely reach the keys. She grabbed one between her third and fourth finger and gently pulled them out. As they fell, they clinked together softly, but the drunk man hardly noticed. She recognized the right key instantly.

Slowly, she poked her hand out of the bars again and

twisted it around, putting the key in the key hole. Then she paused. Which way to turn it?

"Lefty loosey, righty tighty," she said to herself.

She turned the key in the lock and was satisfied when the cage door slowly swung open. She was about to leave it when she had a funny idea. Wouldn't it be hilarious for the man to wake up to a closed and empty cage? She quickly closed the cage door and locked it again. Next, she tiptoed down the hallway and decided on a door to try. She tried to turn the handle, but it was locked. Then she looked down at the ring of keys she was still holding. On the third try, a key went into the lock, and the door opened reluctantly.

She clapped her hands in delight when she saw what was there. A cannon. A real polished cannon. Next to it sat a rack filled with cannonballs, and beside that a jar filled with gunpowder. Oh how she wanted to try it.

"But no," she said. "Daddy told me never to fire a cannon without adult supervision." Then she glanced up and down the hall and smiled. "But Daddy would never have to know."

***

Matt Baker thrust his sword forward only to have it blocked again by the smirking Silam. Beads of sweat formed on his forehead as he lunged again for his enemy who defended with a perfect block.

"Hmm… you aren't as good as I hoped, but still enjoyable," said Silam. Suddenly, out of nowhere, a boom echoed through the air. A cannon ball smashed into the side of *The Metal Giant*. The two men nearly lost their balance as the boat swayed.

***

Fists pounded on the door into the cannon room, and angry voices shouted, breaking Lily's concentration.

"Shut up! I'm trying to fire a cannon!" she shouted at them, but the pounding only got louder. Good thing she had the only set of keys. She reloaded, put in the powder, and lit it with a match. BOOM!!!! It thundered it's way out and into the fray.

"Woohoo!!!" shouted Lily. This was the best day of her life!

***

Another cannonball whizzed through the air and smashed into the bottom of one of the former Trinidad ships. The beast swayed and slowly began taking on water. Before long, it was half submerged in the waves. The pirates, all wearing armor, screamed as they got pulled under the water.

Matt grinned at Silam's horror, "My daughter has a few... well... *unique* skills."

***

Helen stood in a small dark room with a cat who was intently watching a mouse hole. For a second, she wondered what had happened, but then Tommy pulled her out of the room and put her back into the shadows with the boy.

"No!" she said sternly. "It isn't possible! It isn't

possible! Get me out of here!" She had to fight with Tommy to leave the shadowy place. By the time the world stopped spinning, she was standing next to Lily. Lily was hefting a metal ball into a cannon that stood in the corner of the room.

"Just a little more gunpowder," said Lily as she poured something out of a jar into the giant gun. "Up, up, and away!" She lit the fuse, and a second later the air around the cannon exploded.

Then Tommy wrapped himself around her again and sucked her back into the shadows, and back to the boy. "Ugh! No! You're just a purple elephant! You're just a purple elephant!" She pushed out again, out into the time and space of her dream.

When the dream stopped spinning, she saw two things at once, as if she were stuck halfway in two worlds. Two figures lay on the ground in a puddle of their own blood: Riggins and her mother. How many more people were going to die like this? How many more would be taken from her?

Once again, Tommy clutched her and brought her back. "Stop!" shouted Helen at the boy. "You're just a purple elephant!" With that, she jumped out of the dream with all of her force and suddenly broke through.

She landed in a strange place, all mist and shadows. She stumbled forward and took a second to catch her breath. It felt different. Everything here felt different. It wasn't a place. It was… a possibility. She looked at the little clouds of mist around her. Slowly, she focused all of her attention on it. As she started, it quaked for a minute then formed itself into a ship. A very familiar ship. "It's the *Bella Fawn*." It was sinking fast in a sea of shadowy waves, sailors jumping off it and swimming to shore. Not one of them was Matt.

"Where is he?" whispered Helen. For the first time since she'd gotten there, she felt Tommy's presence. "Where is he?"

The ship evaporated, and in its place was the body of a man, crushed under a huge object. Helen couldn't tell what it was, but it didn't seem to matter. The look on Matt's face was very clear. He was dead. She couldn't stop a sob that squeezed it's way out of her. Dead. Another person dead, for her. She buried her face in her hands and cried softly, then a strange resolve came over her.

"Tommy," she said. "I've never been here before, have I?" The dream said nothing. "You have taken me both to the present and the past before." The dream didn't respond. "Is this... the future?" A sudden pang leapt through her body, and in an instant, she knew she was on to something. "But I know you ,Tommy. You may look out for me in the same way I try to treat you well, but you would NEVER let me see the future. You don't trust me any more than I trust you." If a dream could agree, Tommy did. "Then is this, a possible future?" Tommy smiled.

"Then I have to stop it!" said Helen. "I have seen the boy in my dreams. Whether it is you or not, I don't care right now. You know how I can talk to other people in my dreams. Show me how!" Tommy hesitated. "Please Tommy, take me to someone who can help me make a difference."

Tommy finally obeyed.

Helen found herself somewhere red hot. She was

buried deep inside a fire. Pain shot through her left arm. "STOP!!!" Instantly, everything around her froze. She could feel she wasn't alone. "No more pain! No more fire!" she shouted. The two slowly melted away, leaving only a black stillness.

***

Riggins stirred slightly in his sleep. He dreamt of fire, a never-ending fire. His head burned, but his body felt frozen. His arm ached with a pain that wouldn't leave him be. He felt so alone, so utterly alone. Suddenly, he wasn't alone anymore.

A voice rang through his dreams: "STOP!!! No more pain! No more fire!" Instantly, the pain and the burning in his head seeped away. He felt light, and free. "Riggins?" came the voice again. Maybe he was going crazy, but it sounded like Helen. "Riggins, you have to wake up! You have to save him!"

Save him? thought Riggins. *Save who?*

"Matt!" answered the voice. Now he knew he was going crazy. Helen said Mr. Baker, not Matt. "Please, you don't have much time!" came her voice again. "Just WAKE UP!!!"

Riggins opened his eyes. He was in the captain's quarters of the *Bella Fawn*. The pain in his head, arm, and shoulder were gone. He looked down at his left hand and tried to move his fingers. Nothing. His hand and arm were just as useless, he sighed. At least he was right-handed. He stood, a bit shakily at first, in his blood-stained clothes. A loud war cry filled his ears from outside. He stumbled to the window. Outside, pirates swung on ropes from other ships onto the *Bella Fawn*. What on earth was going on?

The voice's words came back to him, "You have to save Matt, there isn't much time."

Was this what he had to save him from? He groaned as he looked back down at his limp arm. It would only be a nuisance in going out to battle. He grabbed his left hand with his right and jammed in into his trouser pocket. That would have to do. He reached for the door with a sigh. Whatever would happen, it would happen now.

***

Emily sat on deck of the *Metal Giant,* watching the two captains fight. One fought for the pleasure of killing while the other thought only of his daughters. One of them was honorable; the other only a murderer. Emily glanced over the edge of the ship. For a second, she assessed the jump, wondering the best way to do it without hurting herself.

"Emily," said her pirate guard with an evil smirk. "Come away from the edge." Emily took one last look over the edge, then bent her head and went back to her guard.

PILLAGERS AND PARENTHOOD
CHAPTER EIGHT

Matt could hear his men shouting behind him, and out in front, he saw two more formal Trinidad ships sunk by Lily's cannon, but he couldn't think about that now. Silam was taking all of his brain power. The pirate thrust, blocked, parried, and slashed almost faster than Matt could see. He kept dodging, blocking, and jabbing as fast as he could.

"You're holding out longer than I expected," said Silam delightedly. "It's been awhile since I had this much fun."

"Mutual, I'm sure," said Matt ducking away from another swipe. His hair was permanently cemented to his head with sweat. *Just a little longer,* he kept thinking to himself. *I just need to hold out a little longer.*

***

Lily fired again. BOOM!!! The cannonball smashed into the last of the former Trinidad ships. She laughed to see the mighty thing go down so easily.

"This is better than fasting from vegetables!" she cried in glee. Suddenly, she heard a thud from behind her. The tip of an axe had made its way through the sturdy door that was the only thing standing between her and the pirates. She gulped. If that door came down, she was dead meat, complete and total dead meat. She bit her lip. Time was running out. It was time to get rid of *The Metal Giant.*

***

Matt swung back again and again. His arms were cramping, his knuckles ached, everything seemed worthless. Silam was advancing now, a satisfied look on his face. *It's done,* thought Matt sadly. *It's finally done.*

***

Lily heaved a cannonball up into the cannon with a groan. Five cannonballs! Five cannonballs, and not a single one had penetrated *The Metal Giant.* It was so frustrating. She added the powder and lit the wick. BOOM!!! She watched hopefully. Was the sixth time a charm? The ball flew through the air straight at the ship and once again bounced off the side. Lily stomped her foot. Another thud sounded behind her. This time a spearhead had made its way through the wood of the door. Why wasn't this working?

Suddenly, something about *The Metal Giant* caught her eye - the huge iron mast that stood tall above ship. It looked heavy... very heavy. Lily smiled.

***

Silam swung his sword. Matt tried to block the shot,

but even as he did, his grip loosened, and his sword flew out of his hand and over the side of the boat down into the water. As he watched it fall, he wondered if he would be next. Silam kicked Matt hard, and he fell to his knees in front of his enemy.

"It seems our game is now coming to an end," said Silam, smirking. He raised his sword high above his head, preparing to bring it down between Matt's shoulder blades, but before he had a chance, the cannon fired again. The cannonball zoomed over Emily's head making her scream and smashed into the mast. Time seemed to slow. The mast teetered for a second, then plummeted straight toward Matt and Silam on the plank.

As it fell, Matt wondered how long it would last. Would the pain be over soon? Would it be a fast death? Just as it came down over them, a hand grabbed Matt's collar and tugged him out of the way. It jerked him back, on top of his savior's body, on the edge of the *Bella Fawn*'s deck. Silam tried to jump after him, but the mast came down on his leg before he reached the ship. For one moment, they looked at each other eye to eye. One shocked, the other terrified, then... Silam was gone. Matt heard a splash and knew that no man could lift a mast so heavy. He turned his head to thank George for saving him but gasped to see Riggin's laying under him.

"Riggins?" asked Matt, scrambling to his feet and helping his friend up. "How? Why?"

Riggins just smiled, "How would you ever get along without me?"

***

"YES!!!" shouted Lily in triumph. Her aim had worked.

Not only had the mast broken a hole in the metal exterior, but it had taken down the captain (she would have liked to take credit for the second part, but in truth she had absolutely no control over it). A shout from the other side of the door brought her back to the here and now. After unhooking the chains that held the cannon in place, he propped open the 'window' where it stuck out of the ship as wide as it would go, and pulled the cannon away from it on its wheels. Slowly, with great effort, she turned the cannon around to face the door. "Just one more piece of business to take care of." Once it was facing the door, she carefully tilted the cannon down.

Then she banged on the walls, "Helen!!!!!!" she shouted. "HELEN!!!!! CAN YOU HEAR ME?!?!?!?!"

For a second there was silence and then a sleepy, "I wouldn't be surprised if all Ildathore could hear you!" Helen was in a room just to the right of the cannon room. This was perfect!

"Helen! Do you have a window in your room? And a solid object?" asked Lily crossing her fingers.

A pause, "Well, I have a window and a lantern. Can that work?"

"Yes!" said Lily, excitedly. "Throw the lantern through the window!"

"What?"

"Throw the lantern out the window!!!!" Lily heard a crash. "Good! Is the hole big enough to get through?"

"I think I can get through it."

"Great! Now when I say go, jump out the window!"

"Lily?"

"No time for questions!" shouted Lily. She put the ball in the cannon for the last time and filled it up with gunpowder. As she lit the match, the door was finally broken down and three pirates stood there. "Hope you can swim!" shouted Lily, and she lit the fuse. She hurled herself out of the cannon's opening as the last enemy ship was blown into two. "JUMP!!!"

***

Emily watched as the ship split apart in an explosion of splintered wood. Even while it did, two tiny forms leaped from windows in the side of the ship. One of them, the smaller, quickly swam away toward the *Bella Fawn*. The other made it most of the way out and then got stuck. Emily watched with horror as the girls head was submerged under water. Suddenly, resolve built up in her; this was her moment. She ran to the edge of *The Metal Giant* and jumped, her skirts bellowing out behind her. She reached the water with a splash and swam as fast as she could to the helpless figure now deep under the surface of the water. She took a deep breath and dove. The girl's dress was caught on a piece of broken glass from the broken window. The girls eyes were closed, her body unmoving.

Emily wrenched on the dress once but it only caught more. She wrenched it again to no end. On the third time, the dress tore free. She hauled her up to the surface as fast as she could. As soon as Emily's head came out of the water, she saw Matt jump from the *Bella Fawn* and swim toward them. She could feel the strength in her giving out.

"Here," said Matt, taking her. With the strength of a man in panic, he swam Helen to the shore with Emily and Lily following as fast as they could. By the time they caught up to him, Helen was flat on her back in the sand.

"Come on, Helen!" said Matt, pushing down on her chest. No response. "Come on, Helen!" Again and again and again. Finally, Emily turned her head away.

Matt stared down at his daughters face, and with one last effort, pushed down on her chest. Helen coughed, hacking the water up. "That's it!" said Matt pushing again. "Breathe, Helen, breathe!"

Water streamed down her face, and her eyes fluttered open. "Matt? You're alive?"

Matt laughed the heartiest laugh he ever had. "And so are you!" Then he grabbed her and hugged her as hard as he could. And though he never would have expected it, she hugged back.

"I thought you were gone," whispered Helen.

"I'll always come back," answered Matt, holding her close.

Lily cleared her throat quietly, "Can I join?"

Matt grinned and held out his other arm. Lily squealed with delight and ran in to embrace them. Once they were done, Helen smiled at her sister, "Lily, you were amazing with that cannon! Absolutely amazing! How did you do it?"

Lily smiled sheepishly, "Um, Helen, you weren't supposed to tell Daddy it was me."

Matt chuckled and picked her up twirling around, "I'm extremely glad it was you, Little Lil!" Then he put her down, "But never ever do it again."

Lily grinned. Emily slowly started walking away, not sure how to approach the happy family. "Oh, Emily, come back!" said Helen, standing up. "Matt, this is Emily. She was kidnapped by the pirates, too, a long time ago."

"Well thank you, Emily, for saving my daughter," said Matt, nodding to her.

"The pleasure was all mine, Admiral," said Emily, blushing and batting her eyelashes at him. He cleared his throat awkwardly.

"Wait, she saved Lily?" asked Helen confused.

"No, she saved you," said Lily.

Helen turned to Matt, "But I thought you saved me?"

Matt nodded, "I saved you after Emily did."

"But, didn't I save everyone here?" said Lily, now puzzled.

"No," answered Matt, "Riggins saved me."

"Riggins saved who?" asked Riggins, walking over.

"Riggins!" cried both girls at once. They ran and hugged him. He hugged back the best he could with one arm. "But wasn't I saved by Hele..." started Riggins, looking at Helen, but his words trailed off.

"This is going to take months to sort out," said Matt, laughing.

"Then let's get started," said Riggins, pointing back to the *Bella Fawn*.

"Now that sounds like a plan," said Matt. Then, clearing his throat, he turned to Emily, "Do you have anywhere you would like to be taken? It is the least I could do."

"Oh no," said Emily. "My family is gone. With no pirates, I've got nowhere to go."

"Matt," said Helen. "Couldn't she come back with us? We do need a new nanny."

Matt was about to disagree when Emily said, "Oh that would just be a dream come true. I would love to."

Matt sighed, "Then, I guess it's settled." Riggins watched Matt's fumblings with Emily with an amused expression on his face.

"If that is settled then, can we get going?"

"Yes!" said Matt, taking his daughters hands as they walked.

And though many things changed for them on that trip, one thing stayed the same, "Can I steer, Daddy?"

They were the happiest family in the world that night, and for many more after that. Emily did indeed go to live in the Baker manner as the nanny, and she and Helen became fast friends. Riggins, though a bit banged up from the experience, was never looked down upon for his handicap but instead praised for his work in the Navy. As for Matt, he had learned that he would never have the same relationship with Helen as he did with Lily, but after that day, he never stopped trying. But what happened about the boy, you might ask, the one in Helen's dreams? Did she ever see him again? Was he even really Tommy? Was he a purple elephant? I'm afraid you'll have to read about that somewhere else to find out. But I suppose I could tell you just one thing more...

On the shore of Syma, a haggard blood-stained figure pulled his way out of the water and onto the beach, hand over hand. The moonlight shone off his wet body. Where had once been a right leg, now there was only a bloody stump. Once completely on the shore, he stopped to catch his ragged breath. He turned himself over on his back and saw the *Bella Fawn* heading home way off in the distance.

"Make a fool of Silam, will you?" he said in a low cutthroat voice. "NEVER! DO YOU HEAR?!?!?! Almotrent mebad elgarnat heb brata! I'll find you, Matt Baker! Wherever you are! It may be years from now by then, and I may have become only a distant memory to you, but I will find you and cut you down like you deserve! I'LL KILL YOU, MATT BAKER, IF IT'S THE LAST THING I DO!!!!!"

SABINA BOYER

STORY FOUR
COURTING THE
ADMIRAL'S DAUGHTER

COURTING THE ADMIRAL'S DAUGHTER
CHAPTER ONE

In the capital of the Trinity Islands, there is a park. It is quite a wonderful park that people around the world come to see. In it are different types of trees from all over Ildathore. The people of that city love the place, but I don't think anyone loved it as much as Mark Kalnem. He lived just on the edge of it, and if you ever walked through the park, you would probably see him with his nose in a book. As a matter a fact, that is exactly how our story starts.

Seventeen-year-old Mark Kalnem sat on a bench in the middle of Blossom Park, a math book propped open on his lap. Next to him on the bench was his bag full of several other textbooks he had already studied. He cringed as a cramp started in his left leg. He sighed and stood up, slinging the bag over one shoulder. *Maybe walking around a little will make it go away,* he thought.

Mark Kalnem didn't walk like the typical seventeen-year-old with a math exam the next day. He didn't shuffle his feet with his nose in the book; he took long strides with his nose in the book. His dark brown curls fell down around his ears and quivered as a slight breeze picked up. His gray eyes darted from one side of the page to another as he tried to suck in the knowledge. He had no idea that he was about to come toe to toe with someone who would change his world forever. Literally toe to toe. As he turned a corner in the path around a large shrub, he tripped over the feet of another walker and sprawled out on the ground, scattering books in all directions.

"I'm so sorry!" said a girl's voice. As he looked up at her, he had to squint because of the sun. "Here, let me help you pick up your books."

"Oh, thanks! And don't mention it, the tripping thing I mean. It was my fault as much as yours," said Mark as the girl got down on her knees beside him. Together they scrambled around on the ground, grabbing all of the pens and bookmarks and notes that had fallen out from between the pages of his textbooks.

Once they had stuffed them all back in the bag, the girl sprang up, and Mark followed more slowly. He still hadn't gotten a good look at the girl's face. Before he got a chance to, she turned and walked away quickly like she had somewhere to go. All he saw was her waist-long gray hair.

***

That night, Mark put on a semi-dressy coat and walked through the streets of the capital to his best friend Daniel's house. When Daniel opened the door, Mark could already hear the laughter on the other side.

"Where you been, man?" said Dan. He didn't look like anyone else Mark had ever met. He was from beyond the maps and had dark brown skin, chocolate colored, and a smile that was always quick to come. His black hair fell in locks down to his shoulders and he liked to shake it when he was happy and called it his 'lion's mane.' Mark didn't know any one else he loved more.

"Sorry I'm a little late," said Mark, clasping his friend's hand. "Had to finish homework, you know."

"Yeah I know," said Dan still grinning, "You're making sure you won't miss any of the extra credit."

"Why the extra credit?"

"Because with how much you study, you must already have the rest memorized!" said Dan, clapping him on the back. Mark smiled, hung his coat on a peg in the hallway, and went into the living room. The house already seemed crowded with people. Some sat on tables, others on chairs, others swung their legs from the loft. "So, you ready for me to announce it?" said Dan, walking up beside him.

Mark raised his eyebrows, "Ready for you to announce what?"

"Yo everyone!" said Dan, jumping up on a table. Slowly, the room quieted down and everyone looked at him. "You might be wondering why I called you all here tonight. Well, I've got something special to tell you. Come on up here, Mark!"

Mark stepped onto the table much more awkwardly, aware that the entire room was staring at him.

"As a lot of you know," said Dan, "Mark and I are two members of a group on campus. We are in a race with the chaps over on Thebel to see who will be the first people to fly!" Several of the people in the room whooped. "But just a few days ago, Mark here came up with the first ever design for the prototype! Give it up for the future first man to fly!" The guests hollered and cheered and stamped their feet, forgetting in their excitement that Mark hadn't actually done it yet. "Mark," said Dan, flashing him a smile, "Anything you want to say, man?"

"Sure..." said Mark. "I just want to say to any of you that are wondering that this is the first time I have ever made a speech while standing on a table." More laughs.

Mark and Dan stepped off their stage, and Dan looked at him, intrigued, "Was that really the first time you ever made a speech on a table, man?"

"Yes," answered Mar, grinning. "How often do you do it?"

Dan cleared his throat, "Well... never mind. So, how long do you think till we can start building the prototype?"

"I'd say about..." started Mark, but then he saw something off behind his friend, and his voice trailed off.

Dan glanced behind him, puzzled, "What you lookin at?"

"Who's that girl?" asked Mark in a hushed voice.

"The blond?" asked Dan. "You know her, that's Suzy Lark."

"No, not Suzy, the other one."

"The brunette?" asked Dan. "That's just Grace. Nice girl, kind of a nerd though.
"No, to the left."

"The redhead?" he asked, cocking his eyebrow, "Man, I don't know who that is. Wait, I don't know who that is... Why is she at my party?"

"The one with gray hair!" said Mark.

"The grandma?"

"She's a grandma?!?!"

"I don't know. I was just trying to come up with a cute name for someone with gray hair." Dan thought a moment. "No, grandma definitely wouldn't work. If you ever tried to put it in a love poem, you'd end up getting slapped."

"She's... beautiful," said Mark, sucking in his breath.

"You think?" asked Dan. "She's alright, I guess, but I prefer more typical girls, like Suzy Lark."

Mark stared at her face, "She has the most stunning violet eyes. Do you know who she is?"

"Lily, I think."

"No," said Mark. "Her eyes are definitely violet."

"Not her eyes. I think her name is Lily." Dan glanced at her eyes. "Man, doesn't that creep you out? If they if they glowed I'd be running for the hills. Do you know her?"

"I bumped into her earlier today," said Mark grinning. "If only I knew how I should introduce myself..."

"You should never introduce yourself to a girl," said Dan with a mischievous smile. "I'll have to introduce you to her." With that, he grabbed Mark by the shirt collar and walked the stunned young man over to the girl.

"Excuse me, Lily," said Dan with his most heartwarming smile.

"Oh, hi, um, Dan," said Lily turning toward them.

Dan motioned to Mark, "I would like to introduce you to a wonderful person, a charming man, an unbelievable inventor, a top notch student, a..." Mark elbowed him in the ribs, "Uh, friend of mine, Mark." With that, he walked away.

Marks cheeks were burning as he shook hands with the girl. "Hey, Mark," said Lily, then she paused. "Didn't we run into each other earlier today?"

Mark chuckled, "Literally." She laughed, too. "So, Lily, I haven't seen you around the university. Are you new?"

"No, actually," said Lily, smiling. "You may not have seen me, but I've seen you. We are in mechanics together."

"Oh, I'm sorry I didn't see you."

"No, trust me, that's the point," explained Lily with a grin, "I come exactly seventeen minutes early and grab the seat farthest back. Unfortunately a lot of them are taken by others with the same idea. Then, at exactly fifteen and a half minutes early, you run in as fast as you can and grab a front seat (like anyone else would try to get the front seat), and you take notes the whole time. At the end, I slip out, and you go up to the teacher to ask questions. No reason you should have seen me."

"Wow, that was extremely accurate," said Mark with a laugh. "Are you stalking me or something?"

Lily chuckled, "Only during mechanics class."

"So, why do you try to get the back seat? Do you not like mechanics?"

"It isn't that I don't like it," said Lily, sighing, "but it's so difficult for me to understand."

"Well, if you ever need help, check out the top floor of the west wing at school."

"Why, what's there?"

Mark grinned, "If you want to know, you'll have to visit."

"Maybe I will."

COURTING THE
ADMIRAL'S DAUGHTER
CHAPTER TWO

"So what did you talk about?" asked Dan, sitting down next to Mark's legs. Mark was laying on a roller, and pushed underneath the left wing of the flying machine prototype. The whole room was filled with models and random pieces and parts, but Dan seemed more concerned with talking than working. "Man, did you ask her out?"

"Of course not!" said Mark from under the wing. "Can you hand me the number two faxiter?"

"Here you go," said Dan putting the tool in his friend's outstretched hand. "Why didn't you ask Lily out? I thought you liked her!"

"I do like her," said Mark, twisting a nobble tighter into place. "But I only met her that night."

"You at least set up a time to see her again, didn't

you?" asked Dan, incredulously.

"I told her to stop by here if she ever needed help with mechanics."

Dan grabbed the roller and pulled Mark out from under the wing. "Are you kidding me, man? The only time you could think of to meet a beautiful girl is to study? I knew you were desperate, but now I think you're insane!"

Mark rolled his eyes and pushed himself back under the wing. "In case you haven't noticed, we aren't in the two thousands any more. People don't just meet and marry on the fly."

"The good old days," said Dan. Mark knew he was grinning even from under the wing.

From the far end of the room, Mark heard a creak as the door opened. "It's about time you got here, Fred!" said Mark, not taking the time to roll out and shake hands. "I need your help to fit this nackbock in place. Dan seems to have given up work to analyze me today."

"Mark," said Dan. There was the mischievous grin sound in his voice again. "It isn't Fred."

"Then who is it?"

"Hi, Mark," came Lily's voice from practically right next to him. Mark froze. Dan grabbed his roller and pulled him out right next to Lily's feet.

"Um, hey," said Mark nervously.

"At least this time it isn't my fault you're on the ground," said Lily with a laugh. She reached down and helped him up. "So, this must be your workshop," she commented, looking around at the piles of papers, tools, and other odds and ends.

"Yeah," said Mark, scratching the back of his head. "Not overly impressive but a good place to get work done."

"I like it," said Lily, picking up one of the tools.

"And I like you," said Dan, putting an arm around her as he flashed a smile at Mark.

Mark rolled his eyes, when was Dan ever going to act his age? "Don't you have somewhere to go, Dan?"

Dan thought a moment, then shook his head, "Nope."

"Dan..."

"I'm kidding!" said Dan with a chuckle. "I've got to run, I'll leave you two to... study."

"Thanks, Dan," said Lily as he left. As soon as the door closed, she laughed, "When is he ever going to act his age?" Mark grinned.

***

"It's just this way," said Mark, leading a blindfolded Lily by the hand. It was two months since they'd first met, and Mark was pretty stinkin' sure they were the best two months of his life. As he led her, her light blue dress fluttered in the wind, and her long silver hair fought its way out of a loose braid. "Alright, we're here," said Mark, taking off the blindfold.

"Oh, Mark!" said Lily. "It's stunning!" He had led her to one of his favorite spots in the park, a beautiful little place completely surrounded and covered by elmanon trees, a peculiar tree that blooms in the fall.

"When you told me you were from Vanya a few days ago, I figured you might want to see a little piece of it," said Mark, giving her hand a squeeze.

"They're exactly how I remember them!" said Lily, her eyes sparkling up at the blooming golden flowers. "I remember how I always used to love fall when I was little because we had one of these trees right outside our cottage. Mom would lift me up into the lowest branch, and I felt like I could see the whole world from up there."

"Then that's where we'll have our picnic!" said Mark with a laugh. "Right up there in the branches."

"Picnic?" asked Lily. "You didn't say anything about a picnic!"

Mark nodded, "Everything is ready. Lily. I was hoping you liked to climb trees." Lily stared at him. "You'll see; let's climb up in this one." The tree he had brought her to was a huge thing with a base so big three people couldn't reach around it. "Follow my lead," he said, sitting down in a swing that hung from the branches above. He swung as hard as he could, and after a few times was so high he had to duck from the branches of the tree. Then, on his next swing, he grinned down at Lily and grabbed onto the branch that was closest to him. She gasped as he scurried up and out of sight into the branches.

"Mark!" said Lily in confusion. "Where are you going?" There was no answer. "Mark?" She said is confusion. Then with resolve, she sat down on the swing and began pumping her legs back and forth. Before long, she was as high as she could go. With another swing, she grabbed onto the branch. A thrill went through her as the swing fell away underneath her. She scrambled up the way he had gone. The branches were so thick and tangled that it was practically impossible to get through, but then, her head came out above the leaves, and she grinned.

A few feet above her, the branches cleared a bit, and the view nearly took her breath away. It stretched out over the park and all the way to the shore. And there, right where you could sit and see the most, sat Mark on a rather large branch, a picnic basket sitting next to him. "And now for our picnic," he said with a twinkle in his eyes. "I'm not the best cook in the world, but even I can handle sandwiches."

Lily laughed so hard she nearly fell off the swing, "Mark, this place is wonderful! It's the most magical place I've ever dreamed of, even in storybooks!"

"Trust me," he said smiling, "It isn't half so magical without you here."

Lily blushed, "Flatterer," but he could tell that she liked it.

They ate their sandwiches in silence, watching the flowers fall every time a breeze blew. When they were done, Mark took her hand, "Isn't it just the most beautiful sight you've ever seen?"

"I don't even know what to say," breathed Lily, taking it all in. "Why haven't we come here before?"

"You're the only one who I have ever told about this place," said Mark, glancing at her.

"Really?" asked Lily. "Then why did you decide to take me?"

"Because," said Mark nervously, "I wanted to ask you something important, and I knew it had to be in a place like this."

"Yes?" said Lily, raising an eyebrow.

"Well, we've been friends for a few months now, Lily. And I'm wondering, if you would, maybe, want to be more than friends?"

"More than friends?" asked Lily. "Mark, are you asking me to court you?"

"Maybe."

Lily smiled and leaned over to him, "In that case... yes."

COURTING THE ADMIRAL'S DAUGHTER CHAPTER THREE

"She wants me to meet her father, Dan! Her FATHER!!!" Mark was pacing the inventing room at the university like a mouse with a cat at every exit.

"So what?" said Dan. "What's the worst that could happen?"

"Worst that could happen?!?! I don't even know him! I don't know anything about her family, Dan! What if he's the king and I don't even know until he answers the door and orders my execution!!!"

"Calm down, man," said Dan, grabbing Mark by the shoulders. "First, I should hope even you should know what the palace looks like before you ring the doorbell, and second of all, Trinity has a queen, not a king."

"Well, at least I have that going for me," said Mark,

breaking away and beginning to pace again.

"I've never seen you this nervous over a girl!" replied Dan, trying not to laugh at his friend's behavior.

"I've never loved a girl this much!"

"This really means a lot to you, doesn't it?" asked Dan.

"YES!!!"

"Well, I'll tell you what, man," started Dan, "How about I go with you to her house for the first time, at least to the gate. Then, maybe I can convince you there's nothing to worry about. She gave you the address, right?"

"Yeah," said Mark. "I'm supposed to go there at four."

"Okay, go home and get ready. I'll meet you here at three thirty, and we can walk together."

***

"Why did Daddy have to insist on meeting him now!?!?! NOW!!!! Of all of the days, why the one when he ends up asking to court me?" said Lily, putting her hand to her head.

Her sister Helen had come into her room to talk about it and was now sitting on her bed. Helen was twenty already, and she was typically the one sixteen-year-old Lily went to for advice about things like this. "You know it's just because Matt cares about you," said Helen, trying to hide a smile.

"But don't you remember what he did to your suitors?" asked Lily, terrified. "That one guy… what was his name?"

"Frank," said Helen with a sigh.

"Yeah, that Frank guy actually peed his pants! In our living room!" Lily flopped down on her bed beside Helen, head in hands.

"Well, one good thing came out of that," said Helen, quietly.

"What?" asked Lily, uncovering her eyes with the slightest amount of hope.

"If I hadn't brought him here to meet Matt and I had gone ahead and married him, who knows, I might have woken up one morning with a puddle in my bed."

"Not funny," said Lily, burying her face in the pillow. "I'm doomed!"

***

Mr. Tickleten, an old friend of Lily's family, came up the long walkway to the house. As he did, he looked over puzzled at a man with long black hair, one hand in his pocket, pushing a cannon around toward the back of the house. "Riggins!" called Mr. Tickleten, "What are you doing?"

"Taking a cannon into the backyard, what else?" said Riggins, pushing hair out of his face.

"Well, I was able to see that with my very own eyes," said Mr. Tickleten, "I meant, why?"

"Matt's orders!" said Riggins. "Lily's first suitor is visiting today. He would roll the cannon there himself, but he's sharpening his sword currently."

"Oh, good grief," muttered Mr. Tickleten. "So it's that time again."

"Afraid so," called back Riggins.

Mr. Tickleten shook his head in amusement. He walked quickly, his gray hair flopping as his short legs took the steps. When he reached the door, he gave it a push and paused. Then he knocked.

"Come in!" called Matt from inside.

"I can't," said Mr. Tickleten. "It's too heavy."

"Oh sorry," called Matt again. "Lily is bringing her suitor over tonight, and I decided to make a few adjustments to the door. Try the other one. It's as light as ever."

Mr. Tickleten shook his head and pushed the other half of the double door open, "So, you really are up to it again, are you?"

"Up to what?" asked Matt in feigned innocence.

"Up to what, indeed," said Mr. Tickleten with a laugh. "Making your daughter's lives miserable."

"Oh, come now," said Matt, "That's a low blow, even for you. I'm not trying to make their lives miserable, I'm just making sure they don't open themselves up to anyone who doesn't deserve them."

"Really? Then what about the brute of the boy, remember him? He was so scared during dinner that he broke the door down in his mad rush to escape."

"He broke the door down?" asked Matt in confusion. "Didn't he jump through the glass in the window?"

"No, the scrawny one jumped through the glass in the window. He had to get five stitches from that!"

"You're actually going to blame me that he had to get stitches because he broke my window with his head?" questioned Matt, raising his eyebrows.

"One hundred percent blame!" said Mr. Tickleten emphatically.

"Okay, so there are two incidents that went wrong. That doesn't make me a bad father."

"What about that other kid, what was his name?" asked Mr. Tickleten. "It's on the tip of my tongue."

"Frank," said Matt. "But he was a wimp! Plus it took me a long time to get the pee stain off of that chair, so I'd say we're even."

"The boy peed on your chair?" laughed Mr. Tickleten. "I must admit I hadn't heard that one. You must tell it to me in more detail sometime."

"Then, who were you talking about?"

"I was talking about the boy with the spiky hair who said he was going to report your behavior to the queen."

"Oh! That one, the embarrassing thing is that he actually did."

"Really?" inquired Mr. Tickleten. "What did she say?"

"She said her father did the same thing but they never fired him as king for it," said Matt with a smile. Then he put his hand to his mouth in thought, "But then again, she still doesn't have a husband."

"See, what did I tell you?" asked Mr. Tickleten. "She will have to suffer old age all alone because of him."

"I was thinking more along the lines that his plan worked," said Matt with a grin. "That's inspiring!"

"Oh, goodness, why do I even try?"

"Come on, I know what you're thinking, and it's fine. A little fear will do the whippersnapper good. You aren't going to tell me that you don't actually want me to carry through, are you?"

Mr. Tickleten smiled, "Actually, I was going to ask if I could stay and watch."

"Definitely."

COURTING THE
ADMIRAL'S DAUGHTER
CHAPTER FOUR

"The place is just around the next bend," said Mark, glancing down at his paper with Lily's address on it.

"The NEXT bend?" asked Dan, a grin spreading across his face.

"Yeah," said Mark, "Do you know which house it is?"

"Well, let's turn the bend and see." They had been walking for a good thirty minutes straight out of the capital city, passing big open fields. Mark had gotten much more relaxed at the thought that Lily's dad was most likely nothing more than a farmer. Then they turned the bend. Only one gate stood next to the dirt road. "I knew it!" said Dan. "I knew it!"

All the color drained from Mark's face when he saw a sign written in golden letters that read: *The Baker Estate, Home of Admiral Matt Baker.* "Admiral?" whispered Mark hoarsely. "ADMIRAL!!! That's practically as bad as a king!"

"Mark," said Dan laughing, "I know I told you that you didn't have anything to worry about, but I changed my mind. You're toast, man!"

"Maybe this is the wrong address," said Mark, hopefully. He checked it five times before he finally believed the terrifying truth.

"Don't worry, man. I'll definitely come to your funeral!" said Dan, almost choking with glee. He leaned closer and whispered, grinning, "I'll even do your eulogy."

"Dan! I have to get out of this!" said Mark, grabbing Dan by the shirt collar. "Please just go and tell them I'm not feeling well or that my mom called me home for dinner or that I fell off a cliff and died, just anything!"

"Not a chance, man!" said Dan. "I'm not going in there!"

"I'll pay you ten yerna!"

"I wouldn't do it for a hundred yerna!" replied Dan. "Sorry, man, but this is as far as I go. You're the one in love! Not me!"

"Oh, Dan," said Mark as his friend turned and started to walk away. "Tell my mom I loved her!"

"Will do!" shouted back Dan in another burst of laughter. And with that, he was gone around the bend. Mark's last comfort was gone! Mark took a deep breath. How hard could it be? All he had to do was go in, ask for permission, and come back out. He would survive, right?

"Who are you!" barked a voice on the other side of the gate. Mark nearly had a heart attack. On the other side of the gate stood a tall man with black hair that fell to his shoulders and the darkest eyes Mark had ever seen. Was he the dark-eyed companion, the shadow of a man who seemed to always be at the Admiral's side? He must be; he even had his hand in his pocket.

"Um, hi," choked out Mark. "I'm, I'm Mark. I think Lily is expecting me?" It came out almost more as a question than a statement.

The dark-eyed man looked him up and down, "I didn't think someone as scrawny as you would have the nerve to court her ladyship, but… at least I'm not responsible for your bad decisions." Mark gulped as the man opened the gate and let him in. Then he jumped as the man slammed the gate back shut as soon as he was through and locked it tight. "This way," said the man, leading him down the long, seemingly endless path to the house. *I say house, though if you weren't overly educated about Trinity architecture, you might have mistaken it for a palace.* Huge white pillars held up the massive stone structure on either side of the door. Giant flags flew from the balcony above the door. The windows were ten feet high and arched on the first floor, and over the fifteen foot door hung a golden plaque with the name *Baker* written on it. The walk to the door was far too short for Mark's comfort.

When they reached it, the man nodded and left him there, walking around to the back of the manor. Mark stared at the huge golden knocker. It was made in the shape of a boat being tossed over huge waves. Mark had just reached for it when the massive door swung open, and there, on the other side, stood the admiral. He alone was more terrifying than everything else put together. He was a good six foot four, with huge muscles and massive hands that looked like they had experience cracking bones in half with sheer force. His short brown hair melded into his beard. He was wearing his admiral's uniform with golden buttons and stitching. On his head sat a plumed hat. The man took a step forward so that for Mark to look at him, he had to look straight up.

"Mr. Baker?" squeaked the terrified Mark.

"Yes?" asked the Admiral, staring down at him. "Who are you?"

For the first time, Mark noticed the sword the admiral was wearing. He gulped, "Um, my name is Mark, Mr. Admiral Sir!" He took two steps back in order to bow. As he came back up, he noticed a flicker of a smile on the man's face, but it was gone in an instant.

"So, you're the pipsqueak who wants to court my daughter?" asked the admiral, looking him up and down.

"Yes, sir! I mean no, sir! I mean, well, it's debatable," fumbled Mark.

Again, there was that tiny hint of a smile, but once again it was gone so fast that Mark figured he must have imagined it. "Come in if you have to," said the admiral, turning and going back into the house, "Just make sure to shut the door behind you!"

Was he making headway? Was he really actually making headway? He sauntered through the double doors as casually as he could, grabbed the half of it that was open behind him and tried to swing it as he walked. It moved about a quarter of an inch. He could feel the admiral staring at him. *Really, Mark? How heavy can a fifteen foot door be?* He thought to himself. Trying to regain his momentum, he grabbed it from behind and tried to swing it again, another quarter of an inch. Rather mad now, he grabbed it, put his back into it, and pushed for all he was worth. Slowly, very slowly, it moved bit by bit until it finally latched in place. He wiped the sweat from his brow and was just about to turn and go to one of the chairs near where the admiral was sitting when the other double door swung open with ease. He watched, beet red with embarrassment, as Lily stepped in through it and gently swung it closed behind her.

"Hi, Mark!" she said, giving him her warmest friendliest smile. She looked at his red face, "Are you alright? It looks like you're coming down with something." He heard muffled laughter from one of the seats behind him. Great, so not only did the admiral see that, but he had also invited company.

"I'm not sick, Lily," said Mark, smiling. "It's uh, it's complicated." Another burst of laughter from the unknown guest.

"Lily," said the admiral, standing up. "I think Emily and Helen could use a little help in the kitchen."

Lily looked at him for a long moment then sighed, "If you insist, Daddy." With that she left.

"Come sit down," said the admiral, staring at Mark. Mark obeyed. What else could he do? As he sat, he saw for the first time who the company was. He was a short little man with white hair, a bare face, and eyes that twinkled as he looked around.

"Hello, lad," said the little man. "My name is Mr. Tickleten."

Mark grinned. At least there was one nice person nearby. "Pleased to meet you, Mr Tinkleten."

The admiral turned away to hide a stifled laugh. The little man leaned over with a smile on his lips, "Lad, my name is Mr. Tickleten, not Mr. Tinkleten."

Once again, Mark turned beet red. "I'm so sorry. I didn't know!" By now, the admiral's shoulders were shaking up and down uncontrollably. Once he had gotten control of himself and Mark's cheeks had returned a bit closer to normal color, there was a long awkward silence in the room.

"So, what subjects do you like at the university?" asked Mr. Tickleten.

"I enjoy mechanics a good deal," said Mark, feeling a bit more relaxed. Soon, the two of them were discussing what types of mechanics, what the newest inventions were, politics and all sorts of things. Even though the admiral didn't say much, Mark was pretty sure there had never been anything to be afraid of.

Then, one of the doors opened from the back of the room and the dark eyed man poked his head into the room. "Sir! Requesting permission to speak?"

"Permission granted," said the admiral in his loudest most commanding voice. "What's the problem?"

"Sir, the kid is cutting across your land again."

"The same one as yesterday?"

"Yes, sir!"

"Well," said the admiral, leaning back in his chair. "We gave him a warning. Now it is time for the punishment. You know what to do."

"Yes, sir," said the dark eyed man with a twinkle of amusement in his eyes. Then he was gone. There was a long pause.

Mark cleared his throat, "Exactly what kind of punishment are we talking about here?" Suddenly, an explosion sounded. Dishes rattled, decorations shook, pictures nearly fell off the walls. Mark practically jumped out of his skin!

The Admiral leaned in close to him, "Cannon fire is the type of punishment I enjoy. Sends a message they don't forget." Mark started shaking uncontrollably. "Now," he said standing up and clapping his hands together. "Who's ready for supper?" Mark sincerely hoped he wasn't the main course.

COURTING THE
ADMIRAL'S DAUGHTER
CHAPTER FIVE

Lily knocked quietly on the door to Matt's bedroom. "Come in," he called. She turned the knob and stepped inside. Sitting at his desk, with a quill pen in hand, sat Matt. He was writing carefully in his long beautiful handwriting.

"Who are you writing, Daddy?" asked Lily, coming and sitting down beside him.

He quickly folded the piece of paper before she could see what was written. "Just a letter to somebody."

"Is this the same somebody you're always writing these days?" asked Lily with a sigh.

Matt smiled and put an arm around her, "Yes, the same somebody."

"Why won't you tell me who it is, Daddy?"

"Some things a man simply must keep to himself," he answered, pulling her closer. "Is that why you came in? To ask what I was doing?"

"No, Daddy." She paused. "Why did you have to torture Mark?"

"Torture?" asked Matt with a chuckle. "I would hardly call it torture."

Lily jabbed him in the ribs, "You know exactly what I mean, Daddy. You scared him silly this afternoon... and then telling him about your battles after dinner. And really, the cannon? You fired THE CANNON! That sounds pretty much like torture to me."

"What are you getting at, Little Lil?" asked Matt.

Lily sighed. "I can understand why you did it to Frank, or Joe, or Orlando. They were all twits. But Mark is the kindest, most wonderful man I have ever met."

"Boy," commented Matt. "He's not a man yet."

"Fine, he's the kindest most wonderful boy I have ever met. He didn't deserve to be treated like that."

"Lily," said Matt, "It isn't my job to know right away who the good ones are and who the bad ones are. My job is to protect you. I don't want to see you give your heart to anyone who isn't willing to brave a lot worse things than me for you. If they get through their fear and come back to court you, then I'm glad you found someone special. But if they don't come back, then they don't deserve you, and I don't want you to be drawn in by someone like that."

Lily snuggled closer to him, "Do you think Mark will come back, Daddy?"

"I wouldn't be a bit surprised," said Matt. "Didn't you see him at dinner? He couldn't keep his eyes off you the whole time."

"Really?" asked Lily, looking up at him.

"Really," assured Matt. "Don't worry, he'll come back."

***

"No! No way! No way!" said Mark, sitting down on the wing of the flying prototype.

"Calm down, man!" said Dan, trying to comfort him. "Surely it isn't as bad as all that."

"Not as bad as all that? Not as bad as all that! You're right! It was worse!" said Mark, standing up and beginning to pace again. "I was wimpier than a girl, I jumped like a frightened kitten twice, and a kid got shot by a cannon!"

"Come on, I hardly think they would shoot a kid with a cannon," said Dan, rolling his eyes.

"Well, I don't know, but they shot something!" retorted Mark. "Then after dinner he started sharpening his sword! It was huge! And every time the sharpener made it's way down the length of the sword, he glanced up at me! I could just tell he wanted to carve me like a turkey!!!"

"Okay, it was a bad first experience," said Dan. "So, when are you going back?"

"Going back?" asked Mark. "No, no way, I'm not going back. No chance!"

"What?" said Dan, lifting an eyebrow. "I thought you liked the girl."

"Like the girl? I don't like her, Dan. I love her," said Mark, getting a far away look in his eyes. "She's the most amazing person I've ever met in my life!"

"So you're going back?" pushed Dan.

Mark sighed. "No, I'm not. I've made up my mind. I just can't do it."

"I see," said Dan. "So, when are you gonna tell her?"

"Next time I see her, I guess," replied Mark.

At that moment, Bobby burst into the room holding a metal piece in his arms, "I found it, I found it!"

Mark jumped to his feet, "Let me see, Bobby!"

"Here!" said Bobby, handing it to him.

"Is it the right one, man?" asked Dan, standing beside him.

Mark ran his fingers along the metal part, examining it carefully. Then, he grinned, "Yes, it is!"

"Does that mean..." started Dan, his voice trailing off.

Mark nodded. "Tomorrow is take-off, boys!"

***

"Matt?" said Riggins.

Matt looked up from the book he was reading, "What is it, Riggins?"

"The ship leaves in an hour. Are you coming?"

"Oh, that's right," said Matt, standing up. "Just let me get my uniform on, and I'll be ready."

"Alright," said Riggins, turning to go, then he changed his mind. "Matt, are you sure you want to do this? You could always change your mind."

"No, I've got to," said Matt. "Trust me, Riggins, I know I'm making the right choice."

"Whether or not you are, it isn't like I could do anything about it," said Riggins. "You are the admiral after all... unfortunately."

Matt laughed, "I suppose you still think that you would be better suited to the job, eh?"

"I think that is quite the understatement," replied Riggins, his eyes glowing.

"Whatever you need to believe is fine," said Matt, grinning. "I assume we are still getting to the dock by the same route?"

"Yes. We will take the *Bella Fawn* from here to island of Ableton and then take a stage across the island to the port that *The Last Straw* will leave from."

Matt nodded, "Sounds good, but I still have no idea

why *The Last Straw* is such an exceptional name for a ship."

***

Lily ran across campus, a copy of *The Trinity Gazette* in hand. Her book bag flopped against her back as she did, and her hair fell farther and farther out of her bun. By the time she reached the inventing room, she was out of breath and sweating. Only one person was in the room. Bobby, with binoculars to his eyes, was looking out the window. She vaguely noticed that all of the parts to the prototype were gone, but she hardly had time to think about it. "Bobby!" said Lily, rushing up. "Did you hear the news?"

"Um, news?" asked Bobby, turning around.

"Yes, the news!" said Lily. "The people on Thebel plan to set a man in flight TOMORROW! We're done for!"

"Oh, well. I really don't think that will be much of a problem, Lily," said Bobby sheepishly.

"What do you mean not a problem?" asked Lily. "And what were you just looking at?" She took the binoculars from him and looked out in the direction he had been staring. "Oh no," she whispered under her breath. "Mark!"

COURTING THE
ADMIRAL'S DAUGHTER
CHAPTER SIX

"Alright, man. You know what to do in an emergency, right?" asked Dan nervously as Mark settled himself in the seat of the plane.

"Yes, Dan, I know," said Mark with a smile. "You may remember that I built this thing."

Dan flashed him a smile, "Just making sure being lovesick hasn't gone to your head!"

"Don't worry," said Mark, but he could tell that didn't do anything. The first man to fly, or just another among many to die trying. Those were the only two options left for him now.

"Okay. So remember, no matter what, we'll be down on the ground covering you. You'll just fly to the coast till you can see Ableton, then turn and land. Don't do anything dumb, or I might have a heart attack. There will be someone every few miles who will watch for you to make sure that you are still in the air."

"Yeah, I got it," said Mark. "And I also know not to go any farther because this craft can't hold much fuel, and I know how to work my parachute, and just about anything else you could remind me of."

"How about a helmet?" asked Dan, pulling it out of his bag and handing it to his friend with a wink.

"Thanks," said Mark, taking it and strapping it firmly in place.

"Well, I guess you're ready to go," said Dan, smiling slightly at him.

"Yeah," answered Mark, "I guess I am."

Dan patted his friend's shoulder awkwardly, "Fly safe, man."

Mark nodded, "I'll do my best."

***

Matt stood behind the wheel of the *Bella Fawn* with Riggins beside him, "It will only be a few more minutes until we will reach the other island."

"Probably," said Riggins. "Unless the sea proves to us right now that I'm more qualified to be admiral."

"I see!" said Matt, laughing. "Then let's hope the sea isn't in a bad mood."

***

Mark took a deep breath as Dan stood nearby counting down. This was it, the do or die moment, literally! "Three!" Mark gripped the controls with all of his might. "Two!" He put his finger under the engine switch. "One!!!!"

Mark flipped the switch. The machine started forward with a lurch, hitting every pebble and bump possible. Mark tried to pull up, but he wasn't going fast enough yet. The trees at the end of the field loomed closer. He tried again, still not enough. The trees were almost upon him! He tried one last time. The machine jerked upward just in time and missed the tops of the trees by mere feet.

Now he was above the bushes, above the trees, above the university! He was doing it! He was flying! He heard exited whoops from Dan down below, but he tried to block it out. Focus was all that he needed to do now. He gripped the wheel hard between his knees and pulled the rope that brought up the wheels. The less friction, the more stable the flight. He glanced down at the ground, the first watcher waved up at him, but he was too nervous to wave back.

A bird came up and flew beside him, watching his every move with curiosity. He winked. Soon, the next watcher came into sight. He checked his fuel tank. It was right where they had predicted. He took in a deep breath. This might actually work! He glanced at his compass and slightly changed the direction of the machine.

Here came to next watcher, jumping and screaming with delight like he had a whale in his breeches. This time, Mark ventured a wave. Just one more watcher before the coast. He looked over at the altimeter. Just a tad low. He pulled up a bit. Off in the distance, he spotted the last watcher. He slowly relaxed and simply enjoyed the wind brushing against his face. He raced past the watcher at top speed, whooping at the top of his lungs and wondering how he had ever lived without flying?

Then, as he came upon the coast, he saw a little boat he recognized sailing into Ableton's port. He could tell by the flag that Admiral Baker was aboard. Suddenly, a thought worked its way into his head. If he was willing to risk his life to be the first man to fly, why hadn't he been willing to risk less than that for Lily? The thought caught him off guard. He looked from the little boat, behind him at the landing strip, and back again to the boat. Then he sighed.

"Sorry, Dan," he said under his breath, "but I've got to do this before I lose my nerve."

He glanced down at the fuel monitor, desperately low, but possibly just enough. He sped ahead, top speed, over the water that separated the two islands. As he did, he had only one thought in mind. Skipping rocks. What was the difference between a machine and a rock? As he sped forward, he could see the reading on the altimeter quickly decreasing. He could feel the machine slowly dropping closer and closer to the waves.

Not yet, he thought desperately. *Almost, almost, now!* The machine hit the water flat and jumped back into the air with new momentum. He pushed on as fast as he could as the opposite shore got closer. Down he went again toward to waves, and up he popped! Just one more! One more skip, and he could make it!

He went back down one last time… and up he came again! He let the wheels back down as fast as he could and skidded to a stop on the white beach.

SABINA BOYER

"YES!!!" he shouted to the world, jumping out of the craft. "Yes!!! I'm alive! I'm ALIVE!!!" He had to stop himself from doing a happy dance right then and there. He had somewhere to go. He scribbled a note on a piece of paper and left it in the flying machine. Then, he picked himself up and set off down the beach. Soon, *Bella Fawn* came into sight and then the surrounding village. He picked up his pace.

As he entered the village, he saw down one of the many streets, a carriage whizz off with the admiral riding it. He ran to the stable it had left from. "Excuse me!" he called to one of the workers.

"You're excused. Now beat it," said the man, turning to go inside.

"No, please!" he said, "I have to rent a horse!"

"Sorry, lad. Renting takes money, and you don't look like the type who's stocked up on money."

"Here's my wallet," said Mark, tossing it at the man. "And my watch!" Without waiting for a response, he threw himself up on an already saddled horse. "Thank you!" he shouted down.

"Okay, okay," said the man, fumbling with the wallet. "But why are you is such a hurry?"

Mark whipped the horse forward as he answered, "I have to ask the admiral to court the woman I love before he leaves!!!"

As Mark rode off, the man cocked his head, "Why are you so set on the admiral courting the woman you love? Ha, kids these days."

COURTING THE
ADMIRAL'S DAUGHTER
CHAPTER SEVEN

Matt sat in the back seat of the carriage, next to Riggins. "Nice to see you again, Admiral," called the driver from up in front.

"You too, Pierce," answered Matt with a smile. "It's been a while. Anything new since I last saw you?"

"Well, I can say for sure that nearly everyone on Ableton adores you! You're a hero here."

"Nearly," asked Riggins, suspiciously.

"Well," started Pierce, "Every island has quirky people, and there is a group here who are, shall I say, not your biggest fans."

"I see," said Matt. "Does this group have a name?"

"They're known as 'The Mudders'," Riggins cocked an

eyebrow at the driver. "Great name, I know. They're called that because they cover their whole bodies in mud and ride around on black horses. Why they don't just wear a cool sweatshirt or something, I don't know."

"So, how much do these mud people not like me?" asked Matt.

"Let's just say that they are the reason we didn't tell the island you were coming today," said Pierce, "but as it is, I'd say you're perfectly safe for now."

***

"Come on, Midnight," said Mark, trying to kick his horse forward. The horse wouldn't budge. Mark honestly had no idea if the horse was named Midnight, but it seemed like the obvious choice, and he had to call the brute something. "Come on, Midnight," he said again. "What's so bad about a mud puddle in the middle of the road? Horses aren't afraid of mud!" No response.

"Okay," said Mark, slipping down, "Let's try this the old fashioned way." He grabbed the horse's reins and pulled him forward as hard as he could. The horse jerked his head back, making Mark lose his balance and fall headfirst into the mud. "Oh terrific," he said, standing up. The horse nickered at him playfully and jumped easily over the mud to the other side.

"You couldn't have done that just a bit sooner?" asked Mark, annoyed. Midnight neighed. Mark shook his head and climbed back up on the saddle, trying to forget the mud that still covered his body.

***

Pierce and Matt were still chatting when Riggins spotted something out the window. At first, he wasn't sure what it was, so he kept quiet, but the more he watched, the closer it seemed to get. "Matt," he said quietly, "Check out what's coming up behind us."

Matt looked back with a puzzled expression on his face and then took a deep breath. "What is it?" asked Pierce.

"It's a Dark Mud, riding a black horse straight for us," answered Riggins.

"Well, that's no problem," said Pierce with a grin. "Take these, Matt," he said, giving him a bag and a few matches. "Light the wick at the top of the bag and then shake the contents out of your window!"

"Why?" asked Matt.

"Just do it!" said Riggins.

***

They were in sight! They were in sight! He had almost made it to the admiral! Suddenly, a hand reached out the side window of the carriage and poured something all over the road. *Probably just trash or something*, thought Mark. But as he got closer, he realized each of the little objects had wicks. "What in the world." Without warning, they exploded, and smoke filled the air. Midnight spooked, rearing and bucking, so that all Mark could do was hang on for dear life. Smoke filled his eyes and made them cry it stung so bad. Finally, when it had cleared, Mark saw that the carriage was almost out of sight, but he realized for the first time where it was going. It was heading towards a small town just past a large, green field.

"A carriage might not be able to go on a field," whispered Mark to Midnight patting his mane, "but we sure can!" He whipped Midnight with new spirit. Midnight whinnied with excitement and charged over the field for dear life. Mark held onto the reins tightly but didn't even try to stee. Midnight knew where to go.

Quickly, they started though the first part of the field, jumping over a little stream and dashing past wildflowers. Mark looked up at the town and groaned to see the admiral's carriage reach it. He turned Midnight slightly to the right and aimed their course for the docks. "Come on, Midnight!" he shouted as the air flew past them. "Come on, boy!"

***

Riggins and Matt stepped out of the carriage together and quickly made their way through the city to where the boat was waiting. "I think we lost him," said Riggins.

"Maybe," said Matt, "But that's what concerns me. If there's a killer nearby, I'd like to know where he is, if you know what I mean."

"Unfortunately, I do," said Riggins glancing around. "Let's hurry."

***

Mark pulled Midnight up to a stop at the docks. He tied his reins to a lamppost and patted his neck. "Thanks for the ride. old boy. I'll be back." Then he turned and ran toward the dock.

"Sir!" he cried, running up to one of the sailors on the dock. "Which boat is the admiral on?"

"What happened to you?" asked the man, looking him up and down. Mark glanced down at himself and sighed, he was still filthy and the mud had already started crusting on him.

"Just tell me. Are there any royal ships about to leave?" asked Mark.

"No," said the man, pointing out at the water, "but that one just left." The huge vessel was already a good thirty yards from the dock, but Mark wasn't going to let that stop him now. Without another word to the sailor, he ran and jumped off the dock, swimming as hard as he could for the boat. From where he was, he couldn't see the admiral, but the one with dark eyes was staring at him from on the boat.

"STOP!!!" shouted Mark, still swimming. The dark-eyed man turned and said something to his companion, who nodded. Was it really that easy? Were they stopping? Suddenly, the boat turned so that its side was facing him. Without warning, the cannon doors opened and fifteen angry looking cannons were pointed toward him. *Just great,* thought Mark in disbelief. "I SAID STOP, NOT SHOOT!!!"

The first cannon blasted, and a cannonball landed a few yards to the left of him. This was crazy! He swam left just in time to dodge the next cannonball. "WHAT'S HAPPENING?" he screamed. "HELP!!!!!!!"

"DON'T SHOOT!!!" came a voice from somewhere far behind him. It bellowed louder than Mark's voice ever had a chance. Wait, was that who it sounded like? Someone behind him jumped into the water and swam towards him.

"Admiral?" asked Mark in confusion.

"Mark!" said Matt, swimming up. "What are you doing here?"

"But you went... I thought... didn't you?" Mark didn't know where to start. "Why aren't you on the ship?"

"I'm not going on this journey," said Matt. "Riggins is the captain of this one. I just came to see him off."

"But if that's true, then you weren't going off to possibly never come back and I could have just gone to see you at your house?" asked Mark in disbelief.

"Well, I don't have any idea why you would want to see me after what happened," said Matt, signalling to the boat that they could leave. "But, I guess."

"Oh boy," said Mark with a groan. "But, if you threw stuff at me when I was following you, why did you stop them from shooting now?"

Mat grinned, "The water washed off enough mud that I could see who you were."

COURTING THE
ADMIRAL'S DAUGHTER
CHAPTER EIGHT

Matt and Mark sat by the fireplace of a nearby inn. They had been sitting there for about half an hour now and were finally beginning to sort out all that had happened. As Mark watched the admiral swap stories and laugh heartily form time to time, he wondered what he had ever thought frightening about the big man. "So, you went through all that just to get to me?" asked Matt in amazement. Mark nodded, taking another sip of his hot cocoa and finally beginning to dry out. He now understood why his mom had never let him go swimming in the fall.

"Incredible," said Matt. "So, why did you do it? You still haven't told me that part."

"Well," said Mark with a sigh. "I saw you heading out in the *Bella Fawn* to Ableton, and I knew I had to ask you something."

"What is it?"

"May I court your daughter Lily?" Mark almost gasped when he realized how easily it had come out. "I knew that I couldn't in good conscious court her without asking you first, and I didn't want to risk you going on a dangerous mission and not coming back. I would have lost Lily because of fear, and I wasn't willing to let that happen."

"So you did all that for Lily," said Matt, a grin creeping over his face.

"Yeah," said Mark, nervously. "So, um, may I court your daughter?"

Matt laughed and slapped him on the back, "Mark, you can court her, you can dance with her, you can even marry her one day! And if you happen to have a brother near Helen's age, who is lonely, let me know!"

Mark's eyes practically popped out of his head, "Really! You're saying yes!?!?"

"Yes. I'm saying yes!" said Matt. "Any boy who would do that for my daughter can court her anytime he'd like!"

Mark grinned. He was pretty stinkin' sure that this was the best day of his life.

***

Lily scanned the crowd of reporters and curious onlookers who had gathered around the university. "Dan!" she shouted at a figure not far away. Dan glanced up at her, a worried expression on his face. "Has anyone found him yet?" Dan shook his head, all traces of amusement gone from his face.

Suddenly, a commotion came from the end of the crowd. "It's him!" someone called. "It's the flying boy!" Lily rushed through the throng as fast as her legs could carry her with Dan close behind her.

As soon as she got out of the crowd and could see who was coming their way, she gasped. Two horses, one brown and the other midnight black were coming toward the crowd, pulling a cart with a very banged-up but still impressive-looking flying machine on it. On their backs sat Matt and Mark, waving to the crowd.

"Look what the admiral dragged in!" cried one of the reporters with glee, looking at Mark's muddy clothes.

"Mark!" shouted Lily, running to him.

"Lily!" said Mark, slipping out of the saddle and racing forward.

When they met and embraced with tears and cheers, even the most stone-hearted of the people in the crowd said the age-old word: "Awwwwwww!"

"You're alive, man!" said Dan, bursting out of the crowd and grabbing Mark's shoulders. "I might shake you to death for the way you scared us, though!"

"I should hope not," said Mark with a laugh. As reporters flocked around him, firing away questions in the hopes of deep inspiring answers, Mark whispered something to Lily, "I can't wait to court you!"

***

Mark and Lily talked all the way home from the

university dance. It was a week after the flight, and they were just about to wrap up their first outing together. When they reached the gate to the Baker Manor, Mark opened it with a bow, "My lady!"

"Thank you, my man," said Lily with a playful curtsy. As they went up the walk to the house, Mark glanced up at the stars, wondering if they had ever looked so beautiful. He was pretty sure they hadn't.

"Did you really think I was dead last week?" asked Mark, slipping his hand into hers.

"I don't know. I guess I thought you might be," said Lily, looking up at him.

Mark chuckled, "There were times when I thought I might end up dead, too."

"But one thing is for sure," said Lily, glancing at him innocently.

"What's that?"

"If I had found out you were dead, I was going to kill you!"

Mark laughed again. Soon, far sooner than either of them would have hoped for, they reached the front porch of the Baker Manor. "So," said Mark awkwardly, "we're here."

"Yep, we're here," replied Lily, looking down at her feet.

"Well, I guess I'll see you tomorrow then," said Mark.

"I guess."

Mark looked down at her face. It was such a beautiful face, so so beautiful. He wondered what it would feel like to kiss her. Slowly, he inched his face closer and closer to hers. She looked at him with surprise at first but then leaned in toward him. Just as their lips were about to touch, the front door swung open. "Hi, kids!" said Matt with a grin.

Instantly, the two jerked away from each other. "Oh, um, I think I got it out of your eye, Lily," said Mark with a nervous laugh.

"Uh, thanks, Mark," piped up Lily, rubbing her eye quickly as if she were looking for something. "Yep, it's gone."

"How brave of you to help get something out of her eye, Mark," said Matt, grinning at him mockingly.

"It was nothing really," responded Mark sheepishly.

"Yeah, I know," agreed Matt. Mark wasn't quite sure how to take that.

"Well goodnight, Lily," he said, hugging her stiffly.

"Goodnight," she said, smiling at him.

Matt stepped away from the door and turned as if on his way to his armchair. "Could you shut the door, Mark?"

Mark smiled broadly, opened the light half of the door and shut it, "You can't get rid of me that easily!"

***

Helen crept out of her bedroom and down the creaky stairs, a bag under one arm. She glanced over at Matt, who had fallen asleep in his chair and snuck through the living room into the kitchen where Emily was waiting. Though Emily was quite a bit older than Helen, she had become her closest friend ever since she had moved in with them as their nanny when the girls were little.

"Are you sure you want to do this, Helen?" asked Emily nervously. "We could always just stay here for a few more years."

Helen knew that Emily was thinking about Matt. The woman had had a crush on him from the start, and her giggles and eyelash batting were enough to make anyone nauseous. "Yes," said Helen. "I can't stay here. I know you don't fully understand it, Emily, but I can't. I can feel the Creator pushing me away from Trinity and pulling me somewhere else."

"Where?"

Helen paused. In truth, she had no idea, but she knew she couldn't stay. "That is why I'm leaving... to find out."

"Well, I don't know about the Creator, but I'll stay by your side no matter what, Helen. You can count on that."

Helen smiled, "I know I can." Then, with one last look around the old house, she put a note on the kitchen table and stole out the back door with Emily into the night.

Matt never saw Helen again after that day, but he did see a lot more of Mark. He was at their house more than his own over the next few years, and Matt and Riggins never got tired of watching his lovesick antics. Did he marry Lily? Well, I suppose it is too early to say that, but I can say that they learned to love each other in those next few years. What happened to Helen, you might ask? I'm afraid that is not a story that I will have the honor of ever telling, though others might...

STORY FIVE
WHEN THE WEDDING BELLS TOLL

WHEN THE WEDDING BELLS TOLL
CHAPTER ONE

Matt stood in the kitchen of the Baker Manor washing dishes while Mr. Tickleton sat in a comfy chair nearby helping himself to a jelly roll.

"These are quite amazingly scrumptious," said Mr. Tickleton.

"Lily made them," said Matt, picking up another plate to scrub. "You know, part of me is starting to wonder why she only goes all out on cooking when Mark comes for supper, but as long as she makes sweets like this, I'm fine."

"I can't believe she is already twenty-two!" cried Mr. Tickleton. "And Mark's a solid twenty-three now. It seems like just yesterday he came here for the first time to meet you." Matt nodded with a smile on his face as he remembered that day. Mr. Tickleton took another bite of the jelly roll. "I'd say Lily's cooking has quite improved over the years. Now, she's almost as good as..." his voice trailed off as he realized his mistake.

"As Helen," finished Matt with a sigh.

"I'm sorry, Matt," said Mr. Tickleton apologetically. "I didn't mean to bring it up. When you get my age, you never know what's gonna fly out next."

"It's fine," said Matt, turning back to the dishes.

Mr. Tickleten cleared his throat, "Still no word from her?"

Matt paused and turned slightly to look at Mr. Tickleten, "You know, when I first saw her letter, I just thought it was a stage. I thought she'd be back in a week or two when her money ran out or when she started missing us. I had hoped back then to see her again, but after six years, you stop holding your breath every time you check the mail. I have to admit that I'm glad she took Emily. It was so unnerving to be flirted with by that woman."

Mr. Tickleten wished he hadn't said anything. Quickly, he changed the subject, "So where are those two, Mark and Lily? I haven't seen them since supper."

"They went out in the garden to have a stroll, but it's more than that, let me tell you."

"More?" asked Mr. Tickleten, full of curiosity.

"Didn't you wonder why I didn't go with Riggins to see the ambassador of Chobot? No, I knew I had to stay here and not miss the fun. A week ago, Mark asked my permission to marry her!"

"He did?" squealed Mr. Tickleten excitedly. "But how

do you know that he's going to do it tonight?"

Matt grinned, "Because he was shaking all through supper."

***

"It's a nice evening," said Mark, quietly giving Lily's hand a squeeze as they sat on a bench overlooking the pond. A thousand little points of light rippled in the water alongside the water lilies, mimicking the stars.

"Yeah," said Lily, squeezing back. "One of the most wonderful evenings I've ever had."

Mark stood and walked right to the edge of the pond. Carefully, he scooped out a lily that was in full blossom and placed it in Lily's hair. She laughed softly. "One for her hair," he said, grabbing a lily not yet in bloom but instead closed up. He bent down on one knee and held it out to her, "And one for her finger." Lily's eyes got wide. She reached out and unwrapped the closed petals, then gasped at what lay inside. "Lily Baker," he said, a smile creeping over his face. "Will you marry me? Please!"

Lily laughed, "Yes, I will! Of course I will!"

Now Mark's face was a full out grin. He stood, taking the little ring out of the lily and slipped it on her finger.

***

The two men watched, peeking out the kitchen window as Lily jumped into Mark's arms and he twirled her around. "That means yes!" said Mr. Tickleten excitedly.

"I knew it!" said Matt with a nod.

"Why isn't he kissing her?" asked Mr. Tickleten.

"They've never kissed," explained Matt. "I caught them before they could the first time, and after that, Mark came up with the idea for them not to kiss till they got married. Why do you think I said he could ask?"

Suddenly, Mark looked over to the manor, and both men ducked. By the time the couple came in, Matt was 'hard at work' doing the dishes, and Mr. Tickleten was feasting on his second jelly roll. "Men, I have an announcement to make!" said Mark, smiling harder than they had ever seen before.

"Congratulations!" said Matt, coming over and patting him on the back.

"I'm so glad for you two!" tubed up Mr. Tickleton.

Mark looked confused, "We didn't tell you the news yet."

Lily crossed her arms with a grin, "You two would never spy on us, would you?"

"What?" asked Mr. Tickleten with fake indignation. "You think a sweet old grandfatherly person like me and a wonderful father like yours would spy?"

"Yes!" said Lily and Mark at the same time.

***

Three months had gone by since the proposal. The whole time, the Baker Manor had been a buzz with wedding arrangements. There were only two weeks left until the wedding, and the manor was as chaotic as ever.

Matt was in the kitchen, helping Mark and Lily choose a cake from the cake samples, when a knock came at the front door. "I'll get that," said Matt, getting up from the table and hurrying off to the door. "May I help you?" asked Matt, opening the door.

"Yes," said the man, pulling a letter with the royal seal out of his bag. "You are Admiral Matt Baker, I presume?"

"Yes, I am," said Matt, taking the letter. "Thank you for the delivery." He pulled several coins out of his pocket and handed them to the man.

"Thank you, Admiral," said the man as he turned away. Matt closed the door behind him and opened the letter carefully. Slowly, he ran his eyes across the lines of text, then sighed.

"Lily!" he called. "Could I speak with you for a minute?"

"Alright, Daddy!" said Lily, coming into the living room. "What's wrong?"

"Well, I just got a letter from the queen," said Matt. "She is asking me to head over to Chobot and make sure that everything is alright. Riggins went there a while ago and hasn't come back. He's probably just sightseeing, and I can't picture it taking more than a few days at tops, but if it makes you nervous for me to go this soon before your wedding, I don't have to."

Lily laughed, "As if I of all people would doubt your ability as an admiral. It's fine. Just be careful."

"Careful with what?" asked Matt.

"The Rocks of Hearth," answered Lily. "It's predicted for the twentieth of this month."

The Rocks of Hearth, my dear reader, is a strange weather phenomenon that occurs once every few years. Although it is one of the most disastrous weather patterns in Ildathore, the entire thing only lasts twenty-four hours or so. When it occurs, so much water evaporates from the portion of water between Chobot and Trinity that massive twisting rocks, typically deep under the waves poke up out of the water. Strange winds blow from Chobot and pound against Trinity, and the clouds that form over the Rocks of Hearth let loose their rain, hail, and lightning. The previous admiral was one of many who had died in it.

"The twentieth?" asked Matt. "Lily, your wedding is the twenty-first. I'll be home long before the Rocks of Hearth"

"Good," said Lily. "And try to bring back Riggins from his sight seeing. I want him in the wedding!"

"Yes, ma'am!" said Matt, kissing her on the forehead. "I'll leave for Chobot tomorrow morning."

WHEN THE WEDDING BELLS TOLL
CHAPTER TWO

Matt sailed alone on *The Bounder,* watching Chobot come into sight. The last day and a half had been a bit lonely, he had to admit, without a crew, but it had been a good time all and all. He had almost forgotten the thrill of sailing on a one-man ship, but even with all the work it took, when he anchored at night, he used the peace and quiet to read and write. He smiled, remembering how Lily always used to ask who he wrote letters to. Too bad he could never tell her.

As he sailed up the coast of Chobot, he saw several homesteads, people laughing, and even family dogs running up and down the beach fetching sticks. Before long, he reached the famous pass into the heart of Chobot. The strange island had a large bay that curved right into its capital city. Chobot was known for the twenty ships linked together by chains that could, at a moments notice, sail across the entrance to the bay and form a wall to the outside word. As Matt sailed into the bay, he double checked to make sure that the Trinity flag was flying. Who knew what might happen if he was mistaken as an enemy.

The capital city of Chobot rose up in front of him as he came ever closer. Finally, he reached the dock. When he got there, he motioned to the owner who was standing nearby. "Hey!" he called in Mayren, the merchant language. "Could you help me tie up my boat?"

"Sure thing," answered the man in Mayren. In no time, the little boat was tied up and the man pulled out a list from his pocket, "Name for the dock reservation?"

"Baker," said Matt. "Matt Baker."

The man looked up at him in surprise then grinned in a way that made Matt feel fidgety. The man put two fingers in his mouth and whistled. The other men came out from the dock house, one holding some kind of club. Matt took a step back.

"You're gonna make my fortune," said the man, staring at Matt greedily.

Matt sighed. It was just gonna be one of those days.

***

Matt was led, blindfolded and tied, by the men from the dock. *Any dock,* he thought to himself. *I could have chosen any dock, and I had to choose that one.* They walked for a while, through narrow, winding streets and across a occasional bridge until finally they stopped. He heard his captor talking to someone in a loud voice. Then, the new man took his ropes, and his blindfold was pulled off. He was standing at the entrance to the palace, a place he knew very well. The man now holding his bonds was a guard, surrounded by several other soldiers.

"Wait," said Matt in Mayren, "you're going to take me in there?" The guard nodded but didn't speak. "Good!" said Matt. "I know your king, the Landamad! He's a friend of Trinity! Trust me! This is just a big mistake! We have an ambassador here! Don't I have rights?"

The soldier fingered his knife in the same way Riggins always did before throwing it at a target. Matt didn't speak again. The soldier led him into the palace and through several corridors until he finally brought him to the White Door, the entrance to where the Landamad lived. The people of Chobot thought that the Landamad was a son of the gods and that everything he was in contact with had to be white and pure. Matt thought he was an average Joe who had a favorite color, but he'd never say that for fear of breaking the good ties between Trinity and Chobot.

The soldier knocked on the White Door. "Come in!" came a voice from the other side. When they entered, the room was just how Matt remembered it. The white floors, the white ceiling, the white walls, the white chairs, everything. Sitting in the center of the chamber was a litter, a small room surrounded by white curtains that could be carried on poles. According to Chobot tradition, no man was worthy enough to see the ruler, and his words had to come through a tube protruding from the litter into the ear of a listening servant who would proclaim them. Whether or not there was actually a person in that litter or if the servant was running the country, Matt had never been able to tell.

"Greetings, guest," said the servant in Mayren, with his ear to the little tube. "I have long desired to speak with you, Admiral Matt Baker."

"It is wonderful to be in your presence once again,

Exalted Landamad," replied Matt according to the custom.

The servant put his ear to the tube again and listened with a puzzled expression on his face. "The Exalted Landamad proclaims that Matt Baker should be tied up in a chair."

The guard nodded, and without hesitation, lashed Matt firmly to a chair. The servant listened again and paused, "Are you sure, my lord?" A response came through the tube, and the servant rose. "The Exalted Landamad proclaims that all are to leave the room for him to be alone with this man, Matt Baker. Even I." The servant left the room with the guard and shut the door behind them.

Matt stared at the litter. "Well, they're gone. What's this about?"

A long low laugh, almost a hum, came from the litter. Then the man inside spoke, "Have you forgotten the past so easily, Matt Baker?" Matt scrunched up his face. That voice sounded so familiar, so hauntingly familiar, though no matter how he tried, he couldn't figure out why. Then the curtain opened, and a man stepped out, "Do you remember me now, old friend?"

Matt's breath caught in his throat, "Silam!" The pirate grinned at Matt's astonishment. He was dressed in a long white robe, but his face was the same as it always had been. The pirate who had captured Helen and Lily. The pirate who had owned Emily and used her as a slave. The pirate who had tried to kill Matt Baker on the *Bella Fawn*. Silam, what a bitter terrible name. "But how are you still alive?" asked Matt. "You drowned under the mast!!"

"Not all of me was crushed by the mast," said Silam. "Only my leg." He pulled the white robe back to reveal a metal stump. "The mast took me to the bottom of the sea that day. My leg was severed by the weight. It wasn't a death in battle, it wasn't a death for love, it wasn't a death worth dying for. So I gathered all of the strength I had and swam to the surface."

"You left your leg there?" asked Matt. He felt nauseous just thinking about it.

"The gods had not determined it was my time to leave this earth. Unfortunately, some of my fellow pirates did not believe the same. When I returned to reclaim my position as captain, I was rejected for robbing the gods of my death and for my crippled leg."

Matt wondered what he should feel... pity, anger, distrust, what? "So what did you do?"

"What do you think?" asked Silam. "I left the pirates of Oslo forever. I searched all of Ildathore for a place where I could once again rule over my own domain, and now I've found one." Matt went pale. "Yes," said Silam with a smile. "Imagine my surprise when I heard that Chobot was ruled by someone never seen and never heard from."

"What did you do to the real Landamad?" asked Matt.

"What do you think?" asked Silam, almost offended. "I snuck through his window at night and murdered him in his sleep."

Matt shivered. He didn't mean to; it just came out. "Well, I'm sorry you were rejected, but I don't think it should warrant that kind of behavior."

Silam laughed again. The same evil, menacing laugh. "You're sorry? You're sorry! I DON'T WANT YOUR

SYMPATHY! I want my revenge!" Silam stared at Matt as hungrily as a cat would a mouse. "You took EVERYTHING from me Matt Baker. My leg, my life as I knew it, and my heart's love."

Matt cocked an eyebrow, "Love? You lost me again."

Silam clenched his fists. "Emily! You took her from me! She was all my heart ever truly desired, and YOU TOOK HER FROM ME!!!"

"Emily?" asked Matt in disbelief. "This is about Emily? You can take her back as far as I'm concerned!"

Silam screamed madly, turning over a table. All of the wisdom of war, all of the calm cool wit that Matt had known in him before was gone. Instead, Matt saw a light of angry insanity in his eyes nurtured by bitterness! "Fool now, Matt Baker! Sure, think this is all a game! Think you'll get out of this one, don't you? Don't you understand? I have dreamt of this moment for years, and no one is going to take it from me now!"

Matt gulped, "So, you're going to kill me? Here? Now?"

"Kill you?" asked Silam, a smile creeping across his face. "Yes, I'm going to kill you. It will be the most painfully long and drawn out process that I can come up with after years of waiting for it. But not yet. I must wait. You will be killed on the first of next month so that I may please the gods and once again receive their favor."

Matt sighed in relief, then paused, "What will you do when you're done with me, Silam?"

Silam smiled again, that evil insane smile. "I'll set out for Trinity, of course. Other than killing you, nothing could give me more pleasure than to watch your stupid daughters meet their deaths by my sword. Haven't you seen it coming? I captured the ambassador first, knowing that once he ended contact, it wouldn't be long before they sent someone after him. You can't imagine my disappointment when someone finally showed up, and it was only that pathetic man with the long, black hair. I locked him up, and then you came into the picture. It's only a matter of time before the lies I have spread about Trinity on this island will truly sink in, and my people will be begging me to set out and deal with you barbarians."

"What did you do with Riggins?"

"Why would you care?" asked Silam. "He's such a spoilsport. Even when I had him whipped, I hardly got a reaction at all. It was ridiculous." Matt smiled at the thought of Riggins' expressionless face and his stone hard eyes. "What are you smiling at?" asked Silam suspiciously.

Matt grinned even harder, realizing the best way to play off of Silam, "Why shouldn't I smile? How do you know I don't enjoy being kidnapped, tied up to a chair and seeing my old nemesis?"

Silam scowled, "Be smart now, Matt Baker! We'll see how long that lasts."

WHEN THE WEDDING BELLS TOLL
CHAPTER THREE

"In here!" said the guard, holding Matt's chains and opening the door into the prison. Matt squinted. Why did prisons always have to be so dark and... well... depressing. The guard pushed him forward, and he stumbled on the stairs. The man laughed. "Move it!" Matt walked through the hall with cells on either side. He tried not to look into the cells at first, but eventually, his curiosity got to be too much for him. There were skeletons, lots and lots of skeletons. Even cat skeletons. Matt tried not to smile at this. Apparently, Silam wasn't a cat person either. At least he had one good quality. The whole time they walked, he only saw one living form, a man in the cell next to the last.

He was a miserable looking creature. His eyes seemed hollow, staring off into space. He was fat, but starving nonetheless. Matt recognized him at once. He was Trinity's ambassador.

"In here!" said the guard, pushing him toward the last cell, directly to the left of the tortured ambassador. Matt resisted a bit. The wall between the cells was solid. Matt wanted to at least see the man through the bars at the front of the cells. "I said, get in there!" The man gave him a hard kick, and Matt tripped into his cell. The door swung closed behind him. Matt watched, desperate, as the guard locked the door to his cell and put the keys on a hook on the wall nearby. Then, he left.

Matt sank to the floor. What was he doing here? He had been in a lot of scrapes in his time, but this was definitely the worst. Well, maybe the worst. Being cornered by a dragon didn't look overly promising at the time, either. He groaned.

"Matt?" said a voice from nearby.

"Yes?" said Matt. "Who is that? It's so dark in here that I can't see a thing."

"Don't worry. The sun will rise soon, I think, and your cell has a little window high on the wall."

"Riggins?" asked Matt. "Is that you?"

There was no response for a minute, then a soft, "Yeah. Unfortunately."

"Riggins! What happened to you? Silam said you were whipped!"

"Yeah, I was, but don't worry. It was a lot worse than it sounds," said Riggins in the dark. "How long has it been since I came here?"

"Nearly two months, maybe a little bit longer."

"Two months?" asked Riggins. "Is that all? It feels like so

much longer."

Matt didn't like the way Riggins voice sounded, "Riggins, are you alright?"

"I'm fine, Matt," said Riggins. "It's just hard. With no news of the outside world, it feels like this dungeon is all there is anymore. Well, not all there is. I'm still pretty stinkin' sure I would make a better admiral than you even having missed two months of practice."

Matt grinned. Yep, he was still the same old Riggins. "I have some news of Lily if you think you might want to hear it."

He could almost hear his friend grinning. "The pipsqueak finally proposed, didn't he?"

Matt spent the night telling Riggins of everything he had missed in the last few months. Riggins interrupted several times to make comments, and as the night went on, he sounded less and less like the tortured prisoner he had become and more like the disagreeable sailor that Matt knew so well.

Finally, the sun poked through the window, and Matt saw his friend's face for the first time. A shaggy beard had grown over the usually smooth face. His long hair had passed his shoulders now and hung down his back limply. His clothes were torn and filthy, but his eyes were sparkling with the same humor that Matt had almost forgotten over the last few months.

"So, what do you think, Matt?" asked Riggins. "I look as dashing as ever, don't I?"

Matt laughed, "Yes, as dashing as ever."

Riggins shook his head, "You don't look that sharp yourself."

"Oh, shut up, you two," came a voice from Matt's left on the other side of the wall. "You both look fine compared to an fat, old man like me, so stop complaining."

"Ambassador Melvin!" said Matt, wishing he could see the poor man. "How are you?"

"Like a man locked up in a dungeon. What did you expect?" asked Melvin. "I've been in here for too long already, so maybe it's time I ask the obvious question. How do we get out of here?"

Matt chuckled, "Hey, I'm the new guy. You two'd have a better idea than I would."

Riggins looked at Matt hard, then glanced down the hall to make sure they were alone, "Matt, do you have a match with you?"

"A match?" asked Matt, confused. "What good would a match do?"

Riggins pulled something out from in his coat, "It could light gunpowder." The thing he held was tiny, only a handful of gunpowder wrapped up in a small cloth. Would a little be enough?

"How did you get that in here, Riggins?" asked Matt, disbelieving. "They took all my weapons."

"Let's just say I disguised it by mixing it with those perfume leaves Lily likes so much. How women can stand this stuff, I don't know."

Matt laughed, "Remind me to make one of those little parcels when we get back to Trinity. So, you don't have a hidden match somewhere?"

"I keep my stash of matches in my other coat," said Riggins with a twinkle in his eyes. "You wouldn't happen to have one, would you?"

"No," said Matt, frustrated with himself for not having one.

"I figured," said Riggins, disappointedly.

Suddenly, the wheel in Matt's head started turning. "The guards come in with lanterns right?"

"Yes..." said Riggins. "I've thought of that, but it's risky. There is a guard on duty outside the dungeon door at all times."

"True, true," said Matt. "When do the shifts change?"

Riggins rolled his eyes, "How many times must you worry about guards changing shifts when I am involved?" Matt smiled. "They change right after the guy comes in and gives us our only meal for the day. It is the last task before the switch."

"And when is the meal?"

"About a half hour before sunset. The switch takes about three minutes to complete, so if we tried to get out of here, we'd only have three minutes to do it."

Matt nodded, "I guess that is cutting it kind of close," said Matt, leaning against the wall. "But there is another problem. We'd never get to Trinity! They have really fast ships and a gate that lowers at the entrance to the bay. I don't know how we could lose them even if we wanted to."

Riggins nodded, then paused. "How long did you say I've been here?"

"About two months, why?"

"What day of the month is it? Is it the twenty-first yet?"

"No, it isn't the twenty-first, but why would we go on the twenty-firs...." Matt's voice trailed off as he realized what Riggins was leading up to. Was it possible? Could it work? "I don't know, Riggins. That seems far riskier than getting a lantern."

"What sounds far riskier?" asked Melvin, unable to contain himself.

"Risky?" asked Riggins. "Of course it's risky, but when was the last time that you let that stop you?"

Matt grinned. "Okay, okay, we'll do it your way. Rest up, you two. We leave on the twentieth!"

WHEN THE WEDDING BELLS TOLL
CHAPTER FOUR

It was the twentieth. Matt had been in the dungeon nearly two weeks now and was beginning to understand the vacantness he had seen in Riggins when he first arrived. The air was tense in the three cells. Each of them secretly wondered what would happen next. Finally, the meal of the day came, and the guard entered the hall. None of the prisoners said a word. "Grub time!" said the guard. First, he tossed a piece of food into Melvin, the ambassador. Matt couldn't see the big man, but he could hear him all the same. The mad scramble for the food. The groan of delight as he bit into it. Convincing.

"You next," said the guard, walking over to Riggins' cell. The guard lifted his lantern to see the state of the man behind the bars. It was now or never. "AAHHHH!!!!" screamed Matt, falling and writhing on the floor. The man turned, and Matt saw Riggins's hands reach out from between the bars and bash the guards head on both sides at once. How Riggins had ever learned the best way to hit a man to make him pass out, Matt didn't even want to know, but he wouldn't complain. As the man crumpled the the ground, his lantern fell from his hands. Matt dove for it, hitting the bars with his face but just barely catching it with the tips of his fingertips before it hit the ground. He sighed in relief and brought it to himself.

"Riggins, toss me the cloth!" Riggins wrapped up the little pouch of gunpowder and tossed it. It was a good toss. Matt caught it and was just about to light it when he realized they had forgotten something. "I need a wick!"

"A what?" asked Riggins, the slight tone of panic in his voice.

"A wick! I can't just light the cloth, or I'll go up to!" Matt was just about to freak out when he noticed Riggins shaking his head, his hair falling over one ear. "Riggins, your hair!"

"My what?!?!" asked Riggins. This time there was no mistaking the panic.

Matt ignored his confusion. He balled his hand into a fist, stood, and punched the window with all of his might. It broke into a million pieces. Matt scooped up some of the bigger pieces of glass and tossed them to Riggins through the bars. Most of them hit the bars and fell short, but a few made it into his friend's cell.

"What was that for?" asked Riggins.

"Make a braid out of your hair and use the glass to cut it off! I can use it as a wick for the powder!"

"Why my hair?" asked Riggins defensively. "Why not your hair?"

"My hair isn't long enough to braid!" said Matt. He glanced down the hall nervously. "Just do it, Riggins!"

Riggins groaned, "I don't know how to braid my hair!"

"How do you not know how to braid hair!?!?!" asked Matt, almost in a shriek.

"How would I know? How would YOU know?" retorted Riggins.

"I have daughters! You can't have two daughter and not know how to braid hair!!!!" said Matt desperately. Out of the corner of his eye, he saw Melvin's hand reach out and grab one of the pieces of glass.

"Walk me through it!" cried Riggins.

"It's easy. Make the hair into three parts, then left over right over."

"Over what!?!?!?"

Suddenly, a hand poked out of the darkness to Matt's left, holding a small braid. "Here," said Melvin. "I have daughters, too."

Matt took it gratefully and looked up at the peg on the wall where the keys hung. This better work. Carefully he wrapped the bundle tightly, with the braid sticking out and lit it from the lantern. The braid burned far faster than Matt expected, and he quickly threw the bundle toward the peg on the wall that held the keys. As it hit the peg, the fire reached the bundle, and it exploded!

When the smoke cleared, Matt saw that the keys lay on the floor directly between his cell and Riggins'. They both dropped to the ground immediately and stretched for all they were worth, but the keys were just out of reach.

"No!" said Matt in despair.

Riggins wasn't about to give up yet. He reached for a few pebbles that had blasted off the wall in the explosion and began throwing them one by one at the keys. Suddenly, Matt heard a noise outside the dungeon door. What was is? A voice?

"Hurry, Riggins!" said Matt.

Riggins hurled another rock, another miss. "How did you get into the queen's service without knowing how to throw?" asked Melvin in terror.

"There aren't many pebbles on a navy ship!" said Riggins, throwing the last of his rocks. It clanged off the keys, sending them right over to Matt. He grabbed them and plunged them into the lock on his door. Within seconds, it swung open, and he leaped to free Riggins. By the time the guard came into the dungeon to see what all the racket was about, he met an unwelcome surprise. Riggins kicked him hard in the stomach. Matt cringed as the man collapsed.

"Please let me out!" called Melvin, clasping the bars with all his might. "Let me out of this cage!" He looked as if he were about to cry.

"Here," said Matt, jumping to open the door for him. As soon as it was open, the man fell to his knees and kissed the dungeon floor.

"Matt, catch!" said Riggins, tossing him the sword of one of the soldiers.

"Thanks," said Matt and put it on. It felt good to wear a sword again. "Let's get out of here!"

Together, they fled the dungeon and climbed back up a stairway into the palace. "Do you know where we are going?" Riggins asked as he followed Matt out.

"Well, I just kind of figured we'd make it up as we go along," said Matt with a grin.

"Terrific." They crept as silently as possible through the narrow halls of the palace. Each time they came to a corner. Matt's heart nearly stopped as he peaked around. But so far, every time, the coast had been clear. It was now quite dark outside, and Matt wished that they had somehow been able to keep the lantern.

"I think I know where we are," said Matt after a while.

"Really?" asked Riggins, obviously doubting.

"Yes!" said Matt.

"For sure?" asked Melvin.

"I think so," answered Matt.

"Without a shadow of a doubt?" pressed Melvin.

Matt paused, "More or less."

"That's a 'no,'" said Riggins with a sigh.

"No it isn't! I really think I know where we are. I've come down this hall every time I've been here."

"Why is that?" asked Melvin.

Matt grinned, "This is the way to the toilet."

Riggins rolled his eyes, "What good do you think a toilet is going to do us?"

"You'll see."

They crept further and further down the hall. Finally, they came to the door that Matt had been looking for. He opened it up, and inside was a toilet with a large tube in the bottom of it that led down to... to... wherever it came out of the palace.

Melvin saw the plan at once. "If it will let me see the sky again, then out of my way!" he said. Riggins and Matt watched in disgust as the large man squeezed into the hole and scooted his way with his hands all the way down. When he finally fell out of the long pipe, they heard a sickening 'plop.' Riggins looked like he was going to throw up.

"You next, old friend!" said Matt, pushing him forward.

Riggins stepped up onto the chair slowly and turned to face Matt. "You WILL pay for this plan one day," he said, jumping in after Melvin.

Matt's entire body was covered in goosebumps as he stepped up onto the chair. "Lily," he said softly. "I hope you know that you are the only person I would ever do this for!"

WHEN THE WEDDING BELLS TOLL
CHAPTER FIVE

Matt, Riggins and Melvin ran as fast as their legs could take them through the town and toward the beach. Matt hated the way that his clothes squished every time he stepped. He had always wondered where the waste in palaces went. Now he wish he had never known. Melvin had tears on his face as he ran, glancing up at the sky every few minutes to thank the Creator.

"Once we get to the beach," said Matt between breaths. "All we need to do is pick up a fishing boat and sail it out of here as fast as we can!"

"Sounds like a plan!" said Riggins. "Though I'm still wary of following you just about anywhere after the last plan you had."

Matt chuckled in spite of himself, "Fair enough!"

Finally, they reached the bay. Riggins jumped in the first untended fishing boat he saw and motioned for them to follow. It was a small thing, barely worthy of the title boat, with no hold and one lone sail.

"Not the sturdiest, that's for sure," said Matt, giving the mast a kick and watching it shudder. "But, it should work." Silently, they untied it from the dock and raised the sail. A little gust of wind caught the sails, and they were off. Melvin sat at the back of the boat, grasping his hands together, praying. Matt was praying, too, but he didn't fold his hands in a time like this. There was too much to do.

"I'll climb up on the top of the sail. You stay down here," said Riggins. Matt watched as he climbed the mast one handed. How the man could still be so much better than him at the ropes with only one working hand was a mystery to him.

"Sounds good," said Matt. All the time, they drew nearer and nearer to the exit from the giant bay. Just when they were about two hundred feet away, a deafening horn blast rose from the castle and echoed off the water. "They know!"

The group of ships on the left side of the bay slowly started to move toward the middle with the chain strung up between them. Then those on the right side caught on and started moving, too. "Hurry!" said Melvin, who was rocking back and forth. Unfortunately, the little sail boat wasn't meant for speed.

Only a hundred fifty feet left to freedom. The two lines came on fast, desperately trying to cut off their escape. A hundred feet. Riggins tacked the sail, causing the boat to shoot forward. Fifty feet. Ten feet. A cannon blasted, and the fishing boat was nearly capsized by the waves it caused. Five feet. One foot! They just barely snuck past the two oncoming ships.

"Thank you, Creator!!!" shouted Melvin, jumping to his feet and lifting his hands to the sky.

"Don't be too relieved yet!" said Riggins, tacking the sails again and turning the boat toward Trinity. "We haven't even reached the hard part."

Melvin turned white and cocked an eyebrow, "But now, all we have to do is get to Trinity." He looked over in the direction they were going and froze. A giant black cloud swirled over a small patch of sea, lightning cracking down from it and striking huge twisted rocks that came up to meet it. "That isn't what I think it is, is it?" asked Melvin, shaking. Both men nodded. "I thought the two of you were smart sailors! Why would you time our escape during the Rocks of Hearth?!?!"

Matt put his hand on Melvin's shoulder and turned him around to look behind the boat, "To help us get away from that." A long line of huge warships was strung out behind them, each with their cannons at the ready. On the first one sat a little white litter with a servant sitting next to it. Matt shivered. "We have a chance of getting through this maze with a fishing boat, but there is no way they would be stupid enough to follow us in."

***

"Your Exaltedness," said a servant into the tube that poked out of the White Litter. "The prisoners are going into the Rocks of Hearth. Should we turn back?"

Silam sneered. So, the little admiral thought he could lose him so easily after all these years? Not likely. "Follow them in," he said into the tube.

"But, your Exaltedness," started the servant in surprise.

"FOLLOW THEM IN!!!"

There was a pause. "It will be as you say."

***

Matt looked at the ships in astonishment. "Riggins! They're still coming!"

"What?" said Riggins from the mast.

"I said, 'They're still coming!'" The wind was howling so hard now that you could barely hear yourself think.

Riggins turned back to see, then shook his head. "What are they doing?"

"Riggins!" said Matt. "We'll have to change plans. If we just skirt around the edge, then some of them will make it through! We have to go down the middle!"

Riggins hesitated, looking out to assess their situation. "You're right. If I stay up here, I'll be able to see over the first layer of fog. I'll tell you where to steer, but I can't focus on doing both at once."

"Got it!" said Matt, grabbing the ropes.

"Please don't let me die...please don't let me die!" said Melvin, falling to his knees.

"We don't plan on it!" called down Riggins. The edge of the fog got closer and closer, and so did the ships behind them.

"You ready for this, Riggins?" shouted Matt up at the figure on the mask.

"Let's put it this way," said Riggins. "Ever since you became admiral, I knew something like this would happen!"

Matt laughed in spite of himself, "Yeah, I'm terrified, too!"

All of a sudden, they were enveloped by fog. It was like being in a room when a candle is suddenly blown out without warning. Matt could barely see his hand in front of his face.

"What are we looking like, Riggins?" asked Matt. The dark made him nervous. For a moment, there was no answer. "Riggins?"

"Gradual left!" called down Riggins's voice. Matt tugged on the rope and could feel the boat moving under him. "Straight!" Matt stopped. The darkness continued to blind him. Matt could hear Melvin whimpering behind him. He hoped the big man wouldn't pass out and unbalance the boat. From behind, Matt heard a crash followed by a chorus of screams. That was one ship down. "Hard right!!!!" shouted Riggins suddenly. Matt strained the rope with all of his might. "Okay, straight!" said Riggins again. Another crash, more screams. "Right!" said Riggins. Matt obeyed. "Left!" How long the constant directions lasted, he couldn't say. A month, a week, a minute?

Then, the darkness started to lessen. Little bits of light poked through the fog. "We are nearing the end!" shouted Riggins.

"But, so is he!!!" replied Melvin, pointing behind him.

Matt looked back. There, not twenty feet behind them, was the lead ship with the the deadly White Litter on it. Matt gulped, "Riggins! One of the ships is still trailing us."

Riggins kept his eyes forward. "Don't worry! I know something they don't!"

"I sure hope so!" said Matt. He peered ahead as hard as he could and suddenly caught sight of what Riggins was talking about. It was a huge arch with rocks all around it to their right. Whether it was big enough for the fishing boat to pass through, Matt couldn't tell, but there was no way the war ship would be able to follow. "Riggins! Should I head for the opening?"

"Not   yet!"   said   Riggins.

"Not yet?" said Matt. "Riggins, it is the only way through!"

"Not yet!" said Riggins again and motioned to the ship behind them. Of course! The fishing boat's sails hid the dense rocks up ahead from view. The longer they could wait before turning, the less time the warship would have to figure out how to avoid the wall.

"I don't know about this, Riggins!" said Matt.

"Matt," called down Riggins. "I promise, I will get you to Lily's wedding. Just trust me!!!" Matt nodded. "Melvin, climb onto the step up on the back of the boat."

"Why?" asked Melvin.

"Just do it! And when I say 'go,' jump off and land next to Matt!" Melvin seemed puzzled, but he obeyed. "Matt, when I say go, turn the boat right with all of your might!"

"Whatever you say," said Matt, bracing himself for the pull to come. They sailed closer to the rocks. Lightning shot down and hit one of them. It crumbled, sending pieces in all directions.

In the confusion, Riggins yelled, "Go!!!" Matt pulled as hard as he could as Melvin and Riggins jumped. They smashed onto the right side of the deck in the same moment. The fishing boat sped right. Another lightning bolt flashed, and the noise of thunder covered the tortured screams.

Only one boat made it out of the Rocks of Hearth that day.

WHEN THE WEDDING BELLS TOLL
CHAPTER SIX

Mark stood in his black suit, waiting for the ceremony to start. The Baker Manor had been transformed into the perfect place for a wedding. The large gazebo in the back gardens had been lit with thousands of candles. No matter where you turned, there were white flowers and lilies. Around the gazebo, tables and chairs had been set up for after the wedding dance. Mark smiled at the thought of it. He had always wondered what it would feel like to take part in the wedding dance, the tradition where the father and the bride begin the dance and make their way slowly to the groom where the bride and groom say a few age old words, exchange the rings, and finish the dance. And at the end was the best part - the kiss!

"You better watch out, Mark," said Dan, coming up to him and patting him on the back. Dan had been made one of the groomsmen which in Trinity meant that he had to help pay for the wedding dress. *It had also become a tradition over the years that the groomsmen would work together to buy the most beautiful dress possible in order to make the groom so stunned at her appearance that he might forget the age old words he was supposed to say.* "All I have to say is that there's not a chance in this world that you're going to remember those words during the ceremony. Lily looks gorgeous!"

"As if I would forget them," said Mark. "I don't understand why I'm not allowed to see Lily on our wedding day before now, though."

"If you did, the prank wouldn't work!" insisted Dan. "Trust me, it's better this way."

"Maybe," said Mark, "but I wish I knew how she was doing. You know, the last time I saw her, she was still insisting that Matt would get here in time for the ceremony, but I guess not. It's going to crush her to have someone else dance the dance with her. I just know it!"

"Relax!" said Dan. "It's your wedding. It will be a day you will cherish forever! As soon as the sun begins to set, the dance will start and you will be able to see your bride."

The sun was already quite low in the sky, and guests were crowding around the gazebo to watch the dance. Mark looked over at the little tent made of flowers that he knew Lily was waiting in, then looked back at the sky. In that instant, the sun began to set. Mark sighed. They would have to go on without Matt.

Just as he thought it, a familiar-looking figure moved through the crowd up to the front. He was wearing an admiral's uniform, a large plume poking out of his hat and a sword at his waist. He walked up to the tent and put his hand through the flower curtain. The crowd waited expectantly. When he brought it out again, there was another hand inside it. As Lily stepped out of the tent, the musicians began to play. Lily smiled so wide and so joyfully that Mark almost laughed. Together, Matt and Lily, with a crown of violets on her head, danced around the gazebo to the tune of the music, ever coming closer to where he stood. As they did, Lily's white dress seemed to float around her legs.

Then, finally, they were right next to him. Matt took Lily's hand and put in in Mark's. There was no hesitation. "Take care of her, Mark," said Matt. Then he stepped away.

Mark looked into Lily's kind purple eyes and smiled harder than he ever had before. "Lily Baker, I love you more than the moon loves the stars and the ocean the sky which it ever reflects. I know my love for you shall never perish if you could love me, too." The entire crowd groaned in annoyance, for, of course, he had said the right thing.

Lily blinked with wonder. "Wow!" she said, forgetting her own words. The crowd roared with laughter at her blunder. Mark slipped the ring on Lily's finger, and she did the same to his. It was done. The musicians started up the song again, and Mark swept Lily around the gazebo with new energy that can come only on your wedding day.

When they finished the last step, Mark moved his face toward hers and kissed her for the very first time. Friends and family whooped and hollered and cheered, but the newlyweds didn't hear. They were too busy kissing.

***

"I can't believe you made it!" said Lily, hugging Matt. "I was so worried about you, but now everything is alright!"

"Well, I wasn't the only one who barely made it," said Matt, motioning to someone else in the crowd.

"It's good to see you, Lily," said a familiar voice.

"Riggins!" cried Lily, running to him and flinging her arms around his neck. "I'm so glad to see you!"

Matt and Mark laughed at the startled expression on Riggins's face. "I don't get it," said Mark. "Why were you two so late in getting here?"

Matt glanced over at Riggins, "It's a long story."

That night, the party continued on for hours. Matt kept an eye always on the couple, though, for an old Trinity wedding tradition states that the bride and groom will secretly run off after the wedding and leave for their honeymoon in a row boat. Matt didn't want to miss his chance to follow them.

Mr. Tickleten, on the other hand, was having a wonderful time. He was completely relieved that Matt had gotten there when he had because he was the person who would have danced with Lilly otherwise, and he couldn't dance! He was just enjoying his third slice of wedding cake when he realized that the couple wasn't at the party anymore.

"Just great!" said Mr. Tickelten to himself. "You had to go and get distracted, didn't you?" He searched the party thoroughly for them first, making sure that they weren't anywhere before setting off to the nearest body of water.

He knew he had to hurry if he was to see them off. As he ran, he regretted his tiny little legs time and time again. Then, finally, he got in sight of the water. It was a beautiful little dock that the Baker Manor had. On it stood Matt, staring off into the distance as a rowboat rowed away. Mr. Tickleten smiled. So, maybe he had missed the farewell, but all and all, it may have been a good thing.

He walked up slowly behind Matt. Matt Baker, the young lad who he'd met all those years ago, the day of the terrible misunderstanding. When Mr. Tickleten finally reached him, the boat was out of sight.

"Hello, Mr. Mapmaker!" said Mr. Tickleten.

Matt chuckled with a sigh. They stood there a few minutes, watching the waves lapping up against the shore.

"Are you sad, Matt?" asked Mr. Tickleten after a while. "Are you sad that she got married?"

"Sad?" asked Matt. "No, I'm not sad. How can I be sad when Lily is so happy? I guess I'm just thinking about the past. It seems like just yesterday when I picked her up in my arms and listened, and she told me all the thoughts spinning in her little head."

"Join the old men's club," said Mr. Tickleten with a laugh. "I remember my kids in the same way. They were all so tiny, but then they all grew up! It's strange to look back on their lives, and when their mother died, I had even more time to think about the past. But, since you never got married, that is probably what you will experience right away."

"Yes," said Matt softly. "Not married." Another long pause followed. "Do you think Lily could really love me as her father even though I'm not?"

"Well, let's see," said Mr. Tickleten. "Do you love me

like your father even though I'm not?"

Matt smiled as he looked down at the little man. "Yes, I do."

Mr. Tickleten grinned so hard he looked like he would burst with joy. "I love you, too."

Matt and Lily stayed close throughout the rest of his life. After her honeymoon, she and Mark moved into The Baker Manor with Matt, and he closed off a little section for himself in the west wing and a small section for Riggins in the east wing, where he became like a second grandfather to Lily's kids. Mr. Tickleten also lived out a happy life, in the home of his own oldest son, but... if you didn't know better, you'd think he lived with the Bakers with how much time he spent there. Did Silam die this time, you may ask? Well, I'm afraid now isn't the time for all the answers, especially that one.

STORY SIX
THE ADMIRABLE ADMIRAL

THE ADMIRABLE ADMIRAL
CHAPTER ONE

Matt Baker sat on a bench in the cemetery of Trinity Church. In front of him was a tombstone whose inscription he had memorized. The grave was only a few months old, but he already knew it well. *Isaac Tickleten, beloved father to both his children and the fatherless.* Gone. In a better place. Moved on. Passed away. Didn't they all just mean the same thing? Dead. Matt wasn't afraid of death. He knew in his heart that the Creator was waiting for those who believed in Him with open doors, but he hated the void that death left for the living. He knew he would see Mr. Tickleten again, but that didn't stop the ache in his heart every time he thought about the loving man.

Matt stood slowly and bent down to place some flowers on his friend's tombstone. "We sure miss you, old friend," he whispered and turned to leave.

***

"Good to see you, Admiral Baker," said King Marcus

from his throne.

"And you, your majesty," said Matt bowing. Queen Ella, just another example of death at work. In her place, she had left her spoiled, ambitious son. Matt cringed at the thought of the future of Trinity. "I have come to tell you I am preparing to embark on my last mission."

King Marcus wore a bored expression and popped a grape into his mouth. "Which one would that be again?"

"I am taking five young men in their twenties out onto the open water to test their skills. By the time we return, I will have chosen a new Admiral to take my place now that I am retiring."

"And what makes you think you can retire?" asked Marcus. "What makes you think I will let you?"

"Every man comes to an age when he knows it's time to slow down," said Matt patiently. "And I think mine is here. Fifty-two is older than it looks, especially when spent on the open sea."

"But what about your oath?" asked Marcus. "You promised to be admiral and serve Trinity until death or the Creator's hand stops you!"

Matt laughed. "The Creator has given me two little grandkids already, and I think that's hint enough."

"But really," said Marcus. "You practically own the sea, just as I own the sun. What makes you want to stop?"

Matt was about to answer when he paused, "Wait, you own the sun? Does the sun know that?"

"As the supreme leader, I own everything!" said Marcus. "And everything shall do as I wish!"

"I see," said Matt with a smile creeping across his face. He was pretty sure that Marcus wouldn't be as successful as he might think with talk like that. "Well, to answer your question, a dear friend of mine died recently, and I realized that I had been out on so many missions that I was never really there for him like I should have been. I need to be there for my grandchildren as they grow up."

Marcus nodded distractedly, "Yes, yes whatever. Where are you taking the five men for the test?"

"The middle of the ocean between Thebel, Trinity, and Chobot. We might stop for provisions on the way back, but other than that we'll stay on the water."

"Alright, do it. Just make sure the next admiral isn't a loser like you turned out to be!"

Matt smiled, "I'll try not to."

***

Solomon saddled his horse with everything he might need. He swung up into the saddle and rode out of the stable. Admiral. Admiral. The word sounded so good on his tongue, but what would it be like to be one? Only one way to find out. As his horse trotted down the narrow streets of Trinity's capital, people stopped to look up at the rider. He was certainly the type of rider one looks up at. His dark, brown hair was neatly combed, his blue eyes shone in the morning light, his coat was expensive, and his horse stepped high and tossed his mane. Solomon had to admit that he enjoyed the attention of passers-by. Just imagine how much attention he would get when he was named admiral. Oh, the sweet glory of it!

When he finally reached the royal dock, he dismounted his horse gracefully and stepped out on the wooden planks in his fancy boots. Another young man was already waiting there. His hair was black and a bit longer than Solomon's, but well combed all the same. His eyes were light green and darted around with an expression of awe filling them with every glance. Solomon wondered if it was his first time at the royal dock.

As the other boy glanced around, his eyes finally came to rest on Solomon. "Oh, hi. Are you one of the other possible admirals?"

"Yes," said Solomon, standing a bit straighter. "My name is Solomon Stark."

"Nice to meet you," said the other, shaking his hand with a friendly smile. "My name is Orlando."

"Orlando," said Solomon. "That is a different sounding name. Are you from Trinity?"

"Yes, actually," said Orlando, "but my grandparents came from lands beyond the maps, and I was named after my grandfather."

"How interesting!" said Solomon. "I do love family histories. We should get together and talk about it after all of this when we have more time."

"Sounds good," replied Orlando.

As they finished speaking, a huge six-masted ship docked near them. Even Solomon couldn't help staring. It was followed by a much smaller boat which came in on the other side of the dock. It was so old that the name on it had almost been wiped out over the years. Bell Kawn? Bela Lawn? *Bella Fawn*! That must be it.

As the two young men watched, the huge ship was tied up to the dock, and a tall muscular man stepped off. He had huge hands and a well kept beard with gray hair that fell around his ears. Both young men bowed in honor. "Feel free to get up whenever you like," said the man with a chuckle.

Solomon straightened and reached out to shake the hand of a legend. "The name is Solomon Stark."

"Pleasure to meet you," said the admiral, grasping his hand. "I'm Matt Baker."

Then the man turned to Orlando who was just smoothing down his shirt. "Orlando Cournesure, and may I say I am so honored to meet you, Admiral," said Orlando with wonder in his eyes.

Matt smiled and shook his hand heartily, "The honor is all mine, Orlando." Then he stepped back and took a look over the two of them. "Well, you both seem made out of admiral material, and I have heard nothing but praise about your talents from the academy. Let's get started, shall we? The other three possibilities are already on the boat. I picked them up on the other island."

Solomon smiled. The other three didn't even come from well known families or grand estates! They didn't even live on Head Island where the capital was! This was just too easy!

Once they were on the boat with the other three, they hardly had time to introduce themselves as Matt made them stand in a straight line and briefed them on the plan for the next week, how over the week's time, they would be tested in their strengths and weaknesses blah... blah... blah... Solomon had read the invitation, and that was all he needed to prove himself. Then, finally, Matt decided it was about time they all introduce themselves. "So one by one, step forward, tell your name, age, and maybe some of your experience as a sailor. Solomon, let's start with you."

Solomon took a step forward and stood about as straight as humanly possible, hands behind his back, like he was reciting some great piece of literature. "My name is Solomon Stark, and I'm twenty-six. I have been in the service of the royal family for about five years as a sailor after graduating with honors from the university."

Matt nodded, "Alright. Who is next?"

One by one, the others did the same, but Solomon wasn't listening a bit. He concentrating on trying to look impressive. Then, the last man's voice caught his ear. "My name is Justin." Solomon's head whipped around, and the look he gave the other man was met with the same hostility. The one thing that could ruin his chances and his week! Why on Ildathore did Justin have to be picked for this!!!

THE ADMIRABLE ADMIRAL
CHAPTER TWO

"Why in Ildathore did Solomon have to be chosen for this!" said Justin to Rodney, another of the young men from the program later that day. Justin and Rodney had been raised near each other and had always seemed to relate to each other well. The ghetto is what outsiders called their childhood neighborhood, but everyone else just called it the dump.

"Wait. Which one is Solomon again?" asked Rodney, his red hair falling over his eyes as he spoke.

"The one with the expensive clothes," said Justin, pointing over at the young man talking to Matt Baker. "He always sabotages my plans, every one of them! Then he struts around like a peacock in those fine clothes and expects respect. What a joke!" Justin cursed under his breath.

"I wouldn't do that if I were you," came a voice from

above them. Both men jumped at the sound. There, in the riggings in the mast above them, hung a man. "I wouldn't curse if I were in your shoes. Matt Baker doesn't like the sound of it."

Justin sighed. He couldn't act too at home here. "Thanks for the tip," he replied. "And, who are you?"

The man slid down one of the ropes with a hand in his pocket and landed next to them. His hair was black and reached down to his shoulders, but his face was smooth and expressionless. The first thing you noticed about him were his eyes. They were so dark they looked almost black. "Wait, I know you!" said Rodney, suddenly. "You're that guy who is always at the admiral's side, the Shadow Companion."

The man's eyes twinkled a bit, "I never understood that name."

"So," said Justin, with a sudden inspiration, "What does Matt Baker most hate?" Riggins cocked an eyebrow. "No need to be suspicious. I was just hoping to know what to most avoid."

Riggins thought for a moment, "Well, like I said, cursing is pretty high on the list. So, you two keep your mouths to yourselves, you got that?"

"Yes, sir," said Justin, bowing. "I will!"

Once Riggins had left them, Rodney turned to Justin, "Okay, I know that look in your eye. What's your plan?"

***

Rodney stood casually talking to Collins, the drabbest

of the young men, with brown hair, brown eyes, and average height. Would Rodney normally talk to him? No, he wouldn't, but sometimes desperate times call for desperate measures. As Solomon walked by, Rodney stuck his foot out just a bit more than usual and tripped him so he landed flat on his face on the deck.

This was just perfect. The large barrel was right behind Solomon. The air rang out with Solomon's voice shouting a string of curses. Solomon's face went white as he glanced around. Matt turned to see what was going on.

"Solomon, I would rather not have that type of language on board this ship, if it isn't too much trouble," called Matt, with a disappointed look on his face.

Collins ran over to Solomon and helped him back to his feet while Rodney snickered quietly.

***

"Did you see the look on his face?" asked Rodney with another burst of laughter.

"Nope," said Justin with a grin. "I was stuck in a barrel, but I can just imagine it."

"What are you two laughing about?" asked a voice from behind them. They turned quickly to see Riggins' stone-faced expression staring back at them.

"Just talking about all the useful life skills that can be learned in 'The Dump,'" said Rodney with another snicker.

"Yes, many useful life skills can be learned there," said Riggins in a perfect imitation of Matt Baker's voice, "but I would suggest you leave them in The Dump for the time being." Both young men went pale. Riggins smiled.

***

Solomon trudged into the hold of the huge warship, still beet red from his embarrassment. As he went in, Orlando looked up from a letter he was writing. "What happened?"

"Justin," said Solomon, sitting down on his cot in frustration. "I can't believe him! He's such a cheater! He never cares about anyone but himself, and he always makes ME his target!"

"Sounds like a wonderful guy," said Orlando, turning back to his letter.

"No kidding," said Solomon with a sigh. He glanced over at Orlando's paper. "Who are you writing?"

"Just someone back in Trinity," said Orlando.

"But, you will probably see them again before you could ever send the letter. Why write it?"

Orlando smiled, "Because it feels almost as if I'm with her again."

Solomon grinned, "Her? Oh, now I get it." Orlando nodded and fingered a chain hanging around his neck. Solomon craned his neck to see a wedding ring hanging on it. "Are you married?"

"I will be in three more months," said Orlando with a smile almost too large for his face. "I can't wait to see her again."

Just then, the door to the hold opened again, and Collins came in, his light brown eyes searching around for them in the dark. "Hey, Solomon. Don't worry about what happened out there. I just overheard Riggins talking to Matt, and he told him what happened. The admiral knows you didn't curse."

Solomon sighed, "Okay, thanks for letting me know." Collins nodded and went back up on deck. "You know, Orlando, it was extremely embarrassing to be reprimanded by Matt out there."

"I can imagine," said Orlando, still writing.

"Too bad Justin didn't know how bad it felt. Then maybe he wouldn't do anything like that again."

Orlando looked up, "I don't know. What do you have in mind?"

"Nothing too bad," said Solomon with a smile. "You know anything about swords?"

Orlando nodded, "I used to help make them in my uncle's shop before I started sailing. Why?"

"I think I'll need your help."

***

"So, gang, it's our third day out at sea, and I think it's about time I see your sword fighting skills." said Matt. "Solomon, why don't you start off with Justin."

"It would be a pleasure," said Solomon, drawing his sword.

"Admiral, do we have any tissues, I mean, for Solomon when he starts to cry?" asked Justin with a smirk, drawing his sword as well.

"That's enough," said Matt with a smile. "Fight at will!"

Justin didn't even have time to prepare before Solomon was advancing on him. Solomon swung. His blow clanged off Justin's blade, which shook unexpectedly. Justin tried to go on the offense, but his sword shifted, and he didn't have time to adjust his grip before Solomon was on him again. Another clang, another thrash. Then the troublesome weapon was out of Justin's hand and clattering to the ground. "Need a tissue?" asked Solomon with a satisfied look on his face. Justin just scowled.

"Okay, you two. Good job! Next off, Orlando and Collins," said Matt.

Collins cleared his throat, "Um, I always used my uncle's sword at the academy, and he had to take it with him this week on a navy assignment. Could I borrow someone else's?"

"Here," said Justin, tossing him his sword. Justin didn't like many people, but he didn't mind Collins. The young man was too open and honest to hate.

"Thanks," said Collins, catching it. As soon as it was in his hands, he paused. "How old is this sword, Justin?" asked Collins.

"Only a few months, why?"

"I think it's about time you look into a new one," said Collins. With one slight movement, he pulled the blade from it's handle. "Typically, it's good not to fight with a broken sword"

"Let me see," said Matt, coming over. He took it from Collins and looked it over thoroughly. "You dodged a cannon ball just then, Justin. Someone could be killed using a weapon like this."

Justin clenched his fists and glanced at Solomon who tried his best to look innocent. "Thanks, Collins," he said, taking the two pieces back. "I'll make sure to get to the bottom of this. You can count on that."

THE ADMIRABLE ADMIRAL
CHAPTER THREE

Matt sat wearily in a chair in the captain's quarters with a sigh. Riggins came in after him and closed the door behind him. "They wearing you out, old man?"

"Why do you have to call me that?" asked Matt. "Just remember, you are the elder here."

"Yes, but I don't have white hair yet," said Riggins.

Matt smiled, "It's gray, not white! I tell you what, Riggins. I don't know how to choose in a situation like this. Orlando would make a wonderful admiral, but he can't seem to take his mind off of affairs in Trinity. Solomon and Justin have a lot of experience, but I don't know what to think of their little 'pranks.' Rodney seems the most skilled, but he hasn't ever been in battle before. Collins seems kind hearted, but he's barely out of the academy, and I don't know how he would react in tough situations."

"So, basically you're telling me that you're stumped. Is that what I'm hearing?"

Matt grinned, "Something like that. I just hope something happens to make things clear to me, or else, who knows who might be the next admiral! You wouldn't happen to be free the next fifty years, would you?"

Riggins smiled slightly, "Sorry, I'm all booked with retirement."

Matt put his head in his hands, "Oh, Riggins, what am I going to do? Can't you decide?"

"Not this time," said Riggins. "But don't worry. You'll know when the time is right."

***

"This way," said Justin, softly. It was the middle of the night, and Justin and Rodney were creeping through the bunk room.

"Are you sure he drank the whole thing?" asked Rodney. "I don't want him to wake up and see what we're doing."

"Don't worry! He drank it all, and I put enough sleeping medicine in it. Trust me." Together, they made it to Solomon's cot and lifted him out of it. Then, trying to hide their snickers, they snuck out on deck.

***

Matt woke up the next morning to the sound of someone knocking on his door. "Yes?" he said, standing up and throwing on his admiral's uniform. Riggins opened the door. "What is it, Riggins?"

"I thought you might want to see something before the rest of the crew gets up."

Matt put on his boots and threw his hat over his disheveled hair on his way out the door. What he saw made him stop dead in his tracks. Tied to the mast, three feet above the ground, was Solomon, snoring gently.

"Good grief," said Matt, cutting the ropes. "This has to stop." Riggins nodded and helped him get the young man down. "Let's take him into the captain's quarters and lay him in my bed." Once they were done, Matt sighed. "I can't do it! I just can't do it! I've tried everything, and I can't make those two work together."

"They better learn soon. Tomorrow is the last full day before heading back," commented Riggins.

"I know," said Matt. "Riggins, would you mind if I took some time to myself this morning?"

"Sure, what do you plan to do?"

"Pray!"

***

Solomon had absolutely no idea what to say when Orlando asked him why he had slept in the captain's quarters. All he could say was, "I can't tell you." At least it wasn't a lie!

All that morning and afternoon, he had caught Justin giving him strange looks. But, was that really surprising? After all, Justin was a strange person. "Solomon!" called

Matt's voice. "I need you to head up to the crows nest and keep watch a little while, okay?"

"On my way!" responded Solomon. He quickly jogged over to the ropes that led up and began climbing. When he was about half way up, he noticed Riggins looking at him. He climbed faster. Once he got up, he glanced back down at the Shadow Companion.

"See anything?" called Riggins up to him.

Solomon scanned the horizon, "No. Nothing. Wait, yes there is something! It's way off in the distance. I think it's a… maybe a volcano?"

"Maybe?" asked Riggins in surprise. "Does it look like a volcano?"

"Well, no," said Solomon.

"Then, what does it look like?"

"It looks like, like a boat," said Solomon haltingly.

"Then why did you say a volcano?"

"Well, sir," started Solomon, "because it's billowing smoke!"

"Wait right there!" replied Riggins. "I'm on my way up." Solomon couldn't help being the tiniest bit embarrassed that the man made it up twice as fast as himself with only one arm. "So, where is this mystery object?"

"Right out there!" said Solomon, pointing. Riggins looked. Sure enough, out on the horizon was the silhouette of a giant metal boat with a large column of smoke billowing from it.

"I'll be," whispered Riggins. "That boat isn't on fire. That's for sure! What's going on?"

***

"Wait, wait, you saw a what?" asked Matt. Justin watched as Solomon and Riggins tried to explain it.

"Matt, you know those new good-for-nothing trains they are starting to have on Trinity?" asked Riggins.

"Yes, Lily can't wait to ride on one!"

"It's that type of smoke that's coming out of the boat out there. The same type of pillar!" Riggins was obviously exasperated with his own words, not being able to describe it. "I don't like it, Matt. I don't like it a bit. It's unnatural!"

"What makes you think that?" asked Justin, standing up. "If it is a faster way to sail, then what could be so bad about it?"

"A lot of things COULD be bad about it," said Matt. "Whether they are or not is still to be seen. You said it was heading for us, Solomon?"

"Yes, sir!" said Solomon. "It was heading right for us!"

"Well, then, it should be here later today if all goes well," said Matt. "When it arrives, we can ask the captain about the smoke."

"Maybe we could buy the ship!" said Justin, who was already thinking up things he could do with such a wonderful vessel.

"I doubt he'll want to sell it," said Matt with a chuckle.

"Should we prepare for battle?" asked Orlando, looking up from a letter he was writing.

"No, no. I don't think there will be a need for anything like that," said Matt. "We don't even know who it is. I say we try making friends before firing!"

"And what if he's looking for a fight?" asked Rodney.

"Then… we'll cross that bridge when we get to it."

THE ADMIRABLE ADMIRAL
CHAPTER FOUR

It was nearly evening now. The mystery ship had stopped smoking and had pulled up alongside the Trinity war ship and was signalling for a meeting. The deck was swarming with sailors in black clothes, but no one looking like a captain had surfaced. "Alright," said Matt. "They've asked for a meeting, and I'm willing to give them one. Riggins, I'd like you to come with me, along with Justin, Solomon, and… " his eyes glanced across the remaining three young men. "And Collins."

Collins looked about as surprised as Justin and Solomon at him getting picked. "Are you sure you want me to come, admiral? I mean, Orlando and Rodney are both fine young men."

Matt smiled, "Don't you want to come, Collins?"

Collins grinned from ear to ear, "I'm on my way!"

Together, the two older men led the three younger

ones onto a plank they set between the two ships. "You raised a meeting flag!" called out Matt in Mayren. "We've come for the meeting. Who here is your captain?"

"I am, Matt Baker," said a sinister voice from nearby. Out from a doorway stepped a figure that only Matt recognized. Riggins might have, but it had been such a long time that he didn't. "So, we meet again, Matt Baker. For the last time!"

"I dearly hope so," whispered Matt under his breath.

The man stepped onto the plank with one leg, and the stump of metal tied to his other leg followed. His beard was overgrown and prickly, and his eyes raged with fire. "I bet you never thought you would see me again, did you?"

Matt sighed, "No, not since the Rocks of Hearth. How has life been to you, Silam?"

Silam smiled terrifyingly, "Awful, but it's getting better all the time. I believe it's about time for your execution, isn't it?"

Matt paused. He could sense the curious eyes of the others on him. "So, you seem to like metal boats a great deal."

"Yes… quite fascinating, aren't they? I got this little fancy on Thebel after our last run-in. Do you like her? Because she sure doesn't like you."

Matt looked him up and down, "Speaking on our last run-in, how did you escape the shipwreck?"

Silam smiled again, his eyes gleaming with a mixture of hate and insanity. "Haven't you learned by now, Matt Baker? As long as you are still at large, I could live for a thousand years, if necessary, with only the thought of revenge to sustain me!"

Matt sighed, "Somehow, that isn't comforting."

***

"Who is Silam?" asked Justin, persistently. The rest of the young men gathered around the admiral were wondering the exact same thing.

"He's a pirate, or was a pirate," said Matt distractedly as he walked below deck, followed by the young men. "Then, he sort of became king, though I'm not sure if it was ever legal. After that, he was shipwrecked in the Rocks of Hearth."

"The Rocks of Hearth!" exclaimed Orlando. "How on Ildathore did he survive that? Was that when he lost his leg?"

"No," said Matt, checking the stocks of gunpowder to make sure they had enough. "That happened a long time ago when a giant metal mast crushed him."

Rodney cocked an eyebrow, "Is this guy even human?"

"We better hope so," said Matt, turning back to them.

"No kidding!" said Solomon. "He said he was going to attack and destroy you once and for all tomorrow at sunset!"

"Don't worry," said Matt with a smile. "He won't destroy me. I have nothing to worry about."

"Why is that, admiral?" asked Collins, going pale.

"Because I am not going to be here by then. YOU are!"

All five jaws dropped. "You mean, you're leaving us to fight the battle on our own?" squeaked Rodney.

Matt grinned, "Now, you've got the idea. Riggins and I are leaving on the *Bella Fawn* straight away. You five wanted to be admirals, and now you will be. Each of you will have to prove your skills and your ability to work together. We will leave the crew to you for you to direct as you think best."

Immediately, the room was in an uproar as excuses and fears filled the air. Matt looked over at Collins who was biting his lip hard but not saying anything. Then Collins stomped his foot, and the others grew quiet.

"This is absolutely ridiculous!" said Collins. "There is no way I can do this."

"Collins, listen," started Matt, but Collins cut him off.

"No! Let me finish! I cannot fight like this. There is absolutely no way I can do it without your help!" he said furiously. Then, he grinned, "Will you loan me a sword, Admiral?"

The other young men watched in astonishment as Matt laughed. "Yes, yes. I do think I can." He drew his own sword and gave it to Collins. The others cleared their throats. When everyone was being a coward, it was easy, but it was much more difficult when there was already a hero.

Justin sighed, "Can I borrow one, too?"

***

Solomon looked off in the distance as the *Bella Fawn* retreated from the oncoming danger. Was he scared? No, now he wasn't. He was glad to finally have a chance to prove once and for all that he was worthy of the title of admiral. He only wished Matt could be there to watch it unfold.

The sun slowly began to set, and he knew it was time for action. "Alright, men!" he said, turning to the others. "The fight is on it's way! Which positions are you best at?"

"Hand to hand!" shouted Justin and Rodney together.

Orlando smiled, "If it's all the same to you, fine gentleman, I think I'll man a cannon."

"Alright," said Solomon. Then he turned to the last young man, "Collins, what about you?"

Collins thought a moment. "I'll climb up the riggings and work from there."

"Sounds good," said Solomon. "I'll take the wheel." He was secretly relieved that the wheel had fallen to him, but he wasn't about to show that. "Okay guys, to your positions!" They all went immediately except for Justin. "Aren't you going to get ready, Justin?"

"Don't you think I know what you're up to, Solomon?" asked Justin cooly. "You plan on the same thing that I do. You think you can show the admiral how much better you are than everyone else. It isn't going to work."

Solomon smiled, "How do you know?"

Justin smirked, "You'll see, Solomon. You'll see."

***

Collins gripped onto the ropes as tight as he could. Why, oh why, had he said he would do the riggings! It was the position he was worst at! *You know why,* said a voice inside his head. *You saw that gleam in Justin's eyes, and you don't like it.*

So what? answered the other part of his brain. *What do you think you can do from here? Just because you can keep an eye on Justin from up here, it doesn't mean you can stop him.* He glanced out at the other ship. The sun was just setting. Whatever happened would happen soon.

He pulled Matt Baker's sword out of its sheath and looked at it. It was the most beautiful weapon he had ever seen in his life, and of all people, Matt had let HIM use it! He relaxed slightly at the thought that Matt trusted him with it. Sliding it back into its sheath, he climbed the ropes higher to get to a better vantage point. Down below, he saw the smoke begin to rise from the metal ship. He wondered how it worked. There was smoke, so obviously there was some type of fire, but how did that make it move?

"Collins!" came a voice from below. Collins looked down to see Solomon waving up at him. "I lead, alright?"

Collins nodded, "Sounds good!"

He wrapped the ropes around his wrists and waited for the first turn. All of a sudden, the doors on the metal volcano popped open, and fifty angry cannons poked out. "Creator, help us!" said Collins under his breath. It was time for the battle to begin!

THE ADMIRABLE ADMIRAL
CHAPTER FIVE

As the first cannon smashed into the side of the ship, Justin was knocked off his feet.. He picked himself up as quickly as possible and tried to balance as the next explosion rocked the ship. He grabbed his sword and looked around wildly at the other crew members who stood ready for battle on the deck. Where was Rodney? The next cannonball fell short of the boat but made it bob in the waves. "RODNEY!!!" shouted Justin as loudly as he could. The other man wasn't on deck. "RODNEY!!!" Justin ran to the door of the hold and slid down on the ground beside it.

He pulled open the hatch and pounced into the hole and ran down the hall. As he did, he tripped over a figure curled up on the floor. "Rodney!" he said. "You have to get up! You have to get out there!"

"The cannons!" said Rodney in a terrified whisper, hugging his knees for dear life.

"Ignore the cannons, you coward!" said Justin, trying to pull him to his feet. But no matter how he tried, the other wouldn't budge. "Fine!" he said angrily, giving Rodney a kick. "You'll see the full extent of how cowards are treated later!"

Justin ran back to the door of the hold, leaving Rodney where he was.

***

Collins looked down as Justin returned to the deck. This wasn't good, not good at all. The young man was flaming mad now. He ran to where the pirates were boarding their ship and began cutting them down one by one, going ever closer to the metal ship. "He's going to board their boat!" he whispered to himself. "I have to stop him!"

***

Justin swung his sword wildly, enjoying the thrill of battle! The men around him were cheering now, each of them sure who the next admiral would be! Finally, the last of the pirates with the nerve to come onto Trinity's ship was cut down. Justin looked at the gap between the two ships. Not to far at all. He took a few steps back, inhaled slowly, and charged toward the end of the boat.

"Stop!!!!" came a voice as two strong arms wrapped around Justin's waist and hurled him onto the deck before he reached the edge.

Justin rose to his feet, cursing the stupid Solomon, but Solomon wasn't the one who had stopped him. "Collins!!!" roared Justin. "What are you doing?!?!"

"You shouldn't go onto the other boat for the sake of killing!" said Collins. "If THEY are advancing, that is one thing, but you might accidentally kill sailors who were willing to surrender if given the chance!"

"Let go of me, pipsqueak!" said Justin, shoving him away. "This is war!"

"No! This isn't war! This is a battle with real men who deserve to live!"

Justin kicked him away and unsheathed his sword as several more pirates jumped onto the deck.

***

Orlando stood behind a cannon below deck and fired again. Once again, the ball hardly made a dent in the great boat's side. Orlando sighed. If only Emma were here. He pulled out the ring that was tucked under his coat and looked at it. So beautiful, but hardly even close to HER beauty.

The sudden rocking of the ship brought him back to reality. "Focus!" he said to himself. "Focus!" A hundred feelings swept over him. Would he describe them to Emma in his next letter? No, he wouldn't speak about the battle, only about how much he missed her. How would he say it? "As I think of you, the love in my heart drives me forward through this difficult time." He glanced out the little window to see the position of the other boat, then he paused. It really DID look like a train from the back where the smoke was rising. He wondered what made it rise. Probably an engine, but couldn't engines explode? His own words from a minute before came back to him now. *As I think of you, the love in my heart drives me forward through this difficult time*. If the boat was that big, its 'heart' couldn't be too difficult to hit.

He aimed the cannon right beneath the large pipe with the smoke coming out of it. Once again, it hardly made a dent. So, that didn't work, but what would happen if he hit the pipe itself? It was worth a try, wasn't it? He reloaded the cannon and aimed carefully. Then, BOOM! The cannonball smashed into the pipe, denting it so badly that the smoke was trapped inside. Well, that didn't do much. He aimed again and was just about to fire when… BOOOOOOOM!!!!!!!! The metal boat exploded in a sea of fire and smoke. Orlando nearly jumped out of his skin. Had he done that?

***

Solomon watched the explosion in awe from behind the wheel. You could barely even see the boat any more with the fire dancing through it. "Hooray!" shouted Justin from not far away, and Collins pumped his fist in the air.

"We did it!" said Solomon in relief. "We actually did it!" Orlando ran from the hold and stood stock still, watching the other ship burn. "Orlando!" called Solomon. "Did you do that?"

"I think so!" said Orlando in disbelief.

"Nice job!" said Solomon. "Those pirates are toast, don't you think, Collins?" Collins didn't answer. Solomon looked around for the young man, but he was gone, and so was Justin.

***

Justin leaped past the flames that licked at him, threatening to burn him alive. As he went, the one thing that kept him going were the words of Silam, the pirate: *Haven't you learned by now, Matt Baker? As long as you are still at large, I could live for a thousand years if necessary with only the thought of revenge to sustain me!* There was only one way to prove who the real admiral should be: by getting rid of that menace for good!

He ducked under the smoldering remains of the mast and continued on through the ship. "Silam," he whispered quietly. "Where are you? Are you ready for your death sentence?"

A groan came from somewhere not far away. Justin walked toward it slowly, ignoring the heat that engulfed him. As he got closer, he drew his sword. There he was, a crippled old man laying on the ground, his wooden stump gone. He was curled in a ball, whimpering to himself as the flames drew closer to him.

"Hello there, Silam," he said, quietly.

Silam's old eyes grew large as he looked up at the oncoming man. "Is it time? Have you come to take me away, oh god of death?"

"Yes," said Justin, brandishing his sword. "You're my ticket to fame!" As he brought his sword down on the old man, another sword hit his and sent it sprawling on the deck. Justin looked up to see a figure step between him and his fallen weapon. "Collins!"

The other man's brown eyes stared at Justin with anger. The admiral's sword was lifted in his hands, and the light of the flames danced and flickered off of it. "No. More. Killing."

Justin looked at the young man in surprise that quickly

turned to anger. "He deserves it!"

"Why should we be the judges for that!" snapped Collins. "Deserving or not, he's a man!"

Justin shook his head and stood. "You don't know what you've started, Collins!" said Justin. "You'll regret this one day!" With that, he turned and jumped from the boat, swimming off in the direction of Thebel in the distance.

Collins sighed and looked down at Silam. The old man's eyes were fixed on the drawn sword in terror. Collins put it back in his scabbard and bent down next to the pirate. "Can you move? Is anything broken?"

"No use!" said Silam, hoarsely. "The gods have predicted my death, and this time, there will be no escape."

Collins smiled, "Don't be so sure."

***

Matt stood at the wheel of the *Bella Fawn,* guiding it as quickly as possible to the burning mass of wood and metal that was slowly sinking. "You see any more survivors, Riggins?" called up Matt. Riggins shook his head from where he hung in the ropes.

"Help, please!!!" came a small voice from not far away. Matt ran to the side of the boat where it was coming from and couldn't have been more shocked. There, in the water, swam a desperate young man with an old pirate draped over his shoulders. "Help!!!" repeated Collins, desperately trying to stay afloat.

"Here," said Matt, reaching down. "Grab my hand!"

"No thanks," said Collins. "I can swim. Can you just take Silam please? He's heavier than I expected."

Matt grinned, "Deal!"

THE ADMIRABLE ADMIRAL
CHAPTER SIX

Collins shook Solomon awake. "Come on, Solomon. Matt says he's ready to pick a new admiral!"

Solomon sat up with excitement and shook the wiped the sleep from his eyes. "Really? He's decided?"

"Yeah," said Collins. "Get up quick and get dressed. Everyone else is already up on deck!"

Solomon bounded out of bed and pulled on his shirt. "Did you guys ever end up finding Justin?"

Collins lowered his eyes, "No, the admiral thinks he could have swam to Thebel's shore. I just hope he is okay."

"Sure," said Solomon. He glanced down at the sheath that Collins wore at his side. It was empty. "Did you already give the admiral back his sword?"

"Well, um," said Collins haltingly. "You know how I said I swam with Silam on my back. He was heavier than he looked, you see, and I dropped the sword to lessen the load."

"You lost the admiral's sword to save his worst enemy?" asked Solomon, astonished. "You're dead meat!" Collins gulped. Once Solomon was dressed, the two of them went up on deck to find Matt and Riggins waiting with Orlando and Rodney.

"Morning, Solomon," said Matt with a smile. "I hope you slept well." Solomon nodded. "Good! Well, as you know, today is the day we sail back to Trinity, and I have finally made a decision." Solomon ran over his acceptance speech in his head. He didn't want to miss a single word!

"You know," said Matt, "I had prayed that something would help me make the right decision, and now I think I have." Matt turned to Rodney. "Rodney, you are a very good swordsman and a talented sailor, but I'm afraid I can't name you admiral."

Rodney nodded slowly. He seemed a bit embarrassed, but also relieved. "As you say, admiral." Then, he stepped back, leaving the three others alone in the row.

"Orlando," said Matt. "You have a big heart and more skill than you might ever need on the open sea, but there is something you need to understand about this job, son. You'll have to give your whole heart to it, and I know for a fact your heart is somewhere else." He reached out and grabbed the chain that hung around the young man's neck and pulled it out to see the ring dangling on it. He leaned in close and said, "Tell the little lady that she is a lucky girl."

Orlando smiled so hard it looked like his face would stay that way permanently! "Not half so lucky as I am." Then, fingering the ring, he stepped back, leaving only Solomon and Collins. Solomon sighed. This was it, speech time!

Matt looked at both boys fondly. "I'd like you to both tell me something that you've done wrong this last week that I don't know about."

Immediately, the thought of Justin's sword popped into his head, but he pushed it away. "Nothing, sir! I have worked hard to remain honorable for such an important time as this!"

Matt smiled sadly at him and then turned to Collins who had gone pale, "And you?"

"Oh, sir," said Collins. "I don't have your sword anymore."

A smile flickered in Riggins' eyes as he watched the young man. "How did you lose it?" asked Matt.

"I-I-I was swimming last night with Silam on my back, and the sword just seemed to grow heavier and heavier! So, I let it drop," the young man's face fell, and he looked at the ground.

"So, you're telling me," started Matt "that you lost my sword to save the life of a man who had vowed to kill me?" Collins nodded. Matt grinned and put his hand on Collin's shoulder, "Everyone, meet your new admiral."

Solomon's eyes practically popped out of his head, but no one could have been as surprised as Collins. He tried to speak a few times but ended up just opening and shutting his mouth noiselessly. Matt laughed. "Thank you, Admiral!" said Collins when he could finally get the words out.

Matt took off his admiral's hat and put it on Collin's head, "Don't mention it, Admiral Collins Halaway!"

Solomon watched dumbfounded as the old man removed his jacket and draped it over Collins's shoulders. Collins beamed! "I'll wear it to the best of my ability, sir!"

Matt smiled, "I know you will, son!"

Collins laughed in spite of himself as Solomon, Orlando, and Rodney walked away, "So, uh, what now?"

"Well," said Matt with a chuckle, "You can either go straight back to Trinity with the others or you can come with me on the *Bella Fawn*. I plan to make one more stop before coming back."

"I'll follow you anywhere, sir!" said Collins, with admiration.

"Feel free to cut the formality, Admiral. Just call me Matt."

Collins grinned, "Collins works for me too, Matt!" Matt laughed as they walked together to the *Bella Fawn*. Together they stepped on board, and Matt stepped back to let Collins take the wheel. "No, thanks," said Collins. "You may remember that I don't know where we're going!"

Matt chuckled again, "Truer words were never spoken." As he stood behind the wheel, his gray hair flew in the wind, and his eyes scanned the horizon as he steered the *Bella Fawn*.

"Isn't Riggins coming?" asked Collins.

"No," said Matt, almost sadly. "He will go straight back to Trinity with the others." Collins didn't ask why; he was too busy watching the sea fly past. He was pretty sure he had never enjoyed a boat ride more in his life. "Here," said Matt, stepping aside. "We are heading South down the coast of Thebel. Steer her for me while I get something from below deck."

"Okay," said Collins. He grabbed the wheel hard with both hands, unaware of how much he looked like a certain young man who had stood in that very spot many years ago, looking ahead to his first adventure on the water.

When Matt came back on deck, he was holding an old quilt which he carried like it was a special treasure. Collins watched curiously as Matt climbed up the riggings to the place where the Trinity flag hung and replaced the flag with the old quilt. Then, he slid back down to the deck. "Here, I can take that back now," said Matt, coming up to the wheel.

"Here you are!" said Collins, stepping aside. "Why did you do that? Where are we going?"

Matt smiled, "We're going to visit an old friend on Thebel. It's been so long that I needed to make sure she would recognize me, so I hung the quilt."

"Makes sense," said Collins, looking off over the waves.

"Something on your mind?" asked Matt, looking over at him.

"I was just wondering," started Collins. "If you could go back and tell yourself one thing when you first became admiral, what would you say?"

"Wow," said Matt. "Do you always ask such tough questions?" He sighed. "I guess I would say, 'Kid, you have no idea what you're getting into. In your time, you will see death, and you'll find life. You'll make friends out of enemies and find enemies in the most unexpected places, but overall, you'll find that life can be so much fuller than you ever expected. Never give up!'"

Collins smiled, "Sounds like pretty good advice to me."

This, I'm afraid, is the last of the legends of Matt Baker for though his later years were full of joy, I'm afraid you wouldn't find stories of that sort as intriguing. Although he deserved worse, Silam lived the rest of his life under house arrest in Trinity. Matt lived to be eighty-six years old, and to the end, he never suffered from the forgetfulness of old age but instead sat in his chair in the Baker Manor every night, telling the most wonderful stories to his grandchildren. How do I know this, you ask? Because I, Rosa, was one of them. I remember how his eyes used to light up when telling about the past. Riggins, also, lived out the rest of his life in his own wing at the Baker Manor, and I don't remember a day passing by without those two sitting out on the front porch playing Battle Fleet and arguing about how unrealistic the game was. When Matt died, it seemed the whole country came to the funeral. He was buried at the mouth of the cave on the Isle of Emily where he always claimed to have met a dragon. His tombstone sums up his life better than I could ever trust myself to do:

Matt Baker

He was born and died a simple man, but all who knew him respected him for it. He loved his family with all of his heart and served his country to the best of his ability. Never was there a better man who walked across the face of Ildathore. If his life had to be summed up in three words, the choice would be easy: Kindness, Bravery, and Love.

STORY SEVEN
THE LEGACY OF A LEGEND

Though the last story seemed nearly complete, there is still a mystery waiting to be solved. If you lived in Trinity, you would have read all of the stories up to this point in the *Trinity Gazette*, where they were published by Matt's granddaughter Rosa. However, I believe there is one more story that deserves to be told. Though it was never written down, this collection of stories could not be whole without it. So, I hope you enjoy the last and final legend of Matt Baker.

THE LEGACY OF A LEGEND
CHAPTER ONE

"Keep her safe!" said Mavino as he handed the hands of his daughter over to the young man.

"I will," answered the man.

Mavino stepped back as the young man danced with his daughter off to the horse that stood, pawing at the ground. Even in the gray high-gated courtyard, he couldn't help but smile. Mila had grown so much in the last few months. Why, she looked just like her mother now. He watched, a lump growing in his throat as the two made it to the horse. The young man boosted Mila up to the front of the saddle and swung up behind her. As he did, the warning bell began clanging from behind. Guards rushed from their posts all over the prison. The large barred gate dropped several inches.

"Go," whispered Mavino, softly.

"Come with us," said the young man, bringing back his

horse and holding out a hand.

Mavino shook his head, tears in his eyes. "Go on! Keep her safe!"

"No, no! You have to come, too!" said the young man, glancing around wildly as the guards came closer.

"I said, 'Go!'" shouted Mavino, slapping the horse's rump as hard as he could. The horse charged forward and passed through the gate just before it broke free and crashed to the ground.

"Papa!" shouted Mila from on the saddle.

"Go on!" shouted Mavino. "And never stop dancing, Mila! Do you hear me, daughter? Never stop dancing! As long as you remember me, I'll always be with you, my daughter! I promise!"

Arrows whizzed through the air, and the young man steered the horse away as fast as he could, not looking back. Mavino heard shouts of "After them!" and "Don't let them escape," but he knew in his heart that they would. He smiled through the tears now streaming down his face as the guard led him back to his cell.

That evening, he sat silently in his cell, scratching away at a piece of parchment with a pen.

"What are you writing?" asked his cellmate, glancing at him.

"A letter," said Mavino.

"What a shocking revelation," said the cellmate.

"Please just let me write!" said Mavino. "After today, I don't know how much longer they'll let me live, and I must finish this letter before..." He couldn't finish the sentence. His cellmate nodded and walked away to give him some space. Mavino sat there for a long time, writing all his thoughts and feelings over the last few days onto that old piece of paper. When he was finally done, he smiled.

"Mavino Larentka?" asked a man, swinging open the door to his cell.

"Yes," answered Mavino.

"It's time."

Mavino nodded slowly and gripped the folded letter in his hand. The guard followed him down the hall and out of the door, ever prodding him forward with his spear.

"Keep moving!" Mavino bowed his head and obeyed. Once they were out the door, Mavino was led into to the execution yard.

The executioner smiled at him, an sickening smile. The guard that led him helped him up onto the cart and fastened the rope around his neck.

"Any last words?" asked the executioner.

Mavino sighed, "If you would let me, I'd like a moment to pray."

The man rolled his eyes. "If you must."

Mavino clenched the paper and closed his eyes. "Oh, Creator, help to guide her down the right path in life. Let her believe in you the rest of her life so I can see her again one day. I don't know if I can bear eternal life otherwise." When he opened his eyes again, there were tears in them, but he was smiling. Slowly he nodded to the executioner.

The man nodded back and climbed onto the horse that was attached to the wagon. "Mavino Larentka, this day, the royalty of Trinity does sentence you to the penalty that you well deserve. For spying and assisting in a prison escape, you are hereby sentenced to death!" With a hard kick, the horse charged forward, and Mavino took one last rapid breath before his feet left the wood of the wagon. A few seconds later, the folded letter fell from the man's limp hand and fluttered to the ground.

***

67 Years Later

"You check over there, and I'll cover this side!" said Sam, jogging over to the corner of the old prison yard, trash bag in hand.

"Man," answered Jake, going over to the other side with a bag of his own. "I can't believe that the new government is finally getting rid of this old prison. It's about time."

"No kidding," replied Sam. "This place has become such a dump. Why people took the time to throw their trash over the wall instead of just finding the nearest trash can and throwing it away, I'll never understand." He sighed and changed the subject. "Are you at all surprised that King Marcus was overthrown?"

"Nah," said Jake, shoving a handful of trash in his sack. "When he started claiming that he owned the sun, you knew things were going downhill. Then, when Matt Baker died two years ago, it was like the country lost its identity."

"It practically did!" said Sam. "I remember going to his funeral with my parents! Practically half the country showed up and cried like they all knew the guy or something."

"Yeah," mumbled Jacob. "As soon as he died, it was pretty obvious that Marcus wouldn't be in power long. Only six months after he dies, and what do you know, Trinity becomes a democracy. I don't know about it myself, but if the new government is getting rid of this eyesore, how bad can they be?"

"True." Sam went over to one of the larger trash piles and scooped it up in the bag. Of all the days they could have been sent to work in the sun, why on a day like today? It felt like the hottest day that Trinity had ever seen! Finally, after a few more hours, most of the trash was gone and the two boys felt pretty proud of themselves. They were just about to turn and leave when Sam said, "Hey Jacob! There is another piece of trash right next to your foot!"

"There is?" asked Jacob, looking down. Sure enough, a small folded piece of paper sat there on on the ground. "I got it!"

"Okay," said Sam, turning and opening the gate to leave. When he didn't hear anything from Jacob after a few seconds, he turned to look at him. He had unfolded the paper and was glancing over it. "Are you coming or what?"

"Sam!" said Jacob. "This isn't just trash! This is a letter!"

"Okay, so a prisoner left a letter here a long time ago. Why does that concern us?"

Jacob looked up with a twinkle in his eyes, "Because it is about Matt Baker!"

"What?"

"Come look!" said Jacob, and Sam ran over. "See, most of it isn't even written in Trinidad, but his name is all over it!"

Sam looked it over, "You're right, but why would an honorable admiral have anything to do with a prisoner who got executed?"

The two boys looked at each other, each with the same idea in mind. Jacob smiled, "I HAVE always wanted to uncover a scandal!" Together the two hot and sweaty boys dropped their bags of trash and raced through the streets of Trinity's capital city. Once they finally reached their destination, they glanced up at the sign to make sure of themselves: *The Trinity Gazette Printing House.*

Side by side, they burst through the door, and Sam waved the paper triumphantly in the air, "We found a scandal!"

Two people turned their way as the others continued to work with the printing presses. One was medium height and rather pudgy with a hairpiece that kept slipping over his eyes, and the other a lanky man in his twenties with a gleam in his green eyes and a spring in his step.

"A scandal?" asked the pudgy one, walking over with the air of someone who thinks himself quite important.

"Yes!" said Sam, quite out of breath. "A scandal involving Matt Baker!"

The pudgy man snatched away the paper and looked over it. "Why, this is just an old paper with his name on it a few times here and there. What is so scandalous about that? Tell me, where did you find this paper?"

"The execution yard in the old prison!"

The young man's eyes nearly popped out of his head, "WHAT!?!?!"

THE LEGACY OF A LEGEND
CHAPTER TWO

"There has to be some kind of mistake!" said the young man, grabbing the paper. Sam and Jacob watched as his green eyes flew across the page. As he read, the pudgy man nodded at the boys and handed them each a few coins. They left content, but the young man still was not. "I'm telling you, Mr. Conerel. There's something wrong with this!"

"Ravenoff, I know you knew Matt Baker, but you also know I'm not going to give up this kind of dirt!" said the pudgy man.

Ravenoff looked up at him with panic in his eyes, "You can't print this, sir! Matt Baker wasn't a criminal, honestly! Besides, you literally can't print it!"

Mr. Conerel lifted his eyebrows, "And why is that?"

Ravenoff's mind searched desperately for an explanation, and finally he landed on one. "Because I know Matt Baker's granddaughter, Rosa. You remember. You printed her story about Matt in the paper, and it got a great response!"

"'The Mapmaker,' yes. And you said she was writing another for us, 'Fathers' or 'Dads' or something. What of it?" asked Mr. Conerel impatiently.

"Well," said Ravenoff. "I happen to know that in his will he made her responsible for any legal matters concerning him after his death, which includes accusations, acquaintances, AND any documents concerning his affairs! You can't legally print anything about this without her consent, and I sure hope you don't want *The Trinity Gazette* to become a tabloid, do you?"

Ravenoff knew by Mr. Conerel's expression that he had won the argument. "I never should have hired an assistant who was in love with Matt Baker's granddaughter."

Ravenoff grinned. Just then, the clock chimed. The first shift of the day was over. Ravenoff folded the piece of paper and stuffed it into his left pocket before grabbing his jacket and heading out the door. As he walked down the street, he couldn't help sticking his hand in his other pocket and fingering the object inside. His raven hair fell over his eyes as a gust of wind kicked up. As the sun beat down, he held his red jacket instead of putting it on. As he left the heart of the capital, the world seemed more alive. He stopped for a minute to grab two twisty breads from a street vendor and swung the bag with them inside back and forth as he walked. Finally, the buildings on both sides of him became scarcer and scarcer until nothing was left but the dirt road he walked on and the trees on either side.

He whistled one of his favorite tunes as his destination came in sight: a large house, maybe a mansion, with huge white pillars in the front that he had played hide and seek around as a little kid. Unfortunately, he had never been a very good hider, and Matt Baker always saw him first though he pretended not to.

He reached the gate and swung it open with the ease of someone who was coming home. The letters on the gate were old but still as beautiful as the day they had been made: *The Baker Manor.* He made his way down the long walk from the gate up the hill to where the house stood. As he did, he glanced at the big oak tree to his left. The remains of his and Rosa's tree house were still inside it, the rope ladder swinging back and forth in the wind as if two little munchkins were scrambling all over it. He climbed the steps to the porch and looked over to where two chairs still sat on either side of a little game table. How many times he had seen Matt and Riggins sitting in them, he couldn't tell. He glanced up at the wing where Riggins still lived before stepping up to the double doors.

Careful to grab the right door, as opposed to the left one that seemed nearly impossible to move, he pushed it open. Inside, he could smell that wonderful smell from the kitchen that he always smelled on Friday afternoons: the smell of Aunt Lily's cheesy sauce. To be fair, Lily wasn't actually his aunt, but he had known her for so long and Matt's relatives were such close friends that to call her anything else now just seemed strange. Ravenoff hung his coat on a peg next to the door and slipped out of his boots before going into the kitchen.

"Good afternoon, Aunt Lily," he said, coming up behind her and putting an arm around her shoulders.

"Sometimes, I think you smell your way here on Fridays, Ravenoff," she said with a jump. "You always get here just as I finish the sauce!"

"Can I help it if I have good taste?" asked Ravenoff, with a smile.

Lily laughed, "If you think a comment like that will get you some extra sauce, you are absolutely right!" She filled two little bowls with the cheesy goodness and put them on a tray for Ravenoff to carry. He took out the two pieces of twisty bread he had bought and set them on the tray. Before he could even get his next question out, Lily answered it, "Rosa is up in the attic."

"Thank you," he said, holding the tray steady and heading to the stairs. As he passed the old armchair in the living room, he paused. In his mind's eye, he could still see himself and Rosa, Charles and little Andy, sitting on the floor around Matt's favorite chair as he told out story after story. He remembered how Riggins used to sit nearby and watch Matt nearly as closely as the children would. Soon, Andy would crawl up on Matt's lap and fall asleep, and Charles would start to nod, but Rosa and he would have to be dragged away when bedtime finally came. He smiled. Some things, even if they make you sad, are still worth the remembering.

He turned and climbed up the stairs, all the way up to the attic, knocking on the door with his foot since his hands were full. He heard a rustling of papers, and then the door opened. There stood Rosa. She looked so much like Lily, but she had a fiery spirit in her. Her violet eyes could look at the same thing a thousand times and always find something new about it. When they were little, she once got him to stand still for two hours so that she could walk around him the whole time and try to memorize every little detail. She looked at him now with the same curiosity, searching out anything that might have changed since the last time they saw each other.

"Hi, Ravenoff!"

"Good afternoon, Miss Rosa," said Ravenoff with such a low, playful bow that he nearly spilled the tray.

Rosa laughed so hard that when she was done, nearly all of her hair had come out of her bun and had fell around the sides of her face. "When will you ever grow up, Ravenoff?"

"When you decide not to eat twisty bread on Friday afternoons," said Ravenoff, waving the tray temptingly in front of her nose. She didn't even try to resist. Ravenoff grinned as she dipped her bread in one of the bowls of cheese sauce and took a big satisfying bite. After he put the tray down, he glanced around to attic. Papers were everywhere, but that was pretty normal. He was pretty sure Rosa hadn't known what she was getting into after she agreed to take care of Matt Baker's matters after his death. It had been two years, and she was still sorting through stuff.

"How's the battle coming?" asked Ravenoff, picking up a paper, pretending to read through it and letting it fall back to the desk.

"Just about the same as always," replied Rosa, taking another bite of twisty bread goodness.

"Well, I hate to be the bearer of bad news," started Ravenoff, "but I found something at work you might want to add to your pile of things to sort out." Rosa looked at him questioningly. "Here," he said, taking the note out of his pocket and giving it to her. "Two kids came into the newspaper office today, saying that they had unearthed some kind of a scandal. I told Mr. Conerel that he couldn't legally print the paper because you were taking care of Matt's legal affairs."

Rosa raised an eyebrow, "I hope you know that there wouldn't have been anything illegal about printing this paper in *The Trinity Gazette*."

"I know," said Ravenoff with a grin, "but I sounded pretty convincing all the same."

Rosa laughed, scanning the paper, "So, where did they find this paper?"

"They said they found it in the execution yard at the old prison," answered Ravenoff, eating another bite of his bread.

"What?" asked Rosa, glancing back at the paper. "Someone is accusing him of being a criminal? How could they?"

Ravenoff shrugged, "Some people just really want their names in the paper, I guess. Are we still on for tonight?"

Rosa smiled. "It depends. Which restaurant did you say we would go to again?"

"Nice try, but you aren't going to get me to blab that easily!" said Ravenoff. "All I'll say is that you just might want get dressed up."

"Dressed up?" asked Rosa with a coy little smile. "And why would I need to get dressed up?" He just grinned. "Ravenoff, tell me! You know I don't like surprises!"

"You love surprises!" said Ravenoff, laughing.

"Only after they happen!" spouted back Rosa. "But I don't like the process of being surprised."

"You know what that really means?" asked Ravenoff, bopping her on the nose with his finger.

"What?" questioned Rosa, looking up into his eyes.

"That you're nosy!"

"Ravenoff!!!"

THE LEGACY OF A LEGEND
CHAPTER THREE

"Keep your eyes closed, or I'll have to blindfold you again!" said Ravenoff with a laugh as he led Rosa down the street.

"Ravenoff, this is foolish! I'm going to look!" said Rosa, but he knew it was an empty threat.

"Go ahead!" whispered Ravenoff, bringing them to a stop. Rosa opened her eyes and started, her hand flying up to her mouth. "I hope you like to dance," said Ravenoff, bowing to her.

"Ravenoff," she whispered, "how?"

"I wrote a poem a few months ago that praised the new government, and it got printed in the paper. One thing led to another, and eventually, they asked if they could pay me back at all. You know what I said?" Rosa shook her head, dumbfounded. "I told them to let me know the next time they would be having a ball." There, in front of them, stood the front gate of the castle. It loomed high above their heads and beyond that stood the castle itself.

"Oh, Ravenoff, I wasn't expecting this! I'm not at all ready! I should have spent more time on my hair and..."

"Relax," said Ravenoff. "I think you look beautiful." Rosa blushed. Hand in hand, they walked up to the gate, and Ravenoff handed the gatekeeper his invitation. The gateman looked at it, then looked the two of them up and down. "It isn't forged," said Ravenoff with a laugh. The man grunted and handed back the paper before opening the gates. When they were opened, what they saw took their breath away. A huge courtyard lay not far beyond them with exotic trees growing up all around it and candles lit on every surface, transforming the dark night into a sky full of shining stars.

"Ravenoff!" whispered Rosa. "It's amazing!" He squeezed her hand, and together, they went into the courtyard. Everywhere, couples were laughing and speaking softly. Before long, they were on the edge of the crowd. Ravenoff left Rosa for a moment and jogged around the people to where a series of musicians were standing. After exchanging a few words, Ravenoff returned to her. She looked at him questioningly, but he only grinned. Then, before they could get anything to eat, a band began to play, quietly at first but growing louder all the time. As if on cue, a large dance floor was cleared as people backed away.

Ravenoff lifted Rosa's hand in the proper way and bowed to her much more seriously than he had earlier. "May I have this dance, Miss Rosa?" Rosa nodded, a smile spreading across her face. Side by side, they stepped out onto the dance floor followed by several other couples. Rosa put her hand on his shoulder, and he rested his on her back as the dance began. In an instant, all of the formality they had possessed a moment ago was replaced by pure energy. All of the dance classes their parents had forced them to attend paid off. Before long, all conversation had died down, and the musicians picked up the pace. Ravenoff swung Rosa around, and her dress whipped around her legs. With no dance in mind, they continued letting the music decide their moves for them. Dancing was just about the only time Rosa let him be the leader in anything, and he quite enjoyed it. She spun, her hair flying around her and as they got close again, Ravenoff brushed it back from her face.

One by one the crowd started clapping to the beat. It was a new style of music by the newest composer in Trinity, Mr. J. A. Z., who happened to be Rosa's favorite. As the tempo increased, they picked up their pace, swinging together and stepping in time. Rosa laughed as they danced faster and faster, having to rush just to keep up with each other.

For a good thirty minutes, the two kept at it excitedly. Finally, the musicians played their last note, and the two struck a pose.

A chorus of cheers erupted from the onlookers, and Ravenoff saw Rosa beaming, as happy as he had ever seen her. There was one thing off the bucket list! Together, they bowed (as Rosa was not the type to curtsy) and left the dance floor, out of breath and rosy cheeked.

"That was amazing, Ravenoff!" said Rosa, laughing at the thought of how they had totally just sabotaged the dance.

"We always said we would dance in the palace!" said Ravenoff. "And now we have!"

"Excuse me," said a voice behind them. "Could you introduce me to your friend, Ravenoff?"

"Oh! Mr. Faltoms, yes of course!" said Ravenoff, turning and shaking the man's hand. "Mr. Faltoms, this is Rosa, a good friend of mine. Rosa, this is William Faltoms, one of the leaders of the new government and the man who invited us."

"Good to meet you, Mr. Faltoms," said Rosa, shaking his hand before he had time to bow.

"After the way you two danced, I'm honored to meet you as well!" said the man. "But please, call me William. I must admit you two far outshined the dancers we hired for later in the evening, but I'm grateful. Once again, you've done me a favor! Is there anything I can do to repay you?"

"Oh, we don't need anything," said Ravenoff, but as he did, he felt Rosa jab him in the ribs.

William laughed, "Your friend seems to disagree. What is it you had in mind, Rosa?"

"It isn't that I'm not grateful for all you've already done," said Rosa, "but I've always wanted to see the Hall of Admirals in the palace. I remember when I was a little girl, a man came to our house to paint my grandfather, Matt Baker's, portrait, but I haven't seen it in years. Do you think we could maybe just take a peek?"

William smiled. "Just the kind of request that I like. It doesn't cost me anything! Of course, my dear. I would be honored to show the two of you the Hall of Admirals." With that, he led them into the palace. It took a long time to get there, and Ravenoff finally began to grasp what Matt always used to say about palaces being more like mazes than houses and how he always wondered how anyone ever got to the bathroom on time.

"Ah, here we are!" said William, swinging open a door. Rosa gasped and immediately left them to walk mesmerized around the room, looking from one portrait to another. William chuckled, "Not the typical girl is she?" asked William.

Ravenoff grinned, "You have no idea!" Absentmindedly, he fingered the object he always kept in his right pocket. Was tonight the night?

"Ravenoff, come look at the picture of Collins, the one Matt picked as admiral. They got it all wrong!" Ravenoff jogged over to where Rosa was standing and laughed at the representation. "You see what I mean?"

"Yes," said Ravenoff, "They got rid of his big nose! It's just normal now."

Then they turned to the empty spot on the wall next to Collins. "Where is Matt's portrait?" asked Rosa. "Shouldn't it be right here?"

"Why, yes it should," said the man with a puzzled expression. "And what's more, it was just this morning! One moment... I'll ask the servant about it." He clapped once, and a man who had been standing in the corner of the room came and spoke something to him softly. "I see," said the man in a rather disappointed tone. Then, turning to the curious faces of the other two, he said, "It seems that the higher powers in our new government have too much time on their hands. They found a tabloid today with a very intriguing title on the front: *Matt Baker Found to be a Conspirator with Executed Criminals!*"

"What?!?!" asked Rosa in horror. "But why would they say that? The paper they found was just an old piece of trash!"

"Either way," said William. "With the new government just starting and all, it seems our leaders decided it wouldn't be a good thing to show support to Matt Baker."

"That's ridiculous!" said Ravenoff. "Since when are the decisions of respectable politicians based on tabloids?"

"Since we became a people's government. I'm sorry, but there is really nothing I can do."

"But there is something we can do!" said Rosa.

"Yeah!" said Ravenoff, then he paused and turned to Rosa. "Like what?"

"I'll write my own article, one that tells the truth!" said Rosa. Ravenoff knew that look in her eye. She was getting fired up. "Ravenoff, let's go talk to Riggins! Surely he will know something about this!"

***

"You're wasting your time," said Riggins, standing up and walking away from them. Luckily, his living chambers weren't very big.

"Come on, Riggins!" said Rosa, Ravenoff standing behind her.

"Rosa," said Riggins. "I love you like you were my own granddaughter, but I have nothing to say about this! There are some things that shouldn't leave a man's heart for any reason!"

"Riggins," started Ravenoff. "Please, it means a lot to us. All we're trying to do is clear Matt's name so no one can ever accuse him of being a criminal or having anything to do with them! Please help us."

Riggins turned so that his limp arm swung a little though his hand was still tucked tightly in his pocket. His dark eyes looked from first one to the other, then he shook his head. "No kids. I can't, and I won't. Now if you will excuse me." He leaned on his cane on the way to his bedroom and shut the door behind him.

Rosa and Ravenoff went out of the house without saying a word and sat down on the two chairs on the front porch. "It doesn't make sense," whispered Rosa after a while.

"What doesn't?" asked Ravenoff.

Rosa looked up at him, "He wouldn't hide something if there wasn't something to hide, Ravenoff. What if Matt really was... a criminal?" Ravenoff didn't respond for a minute. He didn't want to let on that he was wondering the exact same thing. "I have to find out, Ravenoff," said Rosa. "I have to find out the truth!"

Ravenoff sighed, "Yeah, I know you do. You never were a normal girl, Rosa."

Rosa smiled. "Does that mean you'll help me?"

Ravenoff grinned slowly. "Well, I do have this weekend off."

Rosa laughed, "Perfect! And I know just the place to

start our search!"

THE LEGACY OF A LEGEND
CHAPTER FOUR

"This way," said Rosa, leading Ravenoff through the busy streets of the capital the next day. "I know it's around here somewhere!" Ravenoff doubled his pace to try to keep up with her and watched with pleasure as the townspeople stopped and stared at them as they passed. But then again, the only reason he wasn't looking was because he was used to it.

Instead of a dress, Rosa wore long baggy pants made out of flowery material. The pants had elastic at her ankles so that they couldn't trip her up when she was running, and on her feet were a pair of sandals instead of the typical heeled shoes. Many a time he had seen men ask her how she dared to go outside with such outlandish clothes on, and every time, she had had the same answer: "You wear a dress for a whole day and let me know what you think. Pants are just more practical!"

"Oh, I get it," said Ravenoff when Rosa finally stopped in front of a building. A large sign hung over the door with the words: *Translation Station (and other occupations).*

"Yep!" said Rosa, with a twinkle in her eye. "Come on!" Together they stepped through the door and into a large room with desks all throughout. At some, there were scientists with glass tubes working dutifully on experiments, at others were scribes working hard to translate ancient manuscripts, but Rosa walked past all these to the main one at the end of the room. "We would like to have a paper analyzed and translated please!"

The man looked up from his desk with an amused expression on his face, "Sorry, little lady, but it takes money to do that stuff. Maybe you should head back home and knit."

"I enjoy other hobbies," said Rosa, dropping a handful of gold coins on the desk. Ravenoff almost laughed at the look on the man's face as he tried to regain his composure.

"My apologies. Where is the manuscript?" he asked. Once they handed it to him and he sniffed it. "Let me guess, this was from the old prison on the other side of town, right?"

Ravenoff's eyes nearly popped out of his head. "How did you know that?"

"At the time it was built, the king was very superstitious. He ground up granite and mixed it with the soil in the execution yard so the ghosts of prisoners wouldn't come back to haunt him. See these marks? They're traces of granite. Normally people don't buy extremely expensive stone and grind it into powder just to put it on the ground."

Ravenoff cleared his throat awkwardly, "Yeah, um, I knew that."

"This is readly old, though!" said the man. "You can tell just by the way the paper is holding up. I'd say it's at least fifty years old, quite possibly older. What are you looking to know about it?"

Rosa thought for a moment, "Really we just need to know when this note was written and what it says."

"Gotcha!" said the man. "This writing is some dialect from Thebel, and unfortunately, Murray is the only one here who knows those dialects. I say unfortunately because he's working on a project right now that has to get finished today. Tell you what, if you have time to stick around a half hour or so, I can do the age test right away. Then, I can have Murray start on the translation first thing tomorrow morning."

"Sounds good!" said Rosa. "We can wait!"

***

Ravenoff sat on the old bench next to Rosa, watching her look out the window. It may sound silly, but he loved to do it. Whenever she looked out a window, she didn't look at the whole scene. She looked person by person and her expression would change with each one. As she watched a little girl and her mother walk by, he could see the smile twitching over her lips. Next came a mangy man who looked as if he hadn't checked a mirror in a few weeks. A slight glance of disapproval came from Rosa at this. After that, an old man and his granddaughter came and sat on a bench nearby, tossing bread crumbs to the birds. At first, a smile came over Rosa's face, but it faded away as she watched. Then she turned away from the window. Ravenoff turned away quickly.

"Ah, here we are!" said the man, finally motioning them over to his desk. "Come on, kids. I found some things out that you might want to know." Instantly, the two of them jumped to their feet, despite being called kids, and rushed over. "Alright," said the man. "So surprisingly, it answered a few questions I had, too. First, the ink is extremely old. If I had to bet my life on it, I'd say sixty-six or sixty-seven years old. But then, I got to wondering how that was possible because paper isn't exactly the strongest thing in the world. So, I did some tests on it and discovered it isn't ordinary paper at all. It's made by craftsmen on Thebel who have learned the secret of making a nearly indestructible parchment. Though I don't understand half the process myself, I recognize the craftsmanship when I see it. That ties up a few other loose ends, too, if you think about it."

"Yes!" said Ravenoff. "Weren't Trinity and Thebel in a cold war at that time?"

"Exactly!" said the man. "My guess is that the writer was either a spy or a smuggler that got caught and was hung. That was typically the punishment for such things back in the day." Ravenoff's hand went to his throat of its own accord.

"Is that all you found out?" asked Rosa.

"Yes, that's as much as my tests will tell me, but like I said, Murray can get it translated tomorrow morning."

"That would be great," said Ravenoff. "Thanks for all your help!"

"No problem."

Ravenoff and Rosa left the building and went outside

together. "So, are we giving up for the day?" asked Ravenoff, almost hopefully.

"Not a chance!" said Rosa. "Let's go to the archives at the local history center and figure out who was on duty during the execution."

"Okay," said Ravenoff reluctantly. "But, well, can we get lunch somewhere first? I'm starving!"

Rosa smiled, "Sure."

***

Ravenoff and Rosa sat at a table in the corner of *Sally's Diner*. Ravenoff loved this restaurant. It was simple but fun. The windows had words and designs covering them, and each table had a different flower pattern on the tablecloth. They always sat at the violet one.

"Here you are," said a waiter, walking up, "Which of you ordered macaroni on the side?"

"That would be me," said Ravenoff, watching as the man put the plate in front of him. "Thank you!"

"No problem," said the waiter, putting the other plate in front   of   Rosa.

"So," said Ravenoff, taking a bite. "Are you really going to drag me off to talk to some old guard who helped execute people?"

"Yep!" said Rosa, taking her first bite. "What are friends for?"

"Apparently the definition of the word has changed recently," said Ravenoff with a chuckle. "So, how is sorting through Matt's old papers going?"

"Awful!" said Rosa. "I never knew one admiral could have so many legal documents! You know, the most interesting thing I have found so far is a letter in his handwriting. It was addressed to someone he called 'my dearest.'"

"My dearest?" asked Ravenoff, shocked. "He had a sweetheart?"

Rosa laughed, "Apparently. Funny the things you never learn about someone until they're dead."

"No kidding!" said Ravenoff. As he ate another bite, he noticed a restless look in Rosa's eyes. "Rosa, don't worry about Matt. Riggins is probably just being weird about it. It isn't the first time, you know?"

Rosa smiled, "Yeah, like the time he threatened not to come to Matt's funeral if we buried his favorite blanket with him." Ravenoff cocked an eyebrow. He'd never heard this story before. "You remember that old quilt he always had around. Well, we had thought it would be a nice gesture to bury him with it because he liked it so much. Riggins practically had a fit! He told us right out that he wouldn't come to the funeral if we buried the quilt. So, obviously, we didn't. I think it's still in Matt's old room."

"Sometimes when people get old, they can a make big deal about things," said Ravenoff.

Rosa looked at him curiously, "But, you're still coming with me to talk to the old guard, right?"

"Of course!"

THE LEGACY OF A LEGEND
CHAPTER FIVE

Rosa and Ravenoff walked quietly up the hallway in the nursing home. When they finally reached room thirty-two, they paused. Ravenoff took a deep breath and knocked on the door.

"Come in!" said a voice on the other side. Ravenoff turned the knob, and the two of them stepped in. Sitting in an armchair near the window sat an old man with white hair. "Well, looky here!" he said with a smile as they came in. "Aren't I lucky to get two young visitors today!"

"Hello, Mr. Ontalonger?" asked Rosa, coming in.

"Call me George!" said the man. "My friends do."

"Okay, George," said Rosa, going over to him. "Would you mind if we ask you some questions?"

"Sure!" said George. "The prune juice is in the icebox, and the cups are in the cupboard. Help yourselves!"

"Thank you," said Rosa with a smile. "We were wondering if you could tell us some things about the past."

George's eyes twinkled. "That is my favorite subject these days! What is it you'd like to know?"

"We were wondering if you helped in the execution of any spies or smugglers during the cold war between Thebel and Trinity?"

"Where from?" asked George. "If I recall, there were lots of chocolate smugglers from Chobot still around. Chocolate was a big problem in the years before the war. In fact, one time..."

"Actually, we were wondering about any from Thebel," said Rosa. Ravenoff sighed in disappointment. He had been hoping to hear more about the chocolate smugglers.

"Well, there weren't very many smugglers from Thebel, but we were always on the lookout for spies!" said George. "They were sneaky little rascals. I think we only caught three during the whole war, though. One died of injuries, and another one was hung."

"That's so sad!" said Rosa. "Did you see it happen?"

"Nope!" said George, "I was sent after the third."

"What do you mean by sent after?" asked Ravenoff, sitting down beside the two of them with his glass of prune juice.

"I mean chased. The third one had escaped!" George smiled at the dumbstruck looks on their faces. "Yeah, a young girl she was, only eleven. Thebel ought to have been ashamed of using her as a spy. If I remember right, her and the older man were both sentenced to be hung. The day before it was to happen, she broke out."

"How?" asked Ravenoff. "Did she make a hole through the wall or something?"

"No," said George. "Apparently, we didn't catch a fourth spy. A young man helped her escape. It was all very embarrassing for me, as you can imagine."

"Why?" asked Ravenoff.

"Because I was the guard set to watch the gate," said George sheepishly. "I... well... I fell asleep on guard. The next thing I know, the next watchman is shaking me awake, and a horse is galloping out of the courtyard with a young man and the girl!"

"Did you see who it was?" asked Rosa.

"I couldn't see his face," said George. "Oh, but I do remember that he had sandy brown hair! He was about, I don't know, twenty or twenty-one. I also remember he was a good-looking man and tall with light skin."

Rosa's face went white. Ravenoff put his hand on George's shoulder, "Please tell me, did anyone see the man's face?"

"Yeah, I think so," said George. "The other guard who woke me up. Poor fella. He joined the guard to try to prove himself after his pop passed away."

"What was his name?" asked Ravenoff.

"I never knew his name, and I got the impression not

many people did. Private fellow he was, always kept his emotions hidden behind dark eyes and a stone hard face. We had some nickname we used to call him back then. Riggers, or Ridden maybe?"

"Riggins!"

***

Ravenoff knocked on the door of the Baker Manor. He typically didn't knock, but he'd learned his lesson about knocking in the mornings when he was seven and accidentally saw Lily in a towel! The door swung open, and Lily's husband Mark stood behind it.

"Hey, Ravenoff!" he said, patting the young man on the back.

"Hey, Uncle Mark!" said Ravenoff. "I'm just here to pick up Rosa."

"So, she talked you into sleuthing again, did she?" asked Mark with a laugh.

"Yes, but I have to admit I'm getting curious, too!" said Ravenoff, coming in and sitting down on the couch. Mark came and sat beside him. "I assume Rosa talked to Riggings last night," said Ravenoff.

"Tried to," said Mark, "but I'm sure she'll tell you all about it. She came out huffing and puffing like a little girl who got refused a candy bar."

"But, she isn't a little girl anymore," said Ravenoff, absentmindedly.

Mark smiled, "No, she isn't." Then he looked hard at

SABINA BOYER

Ravenoff. "Ravenoff, is there something you want to ask me?"

Ravenoff sighed and fingered the object in his pocket, "Yeah. There is."

A few minutes later, when Rosa came downstairs, Ravenoff was already waiting by the door with a silly grin on his face.

"What are you smiling about, Ravenoff?" asked Rosa, suspiciously, putting her hands in her pants pockets.

"Just smiling," said Ravenoff. "Let's go!"

The morning was far chillier than the day before had been, and they soon found themselves putting on their jackets. A slight breeze blew and picked up a few leaves, sending them dancing across the road. "You know," said Ravenoff. "Something about weather like this just makes me want to..."

"Dance?" asked Rosa with a wry smile.

"No," said Ravenoff, bumping into her playfully. "It makes me want to capture it all, to capture it and put it down on paper! I want to explain it in a new way and light the imagination of a friend on fire!"

"You're a strange one, Ravenoff," said Rosa. "Half the time, you seem like the same playful schoolboy I knew as a kid, and the other half, you seem so foreign, like a great philosopher trying to sort through the world."

Ravenoff grinned. "What's wrong with being both?"

Rosa laughed, "I never said I didn't like it." Ravenoff

looked up at the trees they passed and said something quietly to himself. "What did you say?" asked Rosa.

"Do you remember that little fall poem we came up with as kids?"

Rosa scrunched up her face and then brightened, "You mean the one about the quarreling siblings?"

"Yeah!" said Ravenoff. "Do you remember how it goes?" Rosa shook her head. Ravenoff looked up like the answer might be written somewhere in the clouds, then started slowly:

> "Summer is a little lady
> As feisty as a young girl may be
> Who always speaks her mind,
> But Winter is a little brat,
> And he's her brother at that,
> And he's anything but kind!
>
> Once when they were both still young,
> They used to have a lot of fun,
> But to Summer's surprise,
> Winter then grew really cruel
> And wanted more of the year for school,
> So Fall is their compromise"

"How on Ildathore do you remember that?" asked Rosa.

"I guess I just remember important stuff from childhood. As for math and science, they gone!" said Ravenoff with a chuckle.

They walked the rest of the way in silence. When they finally reached the Translation Station, it was about eleven in the morning. "There you kids are!" said the man from yesterday. "I think you will find your translation quite interesting!"

"You know what it says?" asked Ravenoff.

"No! Of course not!" said the man, who looked slightly offended. "Murray is the only one who read that letter, and he is the most trustworthy man I've ever met. All he told me was that the two of you would think it was interesting, but don't worry, no one will find out what the letter says."

"How do you know?" asked Rosa. "What will keep this Murray guy from blabbing?"

The man grinned, "He has short term memory loss. Why else would he be so trustworthy?" Then he handed them an envelope with the paper and translation inside. "Have a nice day!"

THE LEGACY OF A LEGEND
CHAPTER SIX

Ravenoff stood next to Rosa who sat on a large tree swing in the park. The limb above her moved a bit, and a tiny shower of flowers rained down.

"Well," asked Ravenoff with a smile, "are you going to read it?"

Rosa took the envelope out of her bag and opened it. Then, she pulled out the translated piece of paper. "Mila..." she paused.

"What is it?" asked Ravenoff.

"There is a footnote that the name Mila can also be translated as 'my dearest,' but because of the way this letter was written, he chose to translate it as Mila."

She cleared her throat and started reading again: *"Mila, in all the days we had in Trinity, you never could have known that I was afraid of the fate that finally met us. In war time, there are only so many things that can be foreseen."*

***

"Father!" said Mila. "Come smell these roses! They're finally blooming! I thought spring might never come!"

"Indeed, Mila," said Mavino. "They are lovely!" He watched as Mila spun around in the garden, letting her pink dress poof out until she looked like a flower herself. With a laugh, he came down off the porch and bowed to her. "Could I have this dance?"

"Of course, father!" she said. Then she put her hand in his and together they danced around the garden. Mavino watched her eyes twinkle as he spun her around, her brown curls bouncing energetically. Finally, when the dance was over, he left her in the garden and went inside.

"Does she know?" asked a hushed voice from the corner. Mavino turned to see Edendure and Silvina looking over at him.

"No, no..." said Mavino, sitting down beside them. "And there is no reason that she should. She's only a child; eleven is too young to learn so much about the world."

"She may find out, though," said Edendure. "Then, she'll wonder if you truly do have something to hide since you haven't told her."

"Yes, she'll find out," said Mavino, coming and sitting down beside them, "... many many years from now. All I want is for her to have a childhood, to grow up how her mother hoped she would."

Edendure remained silent a moment. "Does she even

know what to do if soldiers come to the door? You're putting her in too much danger by letting her remain ignorant! This cold war is no laughing matter. Even now, we are hunted simply for being from Thebel. It's taking politics too far when innocent men and women are slaughtered in the name of power."

"Don't I know it?" asked Mavino. "Too many have been caught already, but it's all the more reason I can't let her know the truth. She could never again have the innocence that all children should have. If soldiers come, I'll make sure to take her into the secret room with the rest of us, but I am sure they won't."

***

"Oh, how blind I was," read Rosa. *"In my delusions, I thought that I could keep you safe by making the world seem beautiful to your young eyes. In my defense, it did work for a little while. You were happy there, weren't you? You spoke of new things in the garden every day around the dinner table. How you lifted all of our spirits! You brought joy to even the most lost of us when you spoke of life and hope. I thought I'd chosen the best for us all, but then… one night…it happened."*

***

"Mavino!" whispered someone into his ear. Mavino stirred slightly. "Mavino, get up! It's happened!"

Mavino sat up and tried to focus on the face that was near his own. "Edendure? What's happened?"

"Soldiers are at the door, Mavino!!!" whispered Edendure in the dark. "Get up!"

Mavino went pale and jumped out of the cot he'd slept

341

on, folded it, and put it under the fake floor board. He followed his friend out of the room and up the stairs to the attic. "Wait!" he said suddenly. "Where's Mila?"

"Maria has gone to wake her!" said Edendure. "Now quickly!" They rushed to the entrance to the room behind the bookshelf where nearly all of the others were hidden already.

Just as Mavino was about to step inside, Maria came running in with wild eyes. "Where's Mila!?!?" cried Mavino.

"I don't know!" said Maria, going pale. "She wasn't in her room!"

"Outside!" said Mavino. "She must be in the garden!" Before Ednedure could grab him, he was running blindly out of the attic and down the stairs. When he reached the bottom, he froze as he saw the knob on the front door turn. Everything seemed to slow down. He watched as the door opened a crack, then, more than a crack. He saw the captain's head turning in his direction, but before he was spotted, someone dashed past Mavino, pushing him into the kitchen. Mavino saw Edendure running toward the captain as the captain raised his sword.

There wasn't a scream, only a thud as his friend's limp body crumpled to the floor. Mavino ran through the back door, out of the kitchen, and into the garden as fast as he could. There was Mila, sitting quietly next to a rose bush. Mavino ran to her, but before he could put his arms around her, a hand fell on his shoulder from behind. A hand in a soldier's glove. Mavino and Mila were dragged back through the house. Mavino covered his daughter's eyes before she could see the puddle of blood. Once outside, they were pushed into a metal carriage, and the door was slammed shut. Mila was too short to see out the window, but Mavino watched as a soldier dragged Edendure's body out the front door and slung him over his horse. His friend's chest rose and fell ever so slightly as the horse started forward. The carriage followed close behind.

"Father?" said Mila in a trembling voice.

"Don't worry!" said Mavino. "Everything will be alright."

"Who are these men?" asked Mila.

"Friends," said Mavino. "Such good friends in fact that they are taking us to a new home."

"They are?" Mila was looking up at him again with those big brown eyes, the same eyes that her mother had always looked at him with.

"Yes, Mila," said Mavino. "Just wait and see." The carriage continued to roll down the cobblestone streets until finally it came to a stop at the prison. Mila didn't say a word as they went through the gates and into the smelly hole of a building. She didn't make a sound as they were shoved into a cell and the door was closed and locked. Mavino grabbed the bars and shook them with all his might. Then, he leaned against the wall with his head in his hands.

"Potential," said Mila, softly.

"What was that?"

"Potential!" said Mila again. "It doesn't look very pretty now, but it has potential as a new home! Look," she said, pointing to the bars. "They were even so nice as to make the wall see-through so we can see our new friends in the other rooms!"

Mavino chuckled slightly and glanced over at the tiny smiles spreading across the faces of the other inmates. "Potential, eh?" asked Mavino. "You'll have to convince me. How would you decorate our new little room here?"

"That's easy!" said Mila. "I'd put the bed over in this corner, and a little oven right... here! That way, we could make cookies."

"Of course!" said Mavino. "Why didn't I think of that?" He looked down at his daughter's bright little face. "What else would we bake?"

***

"Even then, in my hope, I thought that, one day, our lives might go on again as they had been before, that perhaps even Edendure would once again return to health. But as you know, Mila, the Creator had other plans in mind." Rosa looked up from the letter at Ravenoff.

Ravenoff sighed. Happy endings seemed a long way off.

THE LEGACY OF A LEGEND
CHAPTER SEVEN

"Here you are," said Ravenoff, handing Rosa a buttered roll he had picked up from a vender nearby. He glanced down at the paper she still held in her hands, and she seemed to read his mind.

Rosa sighed and started to read again, *"I never would have questioned the Creator under normal circumstances, but, then again, that's like saying I would never talk to someone who wasn't there. As the hours wore on and turned into days, the joy you brought me began to diminish under my despair."*

***

Three minutes. Three minutes of light and air a day. Mavino almost wished they weren't allowed outside at all, for the darkness of the prison was even more unbearable when you knew that there was still a world outside the walls. Even so, the memory of that world weakened in between the trips as hunger and exhaustion set in.

Mila was still planning her house, and whenever she glanced in his direction, he did his best to smile, though his smiles got less and less believable as time went on. Mavino watched as one by one the prisoners in the cells near them were taken by guards and soon replaced with others. He saw them each give one last smile to the little girl, one beautiful and devastating smile. He glanced up at each set of eyes and saw the tears there, and over time, he realized the truth. They were in the part of the prison that was awaiting execution.

Then one day, the door at the end of the hall opened unexpectantly. Two guards came in. One seemed almost embarrassed to be there looked apologetically at the prisoners as he went by. The other was stone hard in every aspect. His face was never moving and expressionless, his hair was black and fell down to his shoulders, but the thing that really stood out were his eyes. Black as coal they seemed, holding no more emotion than a worm. He stared at the prisoners one at a time and didn't let himself glance longer at any one than another.

"Hi there," said the first one, bending down next to the bars by Mila.

Mila didn't respond. She had never learned any language but the one used on Thebel. After all, they had only come for a visit, or so they had thought.

"George!" said the other man. "No talking to the prisoners!"

George turned, "The chief isn't in here, Riggins, what does it matter what I do if he doesn't see me?"

"There is a law in this country, George," said Riggins. "Each of these men and women are here because they broke that law! Are you willing to join them?"

"Okay, okay, I get the picture," said George, standing up.

"Wait!" said Mavino in Trinidad, standing up and grabbing the bars. George turned to him, but Riggins kept walking down the aisle. "My friend! My friend was captured!" George looked between Riggins and Mavino. "Please! He was injured! Do you know of him? Is he alright?"

"You were his friend?" asked George quietly. Mavino nodded. George sighed and shook his head, "He wanted me to tell you that it's only a doorway, and that he knows you'll see him again."

Mavino went pale. "What's just a doorway?"

"Death," whispered George, quietly.

"George!" came Riggins voice from the doorway, "Come along." George turned, leaving Mavino standing there. As the door slammed behind the two guards, Mavino slid to the floor. He sat there for hours as the prison got darker and darker. Mila curled up and slept in the corner, forgetting that that was where she had put her imaginary stove.

Mavino put his head in his hands and tried to block out the world around him, but it didn't work. His shoulders heaved up and down with muffled sobs. How long he went on like this, in the dark, he didn't know. When no more tears would come, he took a piece of paper and a pencil out of his pocket. Bit by bit, he scribbled his story onto it in from beginning to end. He poured out his heart, screaming at the Creator to take them back home. He questioned why this was happening to him. What had he done?

By the time he was done, the first rays of dawn made their way through a tiny hole in the wall. Mavino rolled his paper up tightly and stuck it through the hole. *Okay Creator,* he thought. *I've sent you my message, so there isn't any excuse for not responding.*

A few minutes later, Mila woke up and began to work in her imaginary kitchen. Mavino watched as she placed a tray full of cookies into the imaginary oven. Mavino looked up at the roof. *Please, Creator, just give me a sign that you're still there!*

Suddenly, he heard a noise. He turned and stared as his letter was pushed back by someone through the hole and into the cell. Mavino looked down at the paper and then back up at the wall. The wall must border the outside of the prison. No guard would ever bother picking up trash. He snatched up the piece of paper and unfolded it. On the back were written a few words: *"How can I help you? -M Baker"*

Baker? thought Mavino. He looked over at where Mila was baking another round of sweets. *Was it possible?* He bent over the paper and wrote on it again: *"Save my daughter!"*

***

"It was such an easy thing to write, Mila," read Rosa, *"but it seemed impossible. I thought that I could never save you, but asking for it somehow made it seem more possible. I suppose I needed to believe in something. So, together, Baker and I planned the escape. I got the impression from his letters that he was most likely an apprentice to some company, and a young one, too. Even as I helped*

plot our scheme, I had another plan in mind. A plan to make sure he would keep you safe. It was clear that if you were to escape with your life, I'd have to find a way to get to the back gate without being seen. It would be up to Mr. Baker to find a way to open the gate. How he'd come up with a solution to his end of the ordeal, I didn't know, but I knew that I'd have to plan perfectly for my end to work.

***

Mavino tapped Mila on the shoulder and watched her hair sway as she turned to look at him. "Mila, I was wondering if you'd be able to do something with me that we haven't done in a long time."

"What is that, father?" asked Mila.

Mavino glanced at the door. He would have to time this just right. "I'd like to dance with you."

"Dance with me?" asked Mila. "But this room is so small. Why do you want to dance here?"

"Because," said Mavino, quietly, "In a few days, I am going to take you to a courtyard in this great mansion where you will dance with a young man."

"Really?" asked Mila. "Why don't we go there now?"

"Because," stated Mavino, "Before you dance with him, I will have to teach you a new dance." He looked down and could see the question in the little girl's eyes. "Yes, a very new dance," he answered almost to himself. "One that you will never forget." He smiled at Mila's eagerness, "Now, it's not a difficult dance, and you are a lovely dancer. Shall we try it?" Mila nodded, and the two of them began in the tiny space, Mavino explaining future steps to her as they went along. Every few seconds, he glanced up at the door at the end of the hallway between the cells. Finally, it opened. Mila was right in the middle of a twirl, and Mavino sighed in relief as he saw that the guard who had entered was George and that he was alone.

George stood still and watched Mavino and Mila in silence. Finally, when they had taken a break from their dancing, he began moving from cell to cell, slipping the bowls of food under the bars. When he reached their cell, Mavino stuck his hand through the bars and lightly touched his arm. George drew back. "Kind sir," said Mavino, "I want to thank you for giving me the news of my friend." George nodded slightly as he slid the two bowls of food under their bars. "I was wondering if, perhaps, you could do me one more favor. I can pay you in exchange."

George cocked an eyebrow, "You got money in here with you?"

Mavino smiled as George came closer to taking the bait, "No, but I was able to conceal something even better." He reached into the folds of his clothes and pulled out a tiny little glass container. "In here, is the powder used for making Thebel's famous spiced wine." George stared at it in awe. Such a package was worth more than a year's wages and was said to be the best drink in Ildathore. "It isn't doing me much good in here, but add it to a little water, and you'll have yourself a drink of gold."

As George struggled internally, Mila picked up her bowl and began to eat. Mavino was once again grateful he had never bothered to teach her the language of Trinity. "I can't set you or your daughter free if that is what you want," said George, not taking his eyes off the little container. "A drink of wine today isn't worth hanging from the gallows tomorrow."

"Of course not," said Mavino. "I simply want to have one last chance to dance with my daughter before we are put to death. I know that there is a large courtyard next to the back gate. Could you get us there?" George glanced from the door to the cell and back again. "Truly, kind sir, how hard could it be? Surely there's some kind of door or passage that leads from the courtyard we're always taken to to the larger courtyard. Couldn't you just, somehow, leave a door or two unlocked one of the times when you're on duty?"

"Well..." said George. "I am on guard during that time today... you wouldn't have a problem with it being so soon, would you?" George eyed Mavino suspiciously.

Mavino almost quailed at the thought of having to be prepared by then, but he didn't let it show. "No problem at all." Knowing that there was only about twenty minutes until the time for fresh air, he gave the container to George and said, "I would suggest drinking it sooner rather than later. It's already a bit old, and I'm not sure when it will spoil." He watched as George took it, nodded, and left. Twenty minute left? Twenty precious minutes. Mavino turned to the tiny hole in the wall, scribbled one last message on a piece of paper, hoping beyond hope that the Baker man would pass by soon, and pushed it through the hole.

Then he turned and smiled for his daughter's sake, "Now, let's practice that dance again. The young man is on his way."

THE LEGACY OF A LEGEND
CHAPTER EIGHT

Ravenoff didn't take his eyes off Rosa as she turned the paper around to read from the other side. He had always been told that being moved by stories was something that should only happen to women and that men who let themselves be moved were weak. All the same, he was inthralled by Mavino's story. Something about it seemed to be calling to him. Rosa took a deep breath and started back in on the text.

***

Mavino stepped out into the crisp air with Mila by his side. At his urging, she had brought her prison quilt with them. Mavino didn't want to think about what could happen to her out in the cold without it. As the guards who were supposedly watching them fell to talking amongst themselves, Mavino glanced over at the door on the far side of the courtyard. He hoped that it led where he thought it did! Quickly, he wrapped one arm around Mila and walked towards it, casting a glance over his shoulder.

"Father," she said, glancing up at him, "Is this the way to the young man?"

"Yes, Mila," said Mavino, trying to keep his breathing steady. "But you mustn't let them hear you, Mila. We are playing a wonderful game, and we mustn't let them see or hear us." Mila nodded and said nothing more. Mavino thanked the Creator for her trusting heart. When they reached the door, he held his breath and reached for the knob. The door swung in easily. He smiled. Apparently there were good uses for wine! He lead them slowly on until they reached one more door. He knew where it would lead.

"Remember, Mila," he said. "No talking. You must trust me no matter what, and you cannot make a sound or protest!" Mila looked up at him with those sad questioning eyes that seemed to be a reflection of her mother's. For a second, Mavino's spirit almost broke. It took everything in him to keep him from wrapping his arms around her and never letting go. But then, before he could let himself turn back, he pushed the door open.

It led into the courtyard with the great back gate. George was sitting slumped over at his post. Poor man. He thought he would taste the best wine on earth only to devour heavily drugged water instead. Mavino turned his eyes to the huge gate. It was raised, just as he had hoped and dreaded at the same time. Underneath it stood a tall man, early twenties perhaps, his sandy brown hair whipping around his face in the breeze. Mavino lowered his gaze from the man. He couldn't look into those blue eyes, knowing the trick he was about to play on him, but it was the only way of knowing that Mila would be cared for.

He bowed to his daughter and took her hand. In one

graceful motion, she spun around and began to dance that dance of all dances. He could almost feel the young man's eyes staring at him as the two danced closer and closer to him. He recognized it at once - the wedding dance.

Mavino felt a lump growing larger and larger in his throat as he and Mila danced closer to the stranger. How did he know this man would be a good husband? How did he know Mila would be taken care of? Finally the two stood directly in front of the Baker man. The young man's eyes were filled with resolve. He looked down at this young girl without a word.

"Keep her safe!" said Mavino as he handed the hands of his daughter over the young man.

"I will," answered the man.

Mavino stepped back as the young man danced with his daughter off to the horse that stood nearby, pawing the ground. Even in the gray high-gated courtyard, he couldn't help but smile. Mila had grown so much in the last few months. Why, she looked just like her mother now. He watched, a lump growing in his throat as the two made it to the horse. The young man boosted Mila up to the front of the saddle and swung up behind her. As he did so, the warning bell began clanging from behind. Guards rushed from their posts all over the prison. The large, barred gate dropped several inches.

"Go," whispered Mavino, softly.

"Come with us," said the young man, bringing back his horse and holding out a hand.

Mavino shook his head, tears in his eyes. "Go on! Keep her safe!"

"No! You have to come, too!" said the young man, glancing around wildly as the guards came closer.

"I said go!" shouted Mavino, slapping the horse's rump as hard as he could. The horse charged forward and passed through the gate just before it broke free and crashed to the ground.

"Papa!" shouted Mila from up in the saddle.

"Go on!" shouted Mavino. "And never stop dancing, Mila! Do you hear me, daughter? Never stop dancing! As long as you remember me, I'll always be with you, my daughter! I promise!" Arrows whizzed through the air, and the young man steered the horse away as fast as he could, not looking back. Mavino heard shouts of "After them!" and "Don't let them escape!" but he knew in his heart that they would. He smiled through the tears now streaming down his face as he was led back to his cell.

As they took him away, he saw Riggins grab George by the collar. The sleeping man started, and Riggins shook him and shouted something at him. Mavino whispered softly to himself, "I'm sorry, friend."

***

Rosa swallowed hard before continuing.

"I know it won't be long before my time is up. I only hope you know that I made my choices out of love for you. No matter what the world may one day tell you about my intentions, no matter what they may say I was, I want you to know that. Please don't weep for me. You will still find many joys in life that we were never destined to share. But remember this, I'm not lost to you forever, dear one. As our dear friend Edendure has assured me, death is just a doorway!"

Ravenoff felt the tears make their way down his face, but he didn't care. There were some things in life that were worth crying for. Rosa didn't cry. She folded the paper quietly, put in into her pocket, and took a shaky breath. "Well," she said softly. "What do you make of that?"

Ravenoff was leaning against a tree, deep in thought. "Death is just a doorway." That was all he said. All he could say. That one simple sentence hit him over the head hard and left his thoughts spinning in different directions.

"Do you think it's true?" asked Rosa, looking up at him.

When he spoke, his voice was very soft, and his words came slowly, one at a time. "A man about to die a terrible death who writes words like that isn't lying. He's a man who knows good from evil and who does his best to follow his Lord, and he's a man that I admire with all my heart." Rosa had never seen Ravenoff like that before. He stared off into the distance almost as if he could see Mavino there. Ravenoff spoke again, bringing his thoughts back down to the girl sitting only a few feet from him. "We need to find her, Rosa. We need to give her this letter."

"But how?" asked Rosa.

The familiar grin came back to Ravenoff's face as he wiped the wet trails off his cheeks. "How should I know? You are the one with all of the big snoopy ideas around here. All we really know is that this girl is named either Mila or 'my dearest,' depending on the translation."

Rosa thought about this for a moment, then her face lit up. "Ravenoff! That's it!"

***

"Why did we come back to your messy attic again?" asked Ravenoff, still panting from the run to the manor and straight up the stairs into Rosa's little sanctuary.

"Do you remember when I told you about some of the interesting papers of Matt's I found?" asked Rosa, tearing through a drawer.

"Sort of," said Ravenoff. "I mean, I know you mentioned it."

"Do you remember the love letter I found?" asked Rosa, turning from the drawer and searching wildly through another stack of papers.

"Sure," said Ravenoff.

"Do you remember who it was addressed to?"

Ravenoff scrunched up his face in thought, and then went pale, "You don't mean..."

Rosa stood triumphantly holding the correct paper in hand, "Yes! It is addressed to: My Dearest!"

"Mila," whispered Ravenoff. "Well, what do you know?"

Rosa paused, hesitantly glancing at Ravenoff, her fingers preparing to unfold the paper. Ravenoff sighed. Were love letters meant to be read by others? Was it fair? He stopped to think about it. He thought of all of the undelivered letters that sat in his apartment. He wondered what he would think if someone were to open them without his knowing. Slowly, he smiled.

"Matt was the kindest man I've ever met. He'd probably give up the world if he thought it would help a loving father's last words to be delivered."

Rosa smiled, too, and then unfolded the paper.

THE LEGACY OF A LEGEND
CHAPTER NINE

My Dearest,

A few years. So much can happen in just a few years, Mila. More than I thought possible. To think, a few years ago, my only concern in life was to prove myself to Franklin, Franklin, and Smith. I thought only of finally finding my place, becoming a sailor, and being needed. I was willing to do anything to reach that goal. I signed up to run as many errands as possible to try to show my worth. I was constantly sailing from island to island around Trinity on the Bella Fawn. Near the end of one of those days, I took a break to eat my supper, which I had carried with me that day. I sat down, my back to the prison wall, watching the clouds shift overhead. As I looked back down at my food, I saw a rolled up piece of paper poking out of a hole near me in the wall.

I watched as it got pushed the rest of the way through and fell to the ground next to me. Mr. Tickleten used to tell me how my curiosity would get me in trouble one day. It seems he truly was a sage, though you never would have thought it to look at him. The letter was from your father. I must have read it at least ten times sitting there, my sandwich utterly forgotten. I seemed to see my own father on the other side of that wall, preparing to give his child away, but it was no longer because of selfishness, it was because of love. Mavino should have been a poet, Mila. His words nearly brought me to tears.

I took a pencil out of my pocket and turned the paper over. I was not the type to hesitate. I saw my conscious veer from the path but followed it anyway. After writing on the back of the paper, I rolled it up again and shoved it through the hole. My answer came: **Save my daughter**. I knew right then that both of our fates were set.

I worked night and day on Mr. Tickleten, imploring him to help me. He did. There was far more to the slight little man than what meets the eye. With his help, I got to the open gate with a saddled horse and the Bella Fawn docked not far away. Once the gate was open, I saw the guard fast asleep. I have to admit I felt a bit sorry for him. Hopefully, he wasn't punished too harshly for his part in our schemes. Then, you stepped into my world. The small door opened, and you and your father came out dancing. I knew the dance you danced to. When Mavino glanced at me, I saw his hope. For me, there was only one way to answer.

I assume you know the rest. We rode hard to the Bella Fawn and set sail, chased by the sleeping guard and his regiment for seven full days. If the winds hadn't been with us, I doubt either of us would have lived to tell the tale. Once I had gotten you back to Thebel, we said goodbye. I draped my sailor's jacket around your shivering shoulders, and you laid your prison quilt around mine. Mila Larentka, or is it Mila Baker? If only I knew. Before today, I thought of you simply as an acquaintance, as foolish as that sounds. To think of it, a husband and wife as mere acquaintances. I never understood you until today, Mila, because I knew what Mavino didn't. The moment I saw you and took your hands, I knew you knew. You knew the prison, you knew the danger, you knew the dance. I never understood how you could let him do it. I never knew how you could go along with leaving him there to die while you left to *be free.*

Today, I understood. I saw you again in another young girl. Her name is Helen. You should see her, Mila. She is so much like you. Today, I watched her as she found out that she could never be with her father again. I saw her calm silent pain, her strength, her bravery. She wasn't brave for herself; she was brave for her sister. She was hiding her grief to give her sister joy, to give her something to live for. You let your father give you away… to give him something to die for.

You're stronger than I am, Mila. Right now I'm sitting her, on a ship, the only one awake, and I'm shattered. If only I could see you again, Mila. I know this letter will never get delivered to you, but I implore you from an ocean away all the same. When you look out over the water and see a ship in the distance, look carefully. I'll sail to find you in the Bella Fawn and hoist your quilt as high as the mast can reach in hopes that you will see me.

Matt Baker

Ravenoff read the letter again but not out loud. Neither time did he read out loud. Rosa watched as his eyes flicked back and forth across the page. Then he smiled. He looked up at Rosa and handed it to her.

"How would you like to sail to Thebel tomorrow? I could take a week off from work. We could bring Matt's old quilt so as not to be cold along the way. What are the chances that a certain resourceful young lady who wears pants could find out where Mila Larentka lives?"

Rosa took the letter and read it, then she smiled too, "If we were to go, I'd have to take my favorite ship."

***

The next morning, the two of them and a small crew

climbed aboard the *Bella Fawn*. It was an old ship, but Matt's will had asked that it always be kept in repair. As Ravenoff stepped on, his first thought was of a long weekend away from school. His best memories of this boat were of coming with his parents and Rosa's family and Riggins and sailing over to the Isle of Emily to camp out under the stars. As a kid, he had walked into the forest and felt as if he were entering a fairy tale and was far away from Trinity. Only one small town had been built on the island yet, and at night, he would sneak away from the others and climb up the mountain with a lantern to explore Valley's dragon lair and try to find any treasure that hadn't been collected already.

Matt and Riggins used to take two chairs and set them up right next to the entrance of the cave and sit there for hours, just watching the clouds soar by. Even now, Riggins went there often, though these days he had to hire someone else to sail him there. He kept a chair hidden in the cave and pulled it out to sit beside Matt's grave.

Ravenoff's face clouded as he thought about Riggins. Last night, they had tried to get him to come with them, but he had refused. When they asked him about the jail again, he simply stared at the fire quietly, his stone hard face revealing nothing even in his old age.

Now as Ravenoff put the bag with Mila's quilt in it below deck, he understood why Riggins had insisted for it not to be buried with Matt. When Ravenoff came back on deck, Rosa had taken her place behind the wheel and was barking orders at the crew like a true sailor. Ravenoff grinned. Most of his friends at the university thought him crazy for admiring such a girl. Did it look like he cared?

Absentmindedly, he fingered the object in his right hand pocket as he watched her. It seemed like such a perfect moment. He pulled the object out and then put it back like a coward. Better to wait for another day.

"Rosa!" he called. She turned to him with a kind of playful fire in her eyes. "Do you really think it's right for a girl to be behind the wheel? I'm not sure if these men will take you seriously or not."

Rosa grinned her mighty defiant grin and pointed at him accusingly, "What do you mean to talk back to your captain, idle sailor! Get to your duties and be quick about it!"

Ravenoff enjoyed the day, going from one chore to another like he did as a boy. He had to admit, he wasn't a very good sailor, but he could do his best in simple tasks. At the end of the day, the deck was filled with mirth, and to the delight of the crew, Ravenoff and Rosa practiced their dancing. That night, while Ravenoff lay in a hammock with a crew of snoring sailors around him, he smiled at the thought that he might well be laying in the same spot Matt did on his first journey. Matt was right. It felt wonderful.

***

Ravenoff woke to the watchman shaking him awake. "What?" he murmured nearly rolling out of the hammock.

"Ravenoff," said the man. "Rosa wanted me to wake you after I woke her."

"Why did you wake her?" asked Ravenoff.

"The township we are headed for is in sight."

Ravenoff sat bolt upright. It had been a week since they

left Trinity. In an instant, he half jumped half slid out of the hammock, changed into his clothes, and was up on deck. Rosa was already standing there in her sailor's clothes. She turned to him, and her captain's coat flew slightly in the wind.

"Morning Ravenoff," she said. Was it morning? Ravenoff looked around at the cold, gray air. No use calling it morning if the sun hadn't even woken up yet. Good grief!

"So, they spotted land?" asked Ravenoff. The look on Rosa's face answered him. He stepped over to the edge of the boat and looked out to see a huge expanse of land coming ever closer. He looked over at Rosa again to see her clutching the quilt like her life depended on it. "Are you okay, Rosa?"

Rosa shook her head. "Ravenoff, what if she isn't there any more? What if she's dead? What if she IS there? What if she tells us things that… that I don't want to know about Matt?"

Ravenoff smiled slightly and took the quilt from her hand. "Trust me, if we learn anything about Matt, it will only be that he had an even bigger heart than we knew." Rosa returned the smile but stepped back, and Ravenoff walked to the mast. With a heave, he started up, feeling the eyes of Rosa and the others watching him. He pulled himself hand over hand until he finally reached the top. He pulled down the Trinity flag with care and tied the quilt to the rope instead. Then, with a tug, he hoisted the quilt. As it reached the top, the first rays of daylight lit up the sky. Ravenoff looked at the little shore town hopefully. Not a thing stirred. He stood there for what felt like days but could hardly have been more than minutes. Then, something happened. In one of the houses nearest to the shore, a window was opened and a broom stick held out. There was something tied to it, but... what was it? Ravenoff looked closer as whoever was in the window waved the broom back and forth. Then, as the thing was caught by the wind Ravenoff saw what it was. It was an old beat up jacket, obviously worn out with use. It was made of fine leather, or at least it used to be fine, and on the back was stitched the name of a company. Ravenoff looked closer and broke into a wide grin when he saw the company's name. *Franklin, Franklin, & Smith.*

THE LEGACY OF A LEGEND
CHAPTER TEN

Ravenoff and Rosa stepped off the *Bella Fawn* alone, leaving the crew to tend the ship. As they walked up the beach, Ravenoff felt slightly out of place. He straightened out his jacket, feeling the two letters still in his left pocket with another object in his right, and did his best to smooth down his dark curls. Out of the corner of his eye, he saw Rosa doing the same. When they reached the road up ahead, Rosa paused, staring at the house that had flown the old jacket. Ravenoff took her arm, smiled down at her, and lead them both forward onto the path.

Ravenoff saw Rosa matching his steps as they walked. The last time she had done that was when they had gone to Matt's funeral. She tightened her grip on him. When they reached the gate to the home, they stopped. The entire lawn was covered with flowers, and the path that led through it had rose bushes lining both sides of it. Ravenoff slowly swung the gate in, and at the same time, the door of the house opened. In the doorway stood a lady with gray hair, but it hadn't always been gray. Her age shone in the way she moved rather than how she looked. The wrinkles on her brow looked more like a crown than a nuisance. As her brown eyes settled on them, Ravenoff felt sure that there had been no mistake.

He bowed, as deep of a bow as he could manage, and straightened back up, saying, "My name is Ravenoff, Mila."

The lady smiled at him, but then turned to Rosa. "Ah… you must be Rosa."

Rosa blinked, her gray hair falling across her violet eyes. "How did you know?"

Mila smiled again, with a twinkle of laughter in her eyes, and said, "You look just like your mother." Before either of them had a chance to wonder at this, Mila added, "Please, come in. It won't do you any good to go on standing in the yard."

Ravenoff and Rosa obeyed, hanging their coats by the door as they entered. The house was large but not too large. The decorations were almost all handmade, and it was obvious the hands had been young. As soon as you saw it, you could be sure the home was a home of a grandparent.

Once Mila had made them each a cup of tea, they sat by the fireplace, and Ravenoff told her the story of why they had come from beginning to end, leaving out no details. When he was done, he took the letters from Matt and Mavino out of his pocket and gave them to Mila, "Here, I hope you don't mind that we read them."

Mila took the papers and turned them over in her hands one at a time, running her fingers over every inch of them. Then, she smiled. "I'm surprised you haven't asked me yet."

Rosa and Ravenoff glanced at each other. "Asked you what?" said Rosa finally.

Mila's eyes gleamed. "To tell you the rest of the story."

***

Mila clung to Matt as his horse raced them away from the dreadful prison. Her brown hair whipped around her as she hung on for dear life. Matt shouted something to her over his shoulder, but she couldn't understand it. If only she had taken the time to learn the language of Trinity. A horn sounded behind them, and Mila wondered how long it would be before they were caught. Her prison quilt was still wrapped around her shoulders, and she dare not let it go. Finally, after what felt like hours, Matt pulled the horse to a stop and swung off, helping her down after him. They had reached the harbor where his boat was tied. On the boat were the words: *Bella Fawn*. Of course, she couldn't understand them, but she burned them into her memory all the same.

Matt hurried her on deck and ran to untie the boat from the dock. Mila looked out behind them and saw soldier's horses off in the distance, coming toward them. Matt untied the last rope and ran to the wheel. The sails were unfurled, and a gust of wind sped them forward.

"Come on!" murmured Matt, looking back at the approaching horses. The wind continued to carry them forward until the dock was nearly out of sight. "Now," he said to himself, "let's just hope they don't have very fast ships." They continued on all that day and on into the next. Mila sat close to Matt, keeping her quilt wrapped around her for warmth. As the sky grew dark and the events of the day closed in on her, she curled up in a ball to hide her tears from the man behind the wheel. He saw them anyway.

Matt bent down beside her as she sobbed into her quilt uncontrollably. He tried to comfort her, but his words meant nothing, and he knew it. He had long ago thrown the coat he had worn into the prison into the sea, but he still had his company jacket. He took it off and draped it around her shoulders. She looked up at him so gratefully that he knew he wouldn't feel the cold that night. They raced on for six more days, and with each day, their pursuers grew closer. He stood behind the wheel long after she had fallen asleep, not daring to drop the anchor. As they neared Thebel, a thick mist settled over them until Matt could hardly see a few yards ahead of the *Bella Fawn*.

He squinted ahead all night, praying that he wouldn't wreck them on the shore, but just when he thought he couldn't continue, the first rays of daylight pierced the mist. There on the shore sat the entrance to the Twisted Caves. He shivered. The caves had been a hideout for pirates to hide their ships in for years. He just hoped there weren't pirates in there now. Glancing back, he sucked in his breath as three Trinidad ships emerged from the fog behind him. He gulped. The caves would have to do. Mila sat up, and in an instant, saw what he was doing.

"Why are they still chasing us?" she asked softly. Matt looked at her in regret. She knew he couldn't understand her. Quickly, they sailed on toward the caves.

The mouth of the cavern opened like the jaws of a monster waiting to swallow them up. Mila shivered at the thought. As they entered, the mast scraped against the top of the cave. The warships would never be able to follow. The air around them reeked of alcohol. Matt steered the

Bella Fawn around the bends in the cave as carefully as he could. Before long, the water was so shallow that the ship could hardly move. Matt made for a large crevice in the wall in the cavern that could hide the ship from searching eyes. Once it was in place, he ran to the anchor and let it down with a thud, then turned to Mila.

She looked up at him with terrified unblinking eyes. Matt tried to smile, but it didn't work. He held out his hand to her, "Come on, Mila. We'll have to go the rest by foot." She looked from his hand to his face, then wrapped his coat and her quilt tighter around herself and stood up.

He helped her down and glanced into the shadowy passages ahead of them. Which one would take them to an opening back to the surface he could only guess. Randomly, he headed for the nearest one. As they walked, he took his time, trying to make the most logical decisions, going up instead of down, always trying to keep turned away from the sea. *Surely they didn't follow us in,* he reasoned, and indeed, it seemed unlikely they did. But then…

"Riggins! Wait for me!"

"If you can't keep up, George, that's your problem. I won't stop on account of you!"

Matt froze. He could hear other voices and footsteps coming closer behind him. He grabbed Mila's shaking hand and charged madly into the semi-darkness.

"I hear him!" came a voice from behind.

Matt zig-zagged as much as possible stumbling from time to time but never stopping. Mila could hardly keep up, and it was obvious she could not run for much longer. Then, all of the sudden, there was light up ahead. At first,

Matt thought they had finally found an opening, but then he recognized the light of a lantern coming from in front of them. He stopped dead in his tracks and flattened him and Mila against a wall. Two men came into the passage where they stood. One was rather short and stubby, an eyepatch over one eye and a bottle in his hand. The other, a young man near Matt's age, had a large plume in his hat. A sword was strapped to his belt, and his coat was decorated with gold.

"Artbem," said the short man, "Eckle hag ardenat."

"If you hadn't taken so long I would have left already," snapped the young man. "Eldercaught, ebten eemod arden gan?"

"Eeefnude, elhed brach!"

Suddenly, another man stepped into the lamplight. He was obviously the stranger in this group. The two other men hushed when he came. The new man's skin was lighter, and his accent was different. When he spoke, it was in Mayren, the trade language, and Matt was able to understand.

"Why are the two of you still here? You must leave as fast as you can!"

The young man with the plume in his hat raised an eyebrow. "You think you can tell us what to do?" he whispered in Mayren. "Never! Get on your knees, you dog, when in the presence of your superiors."

The newcomer dropped to his knees respectfully, "My deepest apologies, my lord Silam."

Silam rolled his eyes, "So, what do you want? Be

quick!"

The man lowered his voice, "The caves are swarming with Trinity soldiers. I was waiting by the escape hatch, just yonder through the tunnel, when one of my men told me. You must leave as fast as you can. You can either come with us through the hatch back to the surface or get to your ship without being seen."

Silam thought on this a moment. "Have all of your men gone up the hatch already?" The man nodded. "I don't think it would be wise for anyone else to just now. Someone might discover it; you must come with us." The man tried to protest, but Silam didn't give him a chance. "Move!" He jumped up and obeyed, running down a passageway. Silam turned to the short fellow, "How long until we reach our next slave trading market?"

"About three weeks, sir," said the stocky fellow in very sloppy Mayren.

Silam sighed, "Well, at least I won't have to put up with that idiot for long. Hurry, let's go!" The two ran down the passageway. Matt finally let himself breathe. He listened carefully but couldn't hear footsteps from behind anymore. It either meant that their pursuers had stopped or were now creeping up on them. He grabbed Mila's hand and led her forward down the tunnel the other man had come from. Now all they had to do was to find that escape hatch.

THE LEGACY OF A LEGEND
CHAPTER ELEVEN

Ravenoff's breath caught in his throat, "You mean Matt knew Silam before they ever fought?"

Yes, Mila replied with a smile, her gray hair falling over one eye. Ravenoff leaned back in his chair and whistled long and low; then he glanced at Rosa. Rosa hadn't moved a muscle since the story started.

"What happened next?" she asked, quietly.

"Well," said Mila, "We found the hatch the pirates had mentioned! I thank the Creator we weren't discovered. I felt so... so... lost leaving him. I remember how, before we said goodbye, I gave him my quilt. It seemed the right thing to do, to give him something to remember me by. When I reached the surface again, I wasn't sure where to go. It was my homeland, but there was no home left for me there. I wandered around for awhile until I came to a farmhouse owned by a sweet family that cared for me. A lot has happened since then. I grew up, learned what I could of Trinity culture, including their language, and married a wonderful man."

"You married?" said Rosa, standing up. "How could you? You danced the wedding dance with Matt! He was your husband! You said you knew that!"

Mila looked ashamed, "To me, he was like a dead husband. I thought I could never see him again and that he had married someone else as well."

"But he didn't!" interjected Rosa. "He could have married, he could have had his own wife and family, he could have loved someone, but he didn't, and it's your fault!"

"Rosa," said Mila, "how can you say he didn't have someone to love? He loved you."

Ravenoff looked at her, surprised. "What could you know about Rosa?"

Mila smiled, "Oh, quite a lot. He told me all about you when he came to visit me."

Ravenoff's jaw went slack, and Rosa sank back in the chair, "What do you mean he visited you?"

Mila looked questioningly from one to the other, "What? You mean he never told you?"

"When did he come?"

"The year he retired if I remember right. You really didn't know?" She chuckled at the dumbfounded looks on their faces. "Yes, he came on the *Bella Fawn,* waving that old quilt like a flag in the same way you did."

"Was he alone?" asked Ravenoff.

"Alone? No, at least not completely. He had a young man with him. A nice fellow. What was his name... Coller or... Cling?"

"Admiral Collins!"

***

Matt stepped off of the *Bella Fawn* and onto Thebel for the first time in... well... a lot of years. Behind him, Collins followed like a loyal puppy dog, still in awe of the esteemed admiral.

"Is this where the person you wanted to visit lives?" asked Collins.

Matt grinned. "If not, then we came a long way for nothing." He looked up the beach at the road that led to the old brick house. "Come along, Collins. Let's see if they're home." Together, the two of them walked along the path. Matt felt strange without his admiral's uniform on, but that was something he would just have to get used to again. His collared shirt ruffled in the slight breeze, and his white hair drooped around his ears. "I wonder if she'll recognize me," he said, more to himself than to Collins.

"How long has it been?" asked Collins.

Matt chuckled, "A lot longer than you've been alive." When they finally reached the gate, Matt paused. A giant, smoking, metal ship couldn't make him flinch, but for the first time in decades, he was terrified. He put his hand on the gate, then drew it back. Collins watched him silently. Matt took a deep breath and pushed open the gate.

Flowers lined the path up to the house, but before he could even take a step, the door opened up ahead. In the doorway stood two people, the first a man, slightly built and aging but with kind eyes and the second, a woman that Matt had thought of every day for forty years.

He walked the path slowly and up the steps onto the front porch. She had the same wide, shining eyes. The man beside her watched Matt approach, nervously. When he was standing right in front of them, he stopped. He could not get over her eyes; they were not the eyes of a frightened child anymore, but of a strong woman. He reached out and wrapped his arms around her, burying his face in her hair. "Thank the Creator you're safe!"

He felt her clutching him like she had that first time on horseback. "Matt, I can't believe it's you!" she whispered in Trinidad.

The man standing by cleared his throat awkwardly. "So, you must be the man Mila has told me about."

Matt released Mila and grinned at the man. "And you must be her husband. It's a pleasure to meet you."

The man looked a bit taken aback, "Yes, and to meet you. Won't you come inside?"

Matt looked over at Collins, "What do you say, Admiral? Should we go in?"

Collins's ears went beet red as they all looked at him, "Um, sure." As he went in and sat down beside Matt, he whispered, "I'm so confused."

Matt chuckled, "I'll catch you up on the way back to Trinity."

That night after supper, Matt took Mila onto the *Bella Fawn,* just the two of them. "I can't believe you found me," said Mila. "Matt, oh will you ever forgive me?"

Matt looked over at her, "Forgive you for what, Mila?"

"For marrying!" said Mila. "If only you had, too, I wouldn't feel so horrid about it, but there isn't a ring on your finger. I'm so sorry, Matt, but I thought I would never see you again!"

Matt smiled and looked her in the eyes, "Mila, I saved you so that you could live life to the fullest. That is what your father always wanted for you. Do you think I would have wanted you to be lonely all these years? I couldn't be more happy with what has happened to you. Your husband seems like a very good man, and I can see how much he loves you."

Mila smiled, "But why haven't you married?"

Matt sighed, "In my heart, you will always be my wife, and I could never feel right loving another."

Mila looked up at him, "Matt, why did you come now? Why did you choose to look for me? For forty years, we've been apart. What made you try now?"

"Well," said Matt, "the cold war is finally over."

"It has been for a long time," said Mila. "As admiral, you could have used your connections to find me long before you did. What happened that made you look for me again, after all these years?"

Matt sighed, "I used to know someone like you, so

much like you. Her name was Helen. Every time I looked at her, I felt as if you were there. I suppose that's why I didn't try sooner. I was content; life was comfortable. But then, she left… I let her slip right through my fingers. I thought it was just a stage. I thought she'd be back, so I didn't go after her. I doubt I'll ever see her again. I couldn't lose you, too, Mila, not without knowing you were safe, and happy, and cared for… and you are."

Mila smiled, "Thank you, Matt. I always hoped I could see you again."

That night, they spent telling stories and talking together. The next day, Matt and Collins prepared to set sail. When the boat was ready, or as ready as a beaten up old boat can be, he went to say a last goodbye to Mila. As he walked up the lane, he carried a large box on his back, bent over with the weight of it. Collins waited down at the *Bella Fawn*. When Matt reached the house, it was Arnold, her husband, who let him in.

"Hello, friend," said Matt. "This is a gift for Mila. Where should I put it?"

"Just here on the floor will do," said Arnold. Matt obeyed and set it down with a thud. Arnold looked at him, "Matt, I want to talk to you about last night. I know it's silly of me, and I'm sure you're a good man, but… what exactly did you and Mila do on the ship last night?"

Matt smiled and put a hand on the other man's shoulder, "Arnold, to me, she will always be my wife, but you are her husband. I would never dishonor that."

Arnold smiled, "I didn't think so."

Suddenly, Mila came into the room, "Must you leave so

soon?"

Matt nodded, "I must get back to my life and you to yours. Thank you for letting us stay here for the night."

"Any time," said Arnold. Matt shook his hand and embraced Mila one last time before he left.

Mila looked down at the box, "Arnold, what's this?"

"It's from Matt," said Arnold. "He said it was a present to you."

Mila stooped to take a closer look. There was a note attached to the top. It read:

My dear Mila, I give these to you to tell you that even in all the years we were apart, you weren't forgotten. I'm getting old now, and I have no doubt that my adventure on the waves have come to an end. When you see these, Mila, please remember me.   -Matt Baker

***

"What was inside?" asked Ravenoff.

Mila smiled. "Letters. Hundreds of letters."

Ravenoff grinned at the thought. "So it all worked out then?"

"Not quite," said Mila. "Matt told me that after he sent me up to safety, he was caught and then released by a wonderful man who was one of the prison guards. He always said, even in his letters, that he wished I could meet him one day."

"A prison guard let him go?" asked Rosa. "What was

his name?"

"Riggins."

THE LEGACY OF A LEGEND
CHAPTER TWELVE

Riggins stepped off his little one-man boat and onto the Isle of Emily. It was a peaceful place now, no matter what Matt had said about dragons living there. Only a few little villages had sprung up over the years. Riggins left the boat where it was and started up the mountain slowly. The clouds were low today, and by the time he reached Matt's grave at the entrance to the cave, he was above them. He pulled his jacket close around him and stepped into the cave. An old folding chair still leaned against one wall. He grabbed it and took it out, setting it up beside Matt's tombstone.

"Well, old friend," said Riggins, "Looks like your secret won't stay secret very long. That granddaughter of yours is as nosy as ever." He smiled to himself, "If I didn't know better, I would swear you two were related." He sat there for a long time, watching the clouds go by. Then, behind him, someone cleared their throat. Riggins didn't turn. "Who is it?"

"We brought someone to see you, Riggins. Lily told us you were here."

Riggins turned around to see Ravenoff and Rosa standing there with a older woman. Though years had passed he guessed who she was in an instant. He turned back around without saying a word. From behind, he could hear Ravenoff and Rosa leaving, but he sensed the woman was still there.

"May I join you?" she asked after a while.

Riggins shrugged, "I guess you have just as much right to be here as me. There's another chair in the cave just behind the big rock."

Riggins listened as the woman found the chair. She came up and set it beside him before settling into it. "It's a beautiful place," said Mila. Riggins didn't respond. "So, this is where he met a dragon," she said, looking over at the cave.

"I still doubt it," said Riggins. "There's no reason a dragon would show mercy to him."

"But didn't you ask him about that?"

Riggins looked over in surprise, "What?"

"While we were sailing here from Thebel, Rosa showed me a story she wrote about when you and Matt first started working together. She calls it 'Fathers.' In the story, you asked Matt why the dragon understood him... or something like that. Didn't that happen?"

Riggins looked thoughtful, "You have to understand. That wasn't what I was really asking." Mila looked puzzled.

"You see, what I was asking was… No, you still won't get it. Where should I start..." He paused. "It all started when I was a child. My father was a merchant on the high seas, and when I was eight, his ships sunk in a bad storm. Luckily, he hadn't been on them at the time, but everything we had was lost. Maybe if my mother had still been alive, my father wouldn't have responded the way he did."

Mila looked at him curiously, "How did he respond?"

"Despair." Riggins looked out at the clouds again and sighed. "He started drinking. Before long, he was gone every night. The village drunk. As a result, I was the kid mothers didn't allow their children to play with, the kid everyone ignored. I didn't mind; I was never much for attention. Then, when I was sixteen, my father drank himself to death. At the funeral, I looked around me and saw the legacy he had left behind - empty seats. I was the only one, besides the pastor, who had come. I wondered why I'd bothered. I decided I wouldn't grow up to be like him. I would be someone that people respected. So, I did the only thing I could think of that would get me there."

"What was it?" asked Mila.

"I changed my name to Riggins and got a job at a prison, cleaning the execution yard. It was all awful work at first, but then I got promoted to prison guard. After a few years of that, I knew I was in good shape. The other soldiers did as I said, they stopped talking when I entered the room, they took off their hats when they greeted me. But then, something happened that changed everything."

"What happened?"

Riggins looked up, "You happened, and Matt. The

moment he escaped with you, I knew chasing after you could make or break my position. I risked it. We followed you all the way to the Twisted Caves, and when the men were hesitant, I led them in. We split up, but George came with me. We hunted you two the best we could, but finally we came to a split in the path. He went left, I went right, and.... I guess I got lucky if you can call it luck. I came to an opening in the chamber where the hatch was just as you gave Matt your quilt. I didn't move; I stayed in the shadows. I watched as he hugged you one last time before letting you go. I realized at that moment that I couldn't arrest him. As soon as he turned around, he saw me. We stared at each other a minute, then George called from behind me, 'Is he down there?' I shook my head slowly and turned away, 'No, not here.' I could never forgive myself for that."

"But you did the right thing!" said Mila.

"Did I? Matt seemed to always know his path. For me, it wasn't so easy. For years after that, I continued to look over my shoulder in fear that I would be found out. I dreamt every night of being discovered and hanged for my crime... My funeral was always empty in those dreams. Then, Matt was made admiral. I'd already been at sea for a while by that point, and with every day, I came to hate him more. I disgraced and defied him every chance I got, and he went along with it. Then, he said no. I didn't know what had happened. I decided to go along with him for the time being and hid my anger. Even in submitting, I tried to humiliate him. That night when I asked him the question, I wasn't really asking him why the dragon would understand him. I was asking why I didn't. His answer was more than I expected. I looked at him that night and saw a man I could have been, a good man who hadn't become bitter. That was the night I forgave him."

Riggins looked out at the horizon, "If only I had told him."

"What do you mean?" asked Mila.

"We never spoke of what happened," said Riggins. "Not in all the years since. I never got a chance to tell him that I forgave him. I never thought to say how much he meant to me. I never once told him how... how I would have followed him to the ends of the earth had he asked. But now, it's too late. When a man is young, he thinks himself immortal, but by the time he realizes he isn't, it's typically too late."

Mila smiled and put a letter in the old man's hand. "You may not have told him, but he knew, and he felt the same way."

Riggins looked down at the letter for a moment then put it in his pocket without a word. Ravenoff stood just behind a boulder listening. He knew he shouldn't have, but he was almost glad he did. That last sentence hit him hard. *When a man is young, he thinks himself immortal, but by the time he realizes he isn't, it's typically too late.* He put his hand in his pocket and felt the object inside.

"Typically too late," he said to himself, "but not always."

***

As Ravenoff walked up, Rosa turned to look at him. She smiled. "Hello, stranger."

"Hey," said Ravenoff. "What are you looking at?"

"Just this old cave entrance. I remember the first time

we found it as little kids. Even then, we had to bend down to get through it. I wonder if Valley knew there was another way out of his den."

"Who knows," said Ravenoff. "You know, whenever our families camped here, I used to sneak out every night and crawl through here with a lantern, searching through the cave for treasure." Rosa laughed. "It turns out that the Trinity government didn't leave much behind. But," he added, pulling something out of his pocket. "After all that searching, I finally found this." The object he held was a ring. It was made of silver and looked like a vine that would wrap itself around the finger it was put on. Little golden flowers poked out from in between the leaves.

"Oh Ravenoff, it's beautiful!" said Rosa. "Why didn't you ever tell me about it?"

Ravenoff grinned. "I guess I was waiting for the right time. Why don't you try it on?"

Rosa blinked, "But, it's your ring."

"Yes, but it's made for a woman's finger." He took her hand and slipped it on.

Rosa looked down at it, "It's wonderful, Ravenoff, a real piece of art."

As she went to take it off, Ravenoff stopped her. "Please," he said, "I'd rather you keep it on."

Rosa gasped, then laughed, "Ravenoff Tenter, are you proposing?!?!"

Ravenoff grinned sheepishly. "It depends on what you'd say." Without another word, Rosa stood up on her toes and kissed him. In later years, he recalled that she never actually said yes, but he didn't mind a bit.

***

That night, the Baker Manor was filled to the brim with family and friends who had come together to celebrate the good news of Ravenoff's and Rosa's engagement. Riggins had wished them his best but after a few minutes had retreated from the party to the back porch. He had gotten to the age that he tried to avoid crowds as much as possible.

As he sat there, the shouts and laughter of youth behind him, he looked off into the distance. He could see several waves lapping against the shore from where he sat. In them bobbed the *Bella Fawn* tied to the dock. He smiled. The last time he had stepped foot on that old boat, he hadn't felt alone. It seemed like ages ago. He put his hand in his pocket and pulled out the envelope that Mila had given him. With a sigh, he put it back in his pocket, then drew it out again. Slowly, he opened it and pulled out the letter that was inside. He only ever got through the first few sentences:

My Dear Mila,
If only you could meet Riggins. He may seem hard as stone, but there it so much more behind those dark eyes. He's like the brother I never had.

Riggins clutched the paper and smiled through his tears. "I loved you too, Matt."

The End

THE LEGENDS OF MATT BAKER

ABOUT THE AUTHOR

Sabina Boyer has been a missionary kid to Macedonia for the last nine and a half years. Ever since she was little, she was intrigued by stories of worlds far away. Now, she likes to spend her free time creating her own worlds and filling them with all the wonders of her imagination. This is her first book to be self-published, and she sincerely hopes that you enjoyed reading it as much she enjoyed writing it.

ABOUT THE FLABBIT ROOM

The Flabbit Room is a Christ-centered community of young creators gathered together to share their work and to help and encourage one another. As everyone is created in God's image and God is the Creator, we strongly believe that everyone has been created to be a creator, though in what way varies for each person, whether it is baking, writing, drawing, programming, singing, etc.

We also strongly believe in 1 Timothy 4:12: "Don't let anyone look down on you because you are young, but set an example for the believers in speech, in conduct, in love, in faith and in purity." Our hope is that through this community of young artists and creators, we will set an example of love and kindness as well as creating something true, something noble, something right, something pure, something lovely, something admirable, something excellent and praiseworthy that ultimately points back to our Creator (Philippians 4:8).

We also believe that, as humans, creativity is to be encouraged, fostered, and grown, and also that, in the end, we should use our creativity and gifts to glorify God and shine a light to those around us.

31879642R00236

Made in the USA
Middletown, DE
02 January 2019